DANE

A SKÖLL RANCH SHIFTER ROMANCE
BOOK ONE

A SAMSON

Editor: My Brother's Editor

Cover Designer: Rachel McCarthy

Cover Photo: Emma Jane Photography

Dane (Dān)
a person of Danish ancestry

Ulvmand Family

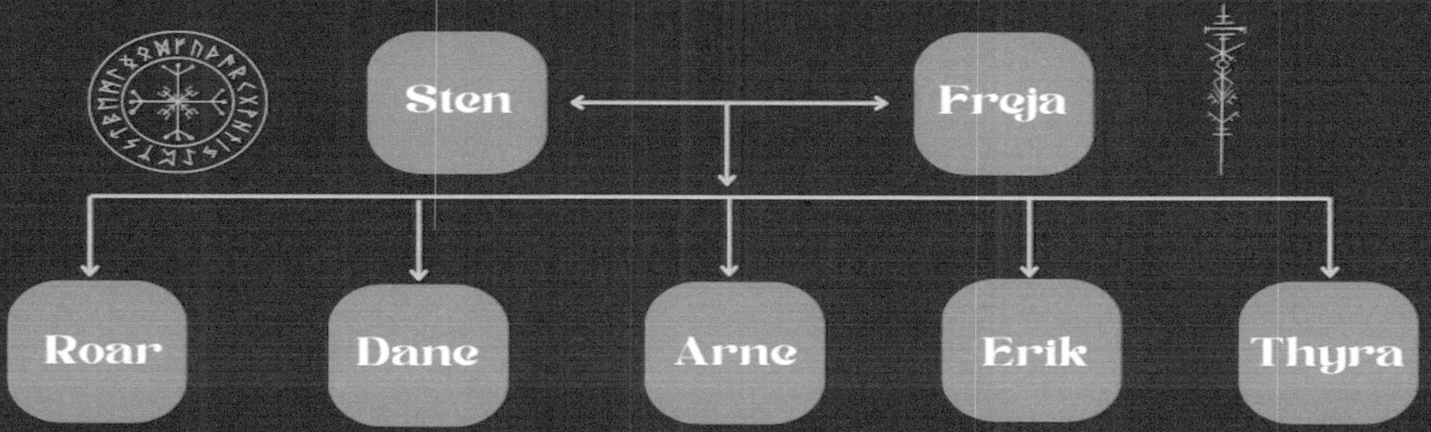

CONTENTS

CHAPTER

ONE

Dane looked up from where he was driving a T-post into the soft ground. He was standing in water up to his ankles trying to stand the fence that had been washed out last week by flooding back up.

His brother, Arne, was at one end trying to stretch the fence line out so his other brother, Erik, could attach the wire as he drove the post back in.

Dane didn't mind hard work. But knowing that he would be right back here putting the same fence up after the next rain made it seem twice as hard.

"Dane!" Arne called from the other side of the washout. "My stomach is eating my backbone. Erik is starting to swoon."

Dane looked over at his youngest brother grinning back at him. He didn't look like he was about to swoon. Besides, he thought, just women swooned. Shaking his head, he sloshed back over to their UTV tossing the T-post driver into the back.

"Can we eat in town?" Arne called to him as he grabbed

up his come-along and made his way back around the washout.

"Can we get chicken-fried steak at Donna's?" Erik asked, climbing into the back of the UTV for the ride to Dane's truck.

"With any luck, there's still some pie left," Arne chipped in, climbing onto the passenger side of the seat.

Dane simply rolled his eyes listening to his brothers discussing the choices for lunch. Driving out of the bottom to the top of the hill, he pulled up next to his truck. Erik hopped out to unhook the trailer holding their supplies from the truck.

"Shotgun," Erik yelled.

"The fuck you do, little brother," Arne yelled back.

Dane wondered why they always had to yell. They weren't ten feet from each other.

"Come on, I don't fit in the middle."

"Tough luck."

It was an argument Dane had listened to all week. None of them fit in the middle. It was a problem when they didn't take the crew cab. Quite simply, they were a family of giants.

Dane was the second son of Sten and Freja Ulvmand. The family had immigrated from Denmark to America around the turn of the twentieth century when Dane's great-grandfather was a boy.

The story was that his family spent one year in Minnesota before wondering why they hadn't escaped the snow and moved south. They weren't the typical immigrant family. They arrived with plenty of money to buy a piece of property in southern Oklahoma to earn a living on. Each family had added to the property until it reached somewhere around eighteen thousand acres.

Dane was still trying to decide if moving back was a good decision. He had earned a degree in soil science assuming he could spend most of his day sitting in a tractor.

What they don't tell the students, though, is that they also need a degree in how to fix those tractors when they break down or what to do when it's too wet to get into the fields. It's not like it should be a surprise to him, he had grown up here. Maybe he was just restless since setting up the same damn fence every couple of weeks no longer appealed to him.

"What are you eating, Dane?" Erik asked as they pulled onto the asphalt road leading to town. Erik was currently attending college, majoring in business. No one, including Erik, knew what he planned to do after graduation.

As the largest of the brothers, he played tight end for the football team. He was home for spring break. Dane was sure he would rethink his choices next spring break. Getting drunk on the beach at South Padre sounded like a much better plan.

"I don't know. Burger maybe," he grunted as his brother tried to find a more comfortable position on the seat next to him. Saying they were a family of giants might have been an understatement. Tall, blonde, and blue-eyed, they all looked alike.

Erik was the biggest of them, though, at six foot six inches. The height wouldn't have been so bad, if his shoulders didn't stretch across half the cab. Dane, at six foot four inches, nor Arne, at an inch shorter than Dane, could sit against the back of the seat because of his shoulders.

"Damn, Erik. Is it you that smells so bad?" Arne asked, shoving Erik over so he banged against Dane.

"I'm sure we all smell ripe. Why did we have to move

here from Denmark again?" Erik asked, shoving Arne back against the door.

"More opportunity, more land, blah, blah, blah," Dane answered, turning up the air conditioner another notch. If March was already this hot, he couldn't bear to think of what it would be in June.

"That's right, it's the blah, blah, blah I keep forgetting." Erik smirked at Dane.

Reaching the restaurant finally, Dane pulled into the dirt lot next to it. He had to agree with Arne, none of them smelled too fresh. He walked into the small diner.

"I need to wash up. Order me a—" Dane found that all of his capacity to form logical thoughts had fled his brain. He stood numbly in the middle of the door, staring at her, his first childhood crush.

Tani Johnston stood at one of the tables laughing with the customers while she took their order. She was just as stunning as he remembered her with her long black hair and caramel-colored eyes. As if in slow motion, she looked up at him, her smile lighting up her whole face.

"Dane Ulvmand? That can't be you, you're all grown up. Hey, Arne. Is this giant Erik?" she walked over to them as Dane stood frozen in place.

"Hey, Tani," Arne answered, jabbing an elbow in Dane's ribs. "I heard you had moved back to town. Didn't I mention it?" he said with a smirk at Dane.

"No, Arne. You didn't." Dane shook his head, clearing his brain so he could speak. It was probably more of a grunt, but whatever.

"You still drink Coke, Dane?" she asked.

"Hmm," he answered, nodding his head. Okay, that was also a grunt. He would have to do something to gain control of his vocabulary so he didn't continue to sound like an idiot around her. "Yes. Grab a table," he said to Arne before turning toward the restroom.

Once he was locked inside, he wanted to bang his head against the mirror until it broke. This was Arne's fault. He should bang his brother's head against the mirror. How could he not warn him that Tani was back in town? Jackass.

Tani had been that perfect girl when Dane was growing up. She was in Roar's class in school, but Dane had a crush on her his entire junior high school career.

Tani was one of those girls who was not only beautiful, but kind. She was a cheerleader, homecoming queen, basketball player, prom queen, academic decathlete, FFA queen, top of her class, and even more queen titles. But she was never the typical stuck-up that came with it. Tani was nice to everyone, including a freakishly large junior high kid.

Dane couldn't even count the number of times he had raced from the junior high to the diner just so Tani would bring him a Coke. He would grin stupidly at her until Roar finally tracked him down, ripping him out of the diner to go home.

Twelve years later, he shouldn't still be struck dumb seeing her, yet here he was. Drying his hands, Dane took a deep breath before opening the door. With a quick look around, he spied his brothers sitting by themselves at a table near the window.

"You should ask her out," Arne said when Dane dropped into the seat next to him.

"Are you out of your fucking mind?" Dane growled quietly back at him.

"I don't think so. Erik, do I appear to be insane?" When Erik shook his head, Arne continued. "You're an adult now,

Dane. She's gorgeous. What's the problem? I'd ask her out myself, but..."

"I'd kill you," Dane growled a little louder this time.

"Yeah, that."

"Okay, Dane gets a Coke," Tani said, stepping up to the table. "A tea for Arne and a Dr Pepper for Erik. Do you know what you want to eat?" she asked, looking directly at Dane.

"Uhh," he said, staring down at the menu. He had probably memorized this menu sometime around his sophomore year of high school. But for the life of him, he couldn't remember a single thing on it.

"I'll do steak fingers," Arne said.

"Chicken-fried steak for me," Erik added.

"My brother, the idiot savant, will have a loaded burger," Arne added. With a smile, Tani left to place their orders. "Christ almighty, get your shit together. How are you going to ask her to suck your dick if you can't even ask her out?"

"Shut up, asshole," Dane said, whipping his head toward the kitchen to make sure she hadn't overheard. "What is wrong with you?"

"What is wrong with you? You've had a thing for Tani Johnston since I can remember. Ask. Her. Out." Arne argued with Dane for a few more minutes until Tani returned to bring their food.

"So Arne, are you home now?" she asked, setting his food in front of him.

"Graduated last May. Dane and I share a house on the ranch. What have you been up to? I heard you moved back in with your dad. How is he?" Arne asked, popping one of his french fries into his mouth.

"For now, yes, and he's good. Erik, what grade are you in?"

"Freshman in college. It's good seeing you again, Tani. You're still just as pretty as I remember."

"You always were a charmer." She sat Erik's plate down in front of him, smiling as he dug in. "What has Roar been doing? Last I heard, he was living in the city."

"He's the controller at the college," Arne answered, his mouth full of food.

"Hey, sweetheart. Can we get refills?" one of the customers across the room asked, drawing Tani's attention away.

"I'll be right there," she called before setting Dane's food in front of him. "I'll be back to check on you in a few." Laying her hand on Dane's shoulder for a moment, she gave him a squeeze as she turned toward her other customers.

Unconsciously, he reached up, touching the place Tani had just had her hand as he watched her walk across the room. Turning back to the table, he caught Erik mouthing the word "pussy" to Arne as he motioned toward Dane with his head. Choosing to ignore him, Dane picked up his burger.

The rest of lunch went by uneventfully. The little diner filled up with customers keeping Tani busy. When new diners started standing by the door waiting for an empty seat, Dane finally rousted his brothers up. Throwing cash down on the table to cover their bill plus a generous tip, he nodded toward the door.

"At least say something to her," Arne said.

Dane rolled his eyes. Taking a deep breath, he turned around to catch Tani watching him. Walking closer, he could only marvel at how beautiful she still was after all these years.

"It was good to see you again, Tani."

She smiled her most brilliant smile at him. Just like in the past, it stole his breath away.

"It was good to see you too, Dane. I can't believe you're all grown up now." She patted his chest as she spoke. Perhaps he would ask her out sometime in the future. After all, he wasn't a love-struck teenage boy any more. No, apparently he was now a love-struck twenty-five-year-old man. "Well, don't be a stranger," she said, finally lowering her hand. With a small wave, she turned back to her tables.

"Not a fucking word," Dane growled when he climbed back into the truck a few minutes later. His brothers had changed positions so he had Arne smashed up against him as he pulled out of the dirt lot this time.

For once, they heeded his advice. The truck remained silent until they arrived back to finish the fence. It seemed neither of his younger brothers were looking for a fight today, much to Dane's disappointment.

All four brothers had gotten into some wicked bloody fights with each other over the years. The only sibling allowed to say what they wanted without repercussions was their sister. She was left alone more because of her propensity to bite than the fact she was a girl. Erik still sported a scar where she had clamped down on him while they were fighting over who got to sit in the front seat on the ride to the city.

"I'm only going to say one more thing, then I'll let it go." So, perhaps Arne was angling for a fight after all. "If you don't throw your hat in the ring, someone else will. Then where will you be? Horny, but still alone," Dane snarled as Arne raised his hands in surrender. "Just something to think about."

Dane was thinking about it. In fact, it was all he had been thinking about. But that didn't mean he wanted it thrown in his face. Asshole, Arne. Except he wasn't really an asshole, he was actually his best friend. The one who had always had his back.

With a sigh, he chunked the post-hole digger back in the UTV. Reaching for the large water thermos, he took a deep drink before handing it to Erik.

"Maybe," he said, swinging into the UTV. "I'll at least consider asking her out."

With a shrug, Arne slapped him on the back as they bounced along the dirt track. They still had to check the rest of the area along the river to see what else had washed out in the last storm. The sooner they had the fence standing, the sooner they could return home. Dane was deep in thought driving along the berm next to the river when he heard Erik speak.

"Dane, pull over. Do y'all smell that?" he asked, sitting up straight. Climbing out, they walked toward the tree line. Keeping an eye out for snakes, they pushed through the trees toward the river. "Oh fuck, look."

Under one of the large bois d'arc trees were the carcasses of three calves. Fighting their way through the undergrowth, Dane found tracks around the tree. Based on the size of the paws it was a large predator.

"Are those bear tracks?" Arne asked, bending down next to Dane. "They're huge."

"I didn't even know we had bears," Erik responded, looking around.

"We haven't in a long time. I'll call the game warden when we get back to see if he's heard anything." Dane reached down, placing his hand in the track. Even by bear standards, it was huge.

"Arne, you need to make sure to carry your gun with you when you're out. It's getting late, let's call it a day, and we'll see if we can track it tomorrow." He led the way back to the UTV keeping an eye out just in case.

"I'm feeding tomorrow, so I'll see if we're missing any more. Erik, you have to head back to school, right?" Arne asked when they reached the UTV.

"Yeah, but not until after lunch. I can help Dane track it in the morning." With a nod, the brothers loaded into the vehicle to head back to the truck, each lost in his own thoughts.

Dane couldn't remember ever seeing a bear on their property. There were stories his grandfather told about seeing them. He would ask his father about it before he and Arne headed back to their house later. If anyone knew how to track an animal, it was Sten Ulvmand.

CHAPTER

TWO

Tani wiped down the last table for the night with a sigh. Her back hurt from a long day of serving customers in the small diner. She was extremely grateful to Donna for giving her the job. She worked at the diner in high school after class and all day in the summers. It was how she saved up enough money to attend the small college in Arkansas where she majored in biology.

When she decided to move home, she applied to teach at the local high school. But they weren't looking for a science teacher right now.

"Hey, Tani. Would you mind locking up?" Donna asked. Tani still had to refill the condiments for tomorrow which would take her another half an hour.

"Of course not. You should have been out of here an hour ago," she answered, returning to the kitchen.

"Thanks, hon. See you tomorrow." Donna left through the back door, locking it behind her.

Taking her tray with the containers of salt, pepper, ketchup, and various hot sauces, Tani walked back into the dining area. She gathered up the containers from the tables and was about to sit down when she heard a knock at the door.

"We're closed," she called out, hoping whoever it was heard her.

"I know," a voice responded. "Can I come in anyway?"

Tani stood to look out the window next to the door. Her heart skipped a beat. Dane was standing at the door waiting. Letting the blinds fall back against the window, she took a deep breath before opening the door.

"Dane, what are you doing here?" she asked. "*How* did you get here?"

"I can drive myself now, you know," he said with a smirk.

She laughed thinking back to a time when Roar would have to show up every day she was working to drag his younger brother home. In the beginning, Roar would be fit to be tied, but something had changed after a while. Roar hadn't seemed to mind too much in the end.

She had often wondered if it was for the same reason that Roar never asked her on a date. In a town as small as this one, you usually dated everyone in your class at some point. But not Roar, he had been friendly but never interested in her.

"You're right." She laughed. "That was a stupid question. But why are you here?" She felt herself blush as she looked up at his brooding face. They were standing entirely too close for her to catch her breath. He had to be almost a foot taller than her now.

Hell, the whole family was tall. They all looked like they had just stepped off the cover of a fashion magazine modeling Icelandic sweaters. Even his mother was tall at close to six feet with her green eyes and stunning long red hair. Roar and Thyra had inherited her looks while the middle brothers were spitting images of their father.

"I thought I would stop by on the way home to see if I can actually complete a sentence. According to Arne, I made an ass of myself earlier. I thought I would prove I'm not still some shy teenage boy." Tani watched as Dane looked around the diner before pinning her again with his glacial gaze. "Would you like some help?"

"Sure," she said, taking a step back. "Would you like something to drink, a Coke maybe?"

"No, I'm good. I don't drink many Cokes anymore. I either gave up the sugar or stayed the chunky kid I was in junior high." She smiled at him wondering how she had missed his voice turning into the sound of thunder.

"You weren't chunky," she stated, drawing a smirk from him. "Okay, you were a little chunky, but I always thought you were adorable."

"Yes, because all men yearn to be thought of as adorable." He chuckled with a shake of his head. Walking around her, he settled in one of the chairs at the table she had commandeered to refill the condiments. "I'll fill the salt shakers."

"Are you upset now since I called you adorable? No fourteen-year-old should be described as virile or sexy." She watched a slow grin spread across Dane's face. "That's better. I don't remember fourteen-year-old Dane being quite so grumpy. Maybe it showed up with the ponytail."

This time Dane rumbled out a laugh.

"You don't like the ponytail?" he asked, pulling his hair out of the band that held it in place. "Better?"

Pulling over one of the salt shakers, he unscrewed the top adding more to it. Had he looked up he would have seen the struggle Tani was having not to run her hands through it. It was long and golden, reaching just below the top of his shoulders.

"I bet if we dirtied you up and then braided your hair in places, you'd look like you just stepped out of an ancient Viking ruin." Tani began refilling the ketchup bottles.

"That's what I looked like before my shower this evening. Pretty sure, though, the Vikings smelled better than I did." Finishing the first shaker, he reached past her, grabbing another one.

Making another mental assessment of him, Tani realized that he had showered since lunch. He smelled like soap, forest, and man. No, this definitely wasn't fourteen-year-old Dane.

"It couldn't have been that bad," she said, standing to place the finished condiments back on their tables. Hearing him snort out a laugh behind her, she stopped to smile at him over her shoulder. He had been watching her. Quickly ducking his head back down, he continued filling shakers.

"I think we have a bear somewhere on our property," he said, changing the subject. "Erik and I are going to see if we can find any sign of it tomorrow morning before he goes back to school."

"Really? I've heard of a bear making an occasional appearance but not in a long time. What makes you think there's a bear?"

Dane told her about finding the large paw prints next to the slaughtered calves this afternoon. Even though the topic was strange, Tani was glad to see him opening up a little more. He described how his father taught him how to track the bear.

"I won't be surprised if Dad decides to come with us tomorrow."

"Yeah, your dad's not one to just sit around," she agreed.

They worked at finishing in silence, having exhausted the topic of bears. Dane finally looked up at her with his eyebrows knitted together. She braced waiting for the question she could read in his eyes.

"Tani, why did you come back here? I heard you were teaching in the city." The city always referred to Oklahoma City, whereas when you said you were going to town, you were referring to the largest town several towns over with a Walmart. She looked around the room for a minute trying to decide what to tell him as he watched her.

"I was teaching ninth-grade biology, but I needed to come home for a while. It's been good being here for my dad again." It wasn't really an answer. Judging by the way Dane narrowed his eyes, he knew it too.

Tani liked Dane, he was a good man from one of the few nice families in the area. But he didn't need to be dragged into the mess her life had become. It was enough to have him look at her like she was special for just a little while longer.

"How long do you think you'll stay?" he asked, letting her off the hook. Everyone had asked her the same question lately. She had no idea how long she would stay but at least a year for sure.

"I'm not sure." Picking up the remaining shakers, she moved through the tables placing a set on each one. When she was done, she looked around checking that everything was ready for tomorrow. Her time with Dane was at an end.

"I see," he added when her attention turned back to him. She watched as he took a fortifying breath, begging him not to ask his next question. "Would you like to go out with me? I know you're closed on Monday if that's best for you. Or Sunday night, whatever."

Tani felt her heart shatter into a million pieces. He had finally gotten up the nerve to ask her on a date, but she was no longer available.

"Sorry, Dane. I can't right now." Turning around, she walked into the kitchen to turn off the main lights. When she returned, she walked over to the front door to wait for Dane. Rising slowly, he met her. "I'm really sorry." She hated seeing the look of disappointment on his face.

"No, it's fine. You should only date who interests you."

When the alarm started to chime, she opened the door pushing him through. She locked up and turned to face him.

"Dane, you are the only man who even remotely interests me. But I just can't date right now." Walking to her car, she opened the door. "I could really use a friend, though." Her back was to him where he still stood by the door. "Can you do that for me? I won't have many left soon."

Feeling her eyes start to burn from the unshed tears, she climbed into her car. She hated to cry, it just made her feel weak. She really didn't want to cry in front of Dane.

"I can do that," he called. "Good night, Tani."

"Good night, Dane." Closing the car door, she drove out of the dirt lot toward home. Looking in the rearview mirror, she could still make out Dane standing in the lot. With a mental shake of her head, she put him behind her. It didn't do any good to think of what could have been. She had a future to figure out that didn't include him.

Pulling into her driveway, she spied her father through the front glass door. He had left the heavy front door open inside. No doubt in anticipation of her getting home.

"It's good to see you're finally home," he said when she

walked inside. "I worry until I see the headlights. How was your day? I heard the Ulvmand boy came for lunch today."

"I forgot how fast news travels here. Three of the Ulvmand boys came for lunch today. Which one are you talking about?" Tani dropped her purse by the front door. Crossing the room, she gave her dad a kiss on the cheek. She slumped down on the couch.

"The one who was sweet on you in high school. He moved home after college to help with his parents' place."

"Dane?" She rolled her eyes when he grinned over at her. Technically Arne had moved home after college also. "Yes, he was there." They watched television for a few minutes before she added, "He came by tonight when I was closing up. Asked me out." She acted completely focused on whatever program he had on so she wouldn't have to meet his eyes. Tani could already feel the red spread up her face, she didn't need to add to it.

"What did you say?"

"I said no. You know I can't date now." He turned back to the television with a grunt. He had been treading carefully around the subject.

"The Ulvmands are good people. Those kids respect their parents, they always have something nice to say, never look down their noses at the rest of us. Would it hurt to go for a Coke with him?" She gave him a look of incredulousness.

"They are good people. The last thing Dane Ulvmand needs is to get embroiled in my mess."

With a shrug, he let the subject go.

Hauling herself off the couch, she headed for her bedroom to shower. Returning to the kitchen when she was done, she heated up some leftovers for dinner.

She only ate lunch at the diner to make sure she didn't

lose any of her paycheck. One meal was provided per shift, even when she worked a double shift like she often did. After that, employees were welcome to start a tab to be paid at the end of the month.

"Did you learn anything else interesting today?" he asked when she sat back down with her plate. Usually he knew more of the town gossip than she did. Chances were, he was still fishing for information about Dane. She shook her head, hoping that would be the end of it. It was easier keeping her life private when she lived on her own in the city.

She now shared the small mobile home she grew up in with him again. It had two small bedrooms, two bathrooms, a kitchen and living/dining room combination. It wasn't huge, but they had always prided themselves on keeping it in good shape. Royal Johnston had even planted fresh flowers outside before she came home to live again.

Royal, or Roy to everyone who knew him, had lived in this town his whole life. The only time he had moved was down the street from his parents when he married Tani's mother. He had worked at the local feed store since high school. To earn extra money, he picked up extra work as a day hand during roundup season.

Tani's mother had decided the life of a small-town wife was not for her. She left before Tani could really even remember her. It had been just the two of them since she was a little girl.

She had known the Ulvmands since she and Roar were in church pre-school together. Her dad meant well, but Dane was now out of her league. Maybe he always had been.

"I'm not the one with all the gossip," she said, steering the conversation away from her. "What did you learn today?" Tani listened as her dad regaled her with the latest gossip.

She learned long ago only about a quarter of all small-town gossip is based on fact. It always amazed her how, with the smallest provocation, your life could be completely rebuilt by word of mouth. The gossip was the one thing she dreaded hitting her over the next couple of months. Her life would provide fodder for the busybodies for years to come.

"That is why Wayne has to hire someone to go get his car back." She nodded her head absently at him with no idea what story he was spinning. "Well, I'd better get to bed. Sweet dreams." Giving her a kiss on the head, Roy headed down the hallway to his bedroom.

It was no wonder she had no idea what had happened to Wayne's car. Her head had been filled with thoughts of another tall, brooding hulk of a man. It was going to be a long night.

THREE

Dane's day started out badly and quickly went downhill. It began when his alarm didn't go off. He was woken abruptly by Arne slapping his stomach as he snored in his bed. Having tossed all night with thoughts of Tani racing through his mind, he was as tired as when he finally fell asleep last night. Pulling on his clothes, he met Arne at the front door. He had slept through breakfast.

"Hopefully this will hold you for a while." Arne handed him a travel mug of coffee and a sausage biscuit. "So based on your scowl, I assume last night didn't go so well?"

Dane looked over at Arne with a growl. If he wasn't currently holding both the coffee and the biscuit, he would seriously have to consider punching Arne in the face.

"Did she shoot you down?"

"She friend-zoned me," he mumbled.

"Ahh, that sucks. Is she dating someone else?"

"I don't know, Arne. Can we please drop it?"

They drove the rest of the way to the main house, where his parents lived, in silence. Pulling up, they found their father outside with his horse saddled. Two more horses were tied next to the tack room waiting for them to arrive.

"Hey, Pop," Arne greeted him. Walking into the feed room, he pulled the feed truck out a few minutes later. With a wave, he headed off toward the pasture.

"Dad." Dane nodded. He pushed a drowsy Erik into the barn. Grabbing his saddle in one hand and the pad in the other, he walked back outside throwing them on his horse.

He worked the cinch strap through the rigging dee on the front of the saddle pulling it snug. The bucking strap in back he left loose enough to not bother his horse but tight enough to hold his saddle down if necessary. Returning to the tack room, he strapped his chaps over his thighs then secured his spurs to his boots.

Snagging a bridle off the wall, he walked back out to his horse. His horse was a large roping horse, bay in color with a laid-back attitude. He took the bit easily, waiting with patience as Dane attached the headstall.

Turning around, Dane found his father and brother sitting on their horses waiting for him. Leading his horse to the truck, he took out his gun, sliding it into the holster attached to his saddle before swinging up into the seat. Within a few minutes, a truck pulled in the gate with a horse trailer.

The men watched as the game warden pulled past them and parked near the barn. After a quick greeting, he unloaded his own fully tacked horse. He fitted a large tranquilizer gun into a specially modified holster on his saddle.

Cody had been the game warden since graduating with Roar's class. He spent most of his days keeping the poachers at bay, but occasionally he got to track predatory animals.

"Mr. Ulvmand, how have you been?" he asked Dane's father.

"Good. You?"

"Good."

Stimulating conversation was not the man's strong suit. Even in high school, he never had a lot to say. Dane actually liked him better because of it. Climbing onto his horse, he motioned for Dane to lead them to the carcasses from yesterday.

"So I hear Tani Johnston is back in town," Cody said, giving Dane a side-eye.

"God almighty! I am not responsible for where Tani lives," Dane growled out. Cody grinned as the horses started down the hill toward the river.

"Just making conversation." They rode in silence for a few minutes before Cody spoke again. "So you wouldn't mind me taking a run at her?" Dane felt his spine stiffen. His glacial gaze worked to bore a hole through Cody's head.

"You might as well," Erik spoke up from behind Dane. "Dane's already struck out."

"Fuck you, Erik." Dane twisted around in his saddle so he could glare at Erik over the back of his horse. Turning back around, he heard his little brother laughing softly.

"You know the rumor has always been that the two of you had a torrid secret affair while she was in high school. That she left heartbroken because you broke up with her." Dane turned in his saddle to look at Cody in stunned silence.

"I was in junior high. She left to go to college. Can the local gossips not find another hobby other than spreading crap about people?" Dane shook his head in frustration.

It's not that he wouldn't have been willing to have an affair with Tani. But he was pretty sure he wouldn't have had much clue how to go about that in junior high school. Now that he was more than capable of one, she wasn't interested. It would be funny if it weren't so depressing.

"Don't feel bad. My senior year of high school, I was supposed to have knocked up half the girl's softball team," Erik said.

"Yeah, I was supposed to have been given the option of joining the Army or going to jail for cooking meth. If they could have seen my chemistry grade, they wouldn't have started that rumor," Cody added. "It's just small-town boredom. Nothing ever happens, so the locals have to make things up."

"I never heard any of this," Sten said from next to Erik. "I don't remember you ever being alone with Tani, however. Don't know when you would have had time for an affair. Besides, Roar was keeping an eye on you. I guess now that you're a grown man, you can do whatever you like."

"Except Tani doesn't want Dane doing her," Erik chirped up. Before Dane could knock him off his horse, his father intervened.

"Erik, what Dane or Tani do is none of your business. You worry about you, and let Dane worry about himself. Need teaches naked women to spend."

"What? What does that even mean?" Dane asked, shaking his head. His father had the tendency to throw out Danish proverbs when he couldn't think of anything else. They rarely had anything to do with the subject.

"I don't know. Your grandfather used to say that to me." With a chuckle, he squeezed his horse into a trot, passing Dane. With a shrug, Erik smiled at him before pushing his horse forward.

Soon they arrived at the site they discovered yesterday.

Leaving Erik with the horses, they pushed their way into the trees to study the scene.

It wasn't long until Cody spotted claw marks on one of the bigger trees. He studied the marks for a while before leading them back out of the trees. He pulled off his cap, running his hand through his hair in thought.

"What do you think?" Dane asked, picking up on the warden's unsettled demeanor.

"This isn't your ordinary black bear you usually find in Oklahoma. They average somewhere around four to six hundred pounds max. This one, based on his reach, has to be around twelve hundred pounds. Big even for a brown bear. It borders on polar bear size, which we obviously don't have around here. I'm going to have to do some research on how to best catch him. Let's see if we can track which direction he went in."

Remounting their horses, they returned to the river. They skirted the side of it until they found more tracks. It was close to lunchtime before they finally lost the trail in the river. They had painstakingly traced him almost to the northern property line before admitting defeat. It took another hour to make it back to the house. Walking past his parents' house toward the barn, they stopped when his mother came out on the porch.

"Did you have any luck?" she called, walking to the fence to stand next to their dog, Odin. It was a ridiculous name for a dog, especially considering it was a female. But Thyra had named her years ago, and no one had the heart to change it. The big lab sat next to his mother as she stroked her head.

"No, ma'am," Dane answered. "But it looks like he's a big one. Bigger than he should be."

"That sounds bad. Cody, you'll be joining us for lunch."

"Yes, ma'am," Cody said with a grin.

It wasn't really a request, it was more of an edict. But it was one Cody seemed happy to follow. Moving on to the horse barn, they untacked their horses, and turned them back out into the trap by the house. They stopped in the mudroom to wash their hands before continuing into the kitchen.

The smell of Freja's cooking filled the house. Dane's family might have immigrated from Denmark, but they learned to cook southern food not long after. His mother was particularly adept at it.

"It's ready. Sit, sit," Freja said, fussing around the kitchen.

Sten led the game warden into the dining room while Dane helped Arne and Erik carry the food to the table. When it was ready, they all took their seats before his father blessed the food.

His mother had made Erik's favorite. The table was laden with chicken-fried steak, mashed potatoes, pickled cucumbers, and rolls. She smiled watching Erik rub his hands together in anticipation. Since his sausage biscuit had worn off long ago, Dane agreed with his brother's enthusiasm.

"So tell me what you found," Arne said, passing the gravy.

"Cody thinks it's some displaced brown bear. It looks to weigh in at around twelve hundred pounds. Are we missing any cows?" Sten asked.

"Not that I've found yet. I still have several pastures left to feed though. How did a brown bear get this far south?" Arne answered.

"I don't know, but I'll call the state office when I get back." Cody stopped eating for a minute to look around the table. "I'm going to need to put out a warning about it. Until he's caught, you need to be very careful. Make sure Odin is inside at night." Everyone nodded solemnly letting him know they took his warning seriously.

"I'll put up flyers listing the area in vague terms so maybe you won't have every yahoo in the county trespassing hoping to bag a bear." Poaching in the area was a constant problem. They chased out enough people illegally hunting as it was. They didn't need to advertise a rare species roaming the ranch.

After dinner, they all went their separate ways. Erik had a three-hour drive back to school, Arne had cattle to feed, and Dane had a windrower to fix. Walking Cody out to his truck, Dane took the opportunity to follow up on the bear with him. After exchanging ideas about trapping it, he started toward the equipment barn.

"Hey, Dane. It's none of my business, but I think you should wait Tani out. You always had a thing for her growing up. This is your chance," Cody said.

"She shut me down."

"That doesn't make sense. She never acted like you mooning all over her in junior high bothered her. I figured if anyone had a chance, it was you."

"Was I really that bad? I thought I was more stealthy than that."

"Oh, yeah, it was bad. We would have given you hell, but every time we started, Roar would shut us down. Well, good luck, maybe she'll change her mind." Climbing into his truck, he waved as he made a U-turn toward the gate.

Had Dane even noticed that his older brother had protected his apparently fragile male ego? It might have been a better idea to let the older boys give him hell. He might not still be carrying whatever this ridiculous torch was for her.

With a sigh, he walked to the equipment barn. Rolling up his sleeves he turned to the large grass cutter. It wasn't really broken, but if he planned on cutting hay next month, he had better get in a service on it now. Most of the basic repairs to the equipment he could do himself. He only called in a mechanic when needed. He'd start with greasing it.

He was wedged awkwardly under the head hunting for his last grease zerk when he heard a voice behind him.

"Hi." Lifting his head up from behind the cutter head, he stared at her in confusion. "I hope you don't mind me stopping by. Your mother said you were out here."

Tani looked anxious as she stood looking around the shop. Dane didn't know what to say, so he chose to remain silent. To be honest, he was debating with himself as to if she was even real. She had sabotaged his thoughts so often lately, it was highly likely that he had finally had a mental break.

"I had the afternoon off," she continued, "so I thought I would come by to apologize for how I left things last night."

"I don't think anything was left unresolved last night. I thought you were perfectly clear," he growled as he turned back to the machine. The last zerk was proving impossible to reach. There was always at least one place on every piece of equipment that you needed a well-trained ferret for.

"But I could have said it better. Yes, I would love to go on a date with you, Dane. Of all the guys in town who have asked me out, you are the only one I would want to say yes to. Unfortunately circumstances are just too...complicated right now."

"That doesn't sound any better," he pointed out. At

least she said she would like to date him, that was a small win, he guessed. With one last push, he finally managed to just reach the grease zerk with his long arms. Did she say she was being asked out by other men?

"Hey, who keeps asking you out?" He hadn't beaten anyone bloody for some time. He could use the practice. She started giving him the list until she stopped suddenly as his growl grew louder.

"Did you just growl at me?" she asked, walking closer to the machine.

"Maybe," Dane said, trying to push himself back out of the tight space. "Not really at you."

"Mmm." Her warm gaze drifted over him. It burned a line of fire into his skin everywhere it touched. He had to divert her attention away from him before he did something rash.

"So what do you have planned today?" he asked.

"Well, I worked the morning through lunch shift. I was heading home when I decided to come here."

Taking a step toward her, he sniffed her hair.

"You smell like french fries."

"Dane Ulvmand, you are a real ladies' man," she teased with a laugh. "Do you mind if I watch you for a while? Dad is still at work, and I don't feel like sitting at home."

"You're welcome here anytime. I brought you two something to drink," Freja said, making them both jump.

Dane spun to look at the door as his mother walked in like he had been caught doing something wrong. His eyes narrowed watching her set down two glasses of tea. She never brought him something to drink, so he had to wonder what she was up to.

"Tani, would you like to stay for supper?" she asked.

"I would, but I usually cook dinner for Dad on the nights I don't have to work. Maybe some other time?"

"We would love to have you any time."

"Thank you, Mrs. Ulvmand."

With a wave, his mother turned to walk back to the house. He studied the empty doorway for a moment trying to work out what she was up to.

"What is that face?" Looking down, he found Tani watching him in amusement.

"Nothing," he mumbled. "Here, you can sit here while I change out the damaged turtles." He pointed to an old office chair. He walked to a large tool chest to hunt for the tools he would need. "Anyone interesting come into the diner today?"

This whole friend thing took a lot of energy. He was always more of a loner growing up. He never had much need for a lot of friends. Arne was the popular kid with an entourage around him at all times in school. Dane could usually be found by himself working on a project of his own making.

Tani had been the only girl he had ever taken much interest in. He did the whole prom thing more because it was expected of him than because he had much interest in dating.

"There was this one odd guy who came in. He was huge, like bigger-than-Erik huge. It's not like he did anything wrong," she hurried to add when he scowled at her. "It just felt like he was watching me the whole time he was there. Oh, he also had a strange accent."

CHAPTER

FOUR

"What did it sound like?" Dane's deep voice sent shivers through her body. Adult Dane had turned into a quiet, sullen giant of a man. When he looked at her, it felt like nothing else in the world mattered to him. It was like she consumed his entire being. It was intoxicating and more than a little daunting. She wondered if everyone felt this way under his glacial gaze or if it was just her.

"I don't know, he didn't say enough for me to decide." She cocked her head to the side looking up at the ceiling. It did remind her of almost every one of the villains in her dad's old James Bond movies. "You know, I think it sounded Russian. Have you ever met anyone from around here who was Russian?"

"No, I don't think so. Was he bothering you?"

"He was just sort of creepy, but he didn't do anything wrong." Sitting in the office chair, she hiked one leg up to her chest while using the other to spin in a circle. It was childish, but nothing was better than seeing if you could spin fast enough staring at the ceiling to make yourself dizzy.

Obviously she was easily entertained. When her stomach flipped over, she decided she had better stop before she had to clean the barf out of Dane's shop. Dane must also be easily entertained, she decided when she found him watching her.

"Dizzy?" he asked with a smirk on his face. Turning around, he began to back the bolts out of the first turtle he was replacing. Tani watched his muscles ripple under his shirt as he tried to bust one of the bolts off.

He stood and crossed back over to his tool chest to pull out a pneumatic driver. She closed her eyes wondering if he ever worked without his shirt in the heat of the summer as sweat slowly ran over his chiseled body.

Opening her eyes slowly, she found him on his knees, bent over as he worked on the machine. He was holding on to the driver as his muscles danced with the strain. With a gentle push of the chair, Tani eased herself around until she had an unobstructed view of his tree trunk thighs straining to support his body as he leaned against the driver.

She took her time working her gaze up his body. The tree trunk thighs led to a rock-hard ass muscled enough to bounce a quarter off she bet. His narrow waist led up to a broad chest with massive shoulders. Was it getting hot in here, or was it just her raging hormones?

"Dane?" she heard over her shoulder. With a quick kick, she pushed the chair back across the floor. Spinning around, she saw Dane's sister walking into the barn with a grin on her face. Damn it, she had been busted. "Hey, Tani. Mom said you were over here. Have you died of complete boredom yet?"

Tani laughed. She didn't know Thyra well, but she had

always been a force to reckon with. She was as headstrong as she was beautiful.

"I thought if I stuck around, he'd give me a ride later," she said, matching Thyra's smile. His sister raised her eyebrow in question. "In the tractor thingy. That thing," she added quickly with a wave at the machine. She could feel herself turning red, but at least Dane hadn't turned around yet.

"I'm sure he'd be happy to give you a ride. You know there's no trainer seat, you have to sit in his lap, right?"

"Thyra, is there something you want?" Dane growled from where he was fitting the new turtle.

"Since you brought it up," Thyra said, turning her attention to Dane. "Can I borrow your truck to drive to practice?"

"No."

"Dane," she whined, "everybody drives themselves. I'm the only varsity player who has to be brought by their parents. I look stupid."

"Last time I checked, you didn't have your driver's license yet," he answered.

"No one else does either, Dane."

Tani watched the exchange between the siblings. She always wanted a brother or sister to share her life with. But her dad never remarried after her mom left. It had always been just the two of them. Dane set the driver on the ground. He turned to study his sister.

"Mom taking you hasn't bothered you before. What's changed?" he asked.

Thyra stood dancing from foot to foot as she considered her answer. Obviously, it had something to do with a boy, but it wasn't Tani's place to point that out.

"Hey, what's up?" Arne greeted them, walking into the shop. "Tani, I didn't know you were here. I hope you've been giving Dane grief." Stopping next to her, he studied the death stares his siblings seemed to be locked in. "So what's going on?" he asked in a singsong voice.

"Well, your sister asked Dane if she could borrow his truck to drive herself to practice. Dane, in turn, told her no because she doesn't have a license. Thyra volleyed back with a 'but everyone else is doing it.' Now they seem to be in a standoff," Tani told him as she watched Dane snarl at his sister.

"Nicely called," Arne said, squeezing her shoulder. "Does this have to do with not looking like a kid in front of the new baseball player?"

"What new baseball player has eyes on Thyra?" a rumbling voice asked from the doorway.

"Oh good, everyone's here," Dane said with a roll of his eyes as Roar walked in the door.

"If anyone should understand your plight, Thyra, it should be Dane," Roar said.

Tani laughed, ignoring the derisive snort from Dane. She jumped out of her chair. "Roar!" she squealed, running to hug him. Sweeping her into a bear hug, he swung her around before setting her back on her feet.

"Mom said you moved back." Holding her out, Roar studied her with his laughing blue eyes. They were similar to Dane's but darker somehow. "You look amazing," he said, pulling her back in for another hug. They had only run into each other a few times since they graduated, and she missed him.

"Dane. Stop growling. I'm not trying to cop a feel. Just hugging an old friend." With a shake of his head, he looked down at her. "He growls a lot."

"I don't growl," she heard Dane grumble.

Roar rolled his eyes, making her laugh. She couldn't

remember the last time she felt so happy. Yes, she knew Dane had the tendency to growl at anyone who came too close to her.

In theory, she should feel offended that he thought he had the right to insert himself in her business like that. In reality, she loved it. It made her feel protected, wanted, valued. She loved her dad more than anything, but she wanted to be part of a big, rowdy family like the Ulvmands.

"Roar, make Dane lend me his truck to go to practice tonight," Thyra said, placing her balled fist on her hips.

"Why would Dane let you do anything that might get you arrested or hurt?" Roar responded in a calm voice. "It's not Dane's job to contribute to your delinquency."

"Spare me the lecture, Roar."

"Stop acting like a brat, and I will," he answered, a little less placating this time.

"How about this," Tani interrupted. She involuntarily gasped when four sets of glacial eyes turned to her. "What if I give you a ride to practice tonight, then one of your brothers can pick you up after? That way you're safe, but having a sibling pick you up will be less of a stigma than having one of your parents do it."

They stood still staring at her for a heartbeat while she wondered if she had outstayed her welcome. Finally, Thyra broke into a grin.

"You're amazing!" she squealed, hugging her. "I have to be there at five. Oh, can Dane pick me up? Arne always flirts with my teammates. It's embarrassing." Spinning, she flounced out of the shop.

"What did I just get volunteered for?" Dane asked.

"I don't flirt with her teammates, they flirt with me. They flirt with Dane too," Arne grouched.

"Yeah, but I bet Dane doesn't even notice. You don't fool

anybody, Arne. You can't help flirting back. It's in your DNA. Now come help me load a chair Mom said I could have." Giving Tani a quick hug, Roar stalked out of the shop. Suddenly, the silence seemed deafening.

"I'll give you a ride any time you want one," Dane said, making Tani's stomach do a double flip.

"What?" she asked, trying to slow down her heart.

"The windrower. You said you wanted a ride." His eyebrows were knit together in his usual scowl.

"Yeah, the windrower. Right."

He watched her for a few more minutes before turning back to the big piece of machinery. She sank back down into her chair with a sigh.

This wasn't going to work. Who was she trying to fool thinking they could just be friends? You can't be just friends with someone when all you can think about is their big piece of equipment. She snorted a laugh at her own joke.

Unfortunately, Dane heard her. He turned around to see what she was laughing at. And she did just what she had been thinking about. She checked out his big piece of equipment. He looked down at the ground to see if he could see what she was looking at before looking back up at her. He shrugged and continued to wrestle with something on the header.

"Damn it." Grabbing a mechanic's creeper out of the corner, he threw it on the ground before lowering himself down on it. "I swear, you have to be seven foot tall to get into this machinery, a rocket scientist to operate it, and a trained weasel to get to the parts that you have to work on."

"Is there anything I can do to help?"

"If I ask for a tool I don't have, can you hand it to me? It should all be in that green chest I've been pulling stuff out of."

She nodded as he laid back on the creeper. Holy hell! If she still had on panties when she got home tonight, it would be a miracle.

The view in front of her might have just melted them off. Dane's T-shirt had ridden up when he laid down. The hem landed just above a rock-hard six-pack. Or she thought it was a six-pack. She couldn't pull her eyes away from the obliques that started just above his pelvic bones and ended somewhere below his belt.

As if the view wasn't enough, it became interactive every time he worked on whatever he was doing under there. She became mesmerized by the tensing of his abs.

She shook her head. She really needed to go before she did or said something to embarrass herself. But she couldn't just leave him under there with no help. That would be unthinkable. She would simply have to soldier on.

Wait, was that a tattoo she could see the edge of just below his shirt on his ribcage?

Rolling closer, she studied it for a few minutes. She pulled his shirt farther up so she could see the rest of it. There was a loud thud from under the header before she heard a moan. With a gasp, Tani realized the thud was Dane's head coming into contact with something.

"Oh my god, Dane. Are you okay?" Slowly pushing out from under the tractor, he sat up holding his head. "Let me see," she said, kneeling next to him. Pulling his hair out of the band he had it secured in, she searched through his hair looking for blood. He flinched when her fingers ran over a goose egg forming. "I am so sorry."

"What were you doing? I thought a mouse or something ran up my shirt."

"I am so sorry, Dane. I saw your tattoo. It looked interesting, so I was trying to see the rest."

"Next time, just ask." Pulling off his shirt, he lifted his right arm so she could see it better. "I have three. This one is a Danish proverb. It basically says there is no rose without thorns. It means you must embrace the gifts given to you, the good with the bad."

Dane turned so she could see his back. Across his shoulders were four runes.

"These spell wolf."

Turning back, he pointed to his left shoulder.

"This is a Norse wolf with other symbols surrounding it. In Norse times, the wolf could represent either destruction or bravery. These characteristics together are the embodiment of savagery bringing out the best and worst in men."

"Hatakachafa," Tani said, reaching out to trace the wolf with her finger.

"What's that?" Dane asked.

"The elders tell a story about the son of a war chief named Hatakachafa, which means nameless. To earn his adult name, he took a raiding party out to fight another tribe only to be slaughtered when they were trapped by the other tribe in a cave they took shelter in.

"After wandering in the cave, he finally emerged in a world he had never seen. He met a white wolf the size of a horse who became his companion. When he found his way home after a year, his maiden had died of a broken heart.

"It is said Hatakachafa kneeled on the hill where he had left her howling until he died. The white wolf learned his howl, teaching his offspring to howl even to this day."

Dane was watching her so intently that she could barely breathe. She gently felt the knot on his head. They were so close all he would have to do was lean forward to kiss her. A part of her yearned for him to do so, but the other half knew they could never be together.

"Tani, are you ready?" she heard Thyra yell from the driveway.

"Yeah," Tani yelled back. She glanced quickly at his bright blue eyes once more before standing up. She wanted to ask him about the necklace he wore with the silver cylinders, but that would have to wait for another time.

"Bye, Dane. I'll be working tomorrow if you need some lunch or dinner." With a wave, she left him sitting on the creeper, staring after her.

"What were you doing with my half-naked brother?" Thyra teased her as they walked toward her car.

"Actually, we were just discussing tattoos. Nothing X-rated, I promise."

"That's too bad. Dane could use a little more X-rated in his life." Thyra laughed at Tani's open mouth as she climbed into her car. "Come on, I have four brothers plus a dad. If you could wring our house out, testosterone would pour out of it. Mom and I have to cover everything in pink just to survive." Tani couldn't help but laugh this time. "I mean, if I had a quarter for every time they told me I couldn't do something, I would be rich by now."

"It sounds like they really care about you," Tani said, pulling out the gate.

"Yeah, they're not bad. At least with brothers, there's no tiptoeing around feelings all the time. They just say what they want. They also fart and belch whenever they want." Tani laughed hard this time. "You want to hear how they react every time I ask for some consideration?" Tani nodded. She couldn't wait to hear this.

"Please, lay it on me."

"Well, Roar just gives a lecture while shaking his head

like you saw earlier. Dane looks at me like I emerged from an alien spaceship." Tani snorted with laughter.

"Wait, it gets better. Arne tells me to ask Dane. Erik is the worst, though. His answer is always "girls don't do that," like the only thing we are supposed to do is sew, cook, and push out babies. Oh, but I have to do it without having sex."

"You are too young to be pushing out babies." Tani was now trying to wipe her eyes with her sleeves.

"Yeah, but I don't want to become an old maid like Dane either. You know, I can't remember him ever dating. Roar had a series of girlfriends, Arne is basically a manwhore, and Erik had a girlfriend all through high school. But Dane, nothing. Maybe he's gay. But if he's gay, wouldn't he have hooked up with a guy by now?"

"I don't think he's gay," Tani offered, trying not to run them into the bar ditch at the incredibly sexy thought of Dane with another man. What was wrong with her? Oooh, a threesome with her and Dane. It was her hormones. It had to be, what else would be the reason for her amazingly naughty thoughts?

"Yeah, probably not. I mean, he had to have undressed you with his eyes at least three times while I was in the shop," Thyra continued. "Don't get embarrassed, but Roar and Arne noticed it too. I heard them discussing it." Tani could feel the red spread up her chest to her face. "You know, y'all would make really pretty babies."

"Thyra!" After listening to Thyra chatter the rest of the way to town, Tani finally pulled up at the ball fields.

"Look, there he is," Thyra said, opening the car door. "You tell me he's not a whole fine jar of eye candy." With a laugh, she grabbed her bag out of the back seat. She waved to Tani and jogged off to chat up the new boy.

Her brothers were right to feel protective of her. She was quite a handful. It would take a real man to finally land the youngest Ulvmand. She would never settle for anything less.

Checking her watch, Tani realized she was going to make it just in time to join her father for supper. With a smile, she backed out of the parking lot to head home.

CHAPTER
FIVE

Dane stood in the door of the shop watching the taillights on Tani's car disappear out the front gate. Turning back into the shop, he pulled his shirt back over his head. Had she been checking him out? Or was it just a figment of his imagination? Fuck, that woman had him tied up in knots.

Looking down at his body, he wondered what she saw when she looked at him. Did the tattoos turn her off? He didn't think so since she had been so intrigued by the wolf on his shoulder. He liked the story she told about the white wolf. If only she knew the secret he barely kept contained under the surface of his skin.

Putting away his tools, he caught his reflection in a small piece of shiny metal attached to his tool chest. He had been told by more than one woman that his eyes made him look cold, like ice. His eyes were almost opaque, they were so blue, as opposed to his siblings who all had slightly darker ones.

Tani had eyes so warm he wanted to dive in and never

come out. The very thought made him hard again. Damn it, he just had that thing finally back under control.

With a sigh, he disconnected the air hose from the driver. He had gotten hard at the very sight of her since the age of thirteen. The first time had mortified him. He had been sitting at the counter telling her about something stupid when she reached over the bar to squeeze his arm with a laugh. For the life of him he couldn't remember what he had said to make her touch him, but he could still feel how absolutely embarrassed he had been at his reaction.

Fortunately Roar walked in, took one look at him and knew exactly what to do. Claiming he needed to speak to Tani about something for school, Roar distracted her long enough for Dane to slink out of the diner. That had resulted in one of the many lectures he received from his oldest brother about women and sex. Dane grinned at the memory. He needed to take Roar to dinner soon just to thank him for having his back growing up.

Once the shop was clean again, Dane grabbed their empty glasses and carried them to the house. The kitchen smelled like homemade mac and cheese cooking. Setting the glasses in the sink, he turned in time to see his mother walk into the kitchen to check on supper.

It was the habit in their family to eat their main meal at noon so they had the energy to finish their work, then eat a smaller meal at night. Arne and he usually ate supper at their house. But sometimes they were lucky enough to be invited to eat something their mother had made.

"I was just about to send Arne to get you," she said. She crossed the kitchen to give him a kiss on the cheek. "It was sweet of Tani to take your sister to town for me. I made an extra dish of mac and cheese for them if you can drop it off on the way to pick Thyra up, please."

With a nod, he leaned back against the sink to watch her get ready for supper. "She's always been such a nice girl."

"Who's a nice girl?" Arne asked, joining Dane next to the sink.

Once the amazing smell of food penetrated into the living room, his mother had to try to work around a pack of hungry men milling around the kitchen.

"Tani," his mother responded.

"It doesn't sound like it. According to Thyra's text, she caught y'all rolling around in the shop half naked," Arne said with a smirk.

"Wait, who was naked in the shop?" Roar asked, stepping into the kitchen. Sten followed on his heels.

"No one was naked," Dane growled.

With a disapproving scowl, Freja took the dinner out of the oven. Taking a bowl off the stack at the back of the stove, she began spooning a large portion into it.

"Well, technically, you don't have to be completely naked." Arne smirked.

"Arne!" she exclaimed.

He at least had the good sense to look sheepishly at her as she handed him his bowl. There were certain things that were never done around their mother without bringing on a swift punishment from their father. No cursing of any kind, no talking back, and under no circumstances did you bring up sex.

"I'm going to say this one time, so pay attention. I asked Tani out, and she said no. She only came out here because she mistakenly thought she had been too mean about shooting me down. I cracked my head on the windrower, so she was simply making sure I was okay. End of story." His family sat in absolute silence staring at him. He assumed they were in shock. He rarely said so many words at one time.

"Are you okay?" his mother asked after a few minutes reaching for his head.

"It was just a bump," he answered, ducking away from her hands.

They ate in silence before Arne couldn't stand it anymore. "So why was your shirt off?"

Dane let out a large sigh, setting his fork back down.

"I was under the windrower on the creeper when she saw the edge of my tattoo. She pulled my shirt up to get a closer look at it. I thought a mouse was running up under my shirt and cracked my head. When Thyra walked in, we were discussing wolves in mythology. She wanted to look at the one on my shoulder." Picking his fork back up, he scooped up another bite. Halfway to his mouth, he realized they were all staring at him again. "What?"

"We just didn't know you knew so many words," Roar said with a grin. Dane would happily flip him off, but he wasn't sure he would make it out of the house alive if his mother saw it.

"Just finish your dinner," Dane growled instead.

"And that took her hands running over your naked chest to accomplish?" Arne asked. Would the punishment for killing his younger brother be worth it? Possibly.

"Leave it the fuck alone, Arne." He heard the snarl his father made. "I'm sorry," he said, looking at his mom. "I'm just going to go. I'll drop off the other dish." Looking over at his father, he skirted around the table, the farthest from where the older man's eyes bore into him. "Can I take you to lunch next week?" he asked, stopping next to Roar's chair.

"Yeah, that would be great."

"Just let me know what day works best for you."

He placed his dish in the sink. Crossing to the stove, he picked up a foil container with a hearty portion of dinner in it.

"Wait, let me cover it so you can get it there," Freja said as she walked into the kitchen. "Just tell Tani I put it in a throw-away container so she doesn't have to return it." She fitted a foil lid to the top crimping the edges of the dish to keep it in place.

"I'm sorry," Dane said again, taking the dish.

"Psst, don't tell your father, but I have heard that word before," she said with a wink. Motioning for him to bend over, she kissed his cheek. "Your head is okay?" He nodded as he pushed back outside carrying the hot pan.

"Hey, wait up. I'll ride with you," Arne called after him. He placed his bowl in the sink. "Thanks for the dinner, Mom. Sorry about winding Dane up, but if I don't do it, he might finally turn into stone." With a kiss on her cheek, he met Dane at the door. Setting the pan on his lap in the passenger seat, Dane waited for Arne to start the truck. "I've always wanted to see what the punishment was for dropping the f-bomb. I'm very disappointed."

"I did it once before. When I was about seventeen," Dane answered.

"No shit? What happened?"

"You know the flagstone patio? Where Mom's reading bench is under the trees in the yard?"

"Yeah."

"I built that. I also mowed the horse trap with a push mower. It took me a week of mowing and building half the night. Didn't have the urge to say that again until today." Dane leveled a death stare at his brother as he drove out the gate. They rode in silence to town pulling up in front of Tani's house.

"Do you need to text her to make sure she's decent?" Arne asked, shutting off the engine.

"I don't have her phone number."

"Seriously? Why are you so bad at this?"

Dane tried another glare, but it was no use. He was pretty sure Arne had become immune to those years ago. With a sigh, Dane opened the door, closing it with his hip so he didn't drop the casserole.

"Good luck, man," Arne offered, rolling down his window.

Dane ignored him as he started up the steps. Pushing the doorbell with his elbow, he waited for someone to answer.

"Dane?" Tani asked.

"Jesus," he heard himself responding. Tani was standing in front of him wearing nothing but a pair of short shorts and a fitted tank top. His brain became absolute mush as he watched her nipples turn to hard peaks under the shirt in the outside air. How he didn't drop the pan was beyond him.

"Dane?" He heard her call again.

Jerking his head up, he looked into her molten eyes. How long had he been staring at her tits? Taking one more quick look down, he closed his eyes. Yep, they still called out to him to be touched. Opening his eyes slowly, he fought to focus only on her face.

"Umm," he said, trying desperately to remember why he was there.

"Very moving. Have you thought of writing poetry?" she asked with mischief in her eyes.

"Who's at the door, Tani?" He heard her father call from inside.

"It's just me, Mr. Johnston. Dane Ulvmand. My mother wanted to send over something as a thank you for Tani taking my sister to practice." Maybe if he could just focus on talking to her father, his erection would settle down again. Except those magnificent breasts wouldn't leave his mind.

Dane let out the breath he was holding when she turned around to lead him into the house. This wasn't much better. Now he was presented with her full hips just perfect for his hands to hold on to as he plowed into her fantastic ass.

Letting out an audible groan, he followed her into the house. If he did that again, Roy Johnston would have no problem chopping him into tiny bits to feed to the dog. Trying to look at anything but Tani, he carried the pan to the kitchen counter.

"Is that your mother's mac and cheese I smell?" Mr. Johnston asked with an appraising look between him and Tani.

"Yes, sir."

"You have perfect timing. I was just about to heat us something for supper," Tani said. His gaze found her again where it settled back on her breasts. They were perfect.

"I need to go," he said suddenly. It took all of his effort to look back up at her face. "I'm supposed to get your phone number, though. Then I need to leave." He could hear her father chuckle behind him as his face grew red. Good Jesus, what was wrong with him?

"I mean, can I have your number so I can make sure you make it home next time?" Why was he assuming there'd be a next time? Though, if he had his way, there would be.

"Hand me your phone." Typing her number in, he heard her phone ping behind him. "There, now I have yours too." Her hand brushed his as she handed it back, lingering a little too long. He was even harder from that one touch than just from watching her ass as she strutted into the kitchen. She was a fucking temptress.

"Uh-huh." With one last look, he spun toward the door. And ran directly into her father's cool glare. "It was good seeing you again, Mr. Johnston." Reaching out, he shook the older man's hand. Clearing his throat, he continued to the door.

"Bye, Dane," Tani called out from the kitchen.

"Bye," he mumbled, pushing outside. He closed the door carefully behind him. His hand ran through his hair as he looked up at the sky. That could have gone better. He was rolling his head from side to side to release the tension when he reached the truck. Climbing back into the passenger side, he ignored his brother's amused gaze.

"Dude, you're pouring sweat," Arne said with a grin.

"Just drive," Dane answered, rolling down his window. If his jeans didn't loosen back up soon, he was going to suffer permanent damage.

Arne backed in against the fence at the softball field so they could watch the end of Thyra's practice. Shoving the door open, Dane hopped out and walked to the back of the truck. He chose to lean against the open tailgate instead of taking a chance of cutting off even more circulation.

"You have to tell me what happened," Arne said, jumping up to sit on the tailgate.

"That old man is going to shoot me in the face next time he sees me is what happened," Dane snapped.

"Fuck. What did you do?"

"I stared at her tits the whole time like I was fifteen.

Except when she turned around so I could stare at her ass." Dane squinted at the field where Thyra had just snagged a fly ball in center field. She was so freakin' fast.

"She had on this tank top with no bra," he continued. "What was I supposed to do? It's not like I had a choice. I have a Y chromosome, for fuck's sake. She was trying to kill me."

Damn, his sister had an arm too. She winged the ball all the way to home plate.

"Were they perfect handfuls? I'd guess a solid D cup at the least." Arne laughed. "Stop growling at me, I'm just giving you shit." Christ, he did growl all the time. Why hadn't anyone mentioned it to him before? "Dane, you've got to cut yourself some slack. This has been the girl of your fantasies since puberty. Of course you're going to stare at her tits if given the opportunity."

Dane stood silently looking over at the stands full of boys watching the girls practice.

"Hey, do you know which one of those little shits has been talking up our sister?" he asked Arne motioning with his head to the stands. Arne hopped off the tailgate and took a step forward so he could look past Dane.

"No, but I'll find out. If he makes one wrong move, we'll bury him," Arne said with a snarl. Dane knew he meant it literally. They had plenty of property to make someone disappear. "Here she comes," he added, nodding toward the dugout gate.

"Hi, Dane. Hi, Arne," several of the girls squealed. Dane ignored them, but he knew Arne could never resist.

"Hey, ladies."

"Get in the truck," Thyra said, walking up to them. "They're jailbait, Arne."

"I was just being friendly," he argued.

"Point out the boy," Dane growled, looking over her head.

"Nope, never going to happen." Thyra dumped her bag in the bed before pulling open the truck door. Sliding into the middle, she waited for her brothers to join her.

Dane sighed. He would find out sooner rather than later. He walked around the truck and climbed into the driver's side this time.

"You always sound old," she admonished him. "Always sighing about something."

"Yeah, you wouldn't say that if you heard what he just did at Tani's house," Arne said, climbing in beside her.

"Shut the fuck up. What is wrong with you?" Dane glared at both of them before starting the truck. He often wished he had decided to live somewhere far away so his every humiliation couldn't be relieved in great detail by his siblings.

"It's cool. I'll just ask Tani later," she said.

Dane snarled at Thyra as he started the truck.

"Stop growling!" she and Arne shouted at him.

"Tani," her dad admonished her.

"What?" Scooping out a big spoonful of mac and cheese into his bowl, she set it on the bar. Taking a seat on one of the stools across from her, he shook his head. He popped a big bite into his mouth.

"You need to stop torturing that boy," he said once he swallowed.

"What did I do?" she asked.

"Tani, that boy was so busy staring at you it's a wonder he didn't have a stroke. If you aren't serious about him, you shouldn't bait him like that." He nodded at her chest.

Looking down at her shirt, she realized she just had on a tank top with no bra. She hadn't even thought about it when she saw who was standing at the front door. It's what she always wore when she was done with her day. She felt the red race up into her face now that she was aware of why he was acting so odd.

"Oh," she whispered.

"You need to tell him," Roy said, taking another bite of macaroni.

"What if he judges me like everyone else will?" She pushed the bowl away from her. Suddenly she had lost her appetite. She couldn't survive if all she saw was disgust or disappointment in his eyes. The shock would be hard enough to witness.

"Then he's not worth knowing," her dad said with conviction. He was wrong though. Dane was very much worth knowing.

When her world crashed down around her, she had fled home with her tail between her legs. Her dad would accept her regardless. But what about Dane? Would he feel the same way? In truth, she missed that sweet, shy smile Dane used to greet her with.

She knew he grew up while she had been away. They both had. But was she prepared for what she saw in him now? Gone was the boy who warmed her heart with his unwavering, if misguided, devotion. In his place, had he become a man she could count on? She couldn't bring him down with her.

Could he ever be happy with just a friendship? She had noticed the way he was always hard when she was around. The way he shivered when she touched him. And how he closed his eyes like he was trying to compose himself. Could they survive a friendship, or would their need to be together crush them both?

"I think I'm going to turn in a little early tonight. I'm kind of tired, and I have the early shift tomorrow," Tani said, reaching for her half empty bowl.

"No need to let this go to waste," Roy said, taking it away from her. "I'll take care of the kitchen. You head on to bed." With a kiss to his cheek on the way by, she started down the hall. "Tani." She turned around at his voice. "Tell him. He might just surprise you."

She continued down the hall, deep in thought. She went through the motions of getting ready for bed as a feeling of dread grew inside her. How did you tell someone so good, so noble, that you had a terrible secret? How did you explain why you're carrying the child of a man you can't even remember?

Climbing into bed, Tani pulled the covers up to her chin. She could feel the tears start to burn behind her eyes. She was tired of crying about it. She had been on her way home from a meeting with her science club students on a Friday night. She decided to stop in at one of the many bars in the tourist district.

Deciding to just have one drink, she almost missed the cute guy smiling at her from across the bar. She thought he was cute, anyway, what she could remember of him. Next thing she knew, he was setting a fresh drink down in front of her. They chatted for a few minutes before she began to feel woozy.

The next morning, she had done everything they said she was supposed to do. She went to the hospital where she was examined and evidence was collected. She spoke to police officers before returning to her apartment. She locked herself inside. The fog she was surviving in lifted, crushing her under the reality of what had happened. For a month she was haunted by nightmares and guilt. Then a pregnancy test came up positive.

Shoring up her resolve, she packed up her apartment, resigned her position, and moved home to the one man in her life she could count on to help her. Her father had taken her in without a second thought.

She got a job at the diner she worked at in high school, kept her head down, turned down all offers of dating, and squirreled her money away to pay for the baby when it arrived.

Tani rubbed her belly with a smile. No matter how it was brought into her life, her baby would never know anything but unconditional love. Today was the first day she had dared to let herself relax again. To laugh as Dane rolled his eyes at her over his siblings squabbling as if she was the only one in on the joke.

For the first time since that night two months ago, she had allowed herself to wish the man in front of her would come closer. She knew she was being selfish. Was it wrong to enjoy feeling adored for just a little while longer? She closed her eyes and dreamed of blond hair and mysterious tattoos and eyes so blue they looked right into your soul.

THE ALARM RANG at five in the morning. Tani could just make it to the diner in time to help prepare for the breakfast crowd. She had figured out early that if she ate breakfast in stages as she got ready in the morning, she could stave off her morning sickness. Dragging into the kitchen, she popped a decaf coffee pod into the coffee maker. She didn't care what the ads said, coffee without caffeine sucked.

"Good morning," Roy said, stopping on his way to the toaster to give her a peck on the cheek. Pulling out two English muffins, he popped them in the toaster before retrieving ham and cheese slices out of the refrigerator. "How are you feeling this morning?"

"Better after a breakfast sandwich, I'm sure," she said, walking back toward her bedroom. She washed her face, pulled on her jeans and a 'Donna's' T-shirt. Roy appeared at her door with her sandwich. "Thanks, Dad." He smiled at her before turning back toward the kitchen.

Even though he didn't have to go to work until eight, he never failed to get up with her to make a quick breakfast. She took a bite of her sandwich and moaned. How did he always get the cheese to melt perfectly?

"When will you be home?" Roy asked as she walked back into the kitchen.

"I should be done at two if nothing changes. I'll let you know if it does." She just had to brush her teeth to be ready. Learning how to put on her makeup while eating breakfast with the other hand was a skill she learned early. Checking her watch, she decided to walk the half dozen blocks since she was running early. She could always catch a ride home if she was tired after her shift.

"I'm heading out. I'll see you tonight." With a wave, she pushed through the front door. She had almost made it to the front door of the diner when she heard a deep voice behind her.

"What time breakfast?" Spinning around, she found the large man from yesterday.

"Oh," she said, surprised. Trying to give him a wide berth while not coming off as rude, she answered. "Sorry, you surprised me. We open for breakfast at six, which is in about half an hour."

"Okay. I come at six," he said in heavily accented English. He definitely sounded Russian or something similar. Standing just a few feet away, she felt a small shiver of fear race through her body. He was well over even Erik's six foot six frame. He had arms the size of tree trunks and a continence even more stoic than Dane's. That was no reason to be afraid of him, she chastised herself. He had done nothing more than ask her when they opened.

"Great, I'll see you then." With a smile, she quickly unlocked the door and slipped inside. Once it was securely locked behind her, she let out a breath.

"You okay?" Donna asked, peering over the counter.

"Yeah, I'm good. That big guy from yesterday just startled me. He asked what time we open." Pushing away from the door, she walked into the kitchen to clock in.

The next half hour, she busied herself helping chop vegetables, mix batter, and anything else Donna needed help with. They were soon joined by Haley, the grill cook. She called out a greeting to Tani as she strapped on her apron. When everything was ready, Donna unlocked the door.

The first group in the door was a group of old retired farmers. She guessed they had gotten so used to rising at dawn, they continued even now. They all asked about Roy. She had automatically grabbed the pot of coffee and filled their cups as they sat down. There would be more drift in over the next couple of hours, so they always took one of the bigger tables. She didn't mind, they ordered breakfast and left a nice tip behind.

Next to show up were the younger guys to grab something to eat before heading off to work. She had almost forgotten the giant from this morning when she saw him duck in under the doorframe. With a nod at her, he found a small table in the corner and sank down stiffly. She gave him a moment to look at the menu before approaching the table.

"Hey, you made it. What can I get you?" He stared blankly at the menu before closing it. It occurred to her that he might not be able to read English based on his limited vocabulary. "Donna makes a pretty good three-egg omelet," she said.

"Yes, eggs," he answered, looking at her. He was so tall that, even seated, they were almost eye to eye.

"What would you like in it? Ham, sausage, cheese?"

"All," he answered, his gaze never leaving her. She felt the hair on the back of her neck rise. His stare wasn't like when Dane stared at her. Dane watched her like his very being was wrapped in her happiness. This felt more like a predator sizing up his prey.

With a mental shake, she put on her best smile. He had done nothing to deserve her apprehension.

"Fully loaded, a man after my own heart. I'll take care of it." With another smile, she turned to walk into the kitchen. "Hey Haley, I need a fully loaded omelet, hash browns, biscuits, and throw on some gravy. I have a feeling that guy needs a lot to fill up."

"He's definitely bigger than even your boyfriend," Haley said, looking over at his table.

"Dane's not my boyfriend," Tani said, picking up the fresh pot of coffee.

"Never mentioned his name," Haley said with a grin. She began cracking fresh eggs in a bowl.

With a roll of her eyes, Tani walked off to refill the coffee at her other tables. She visited with the locals as she worked her way around until she was back to the giant. "Your breakfast should be out in just a minute." She didn't know how much he understood, but he nodded just the same without taking his eyes off her.

"Tani, orders." She breathed a sigh of relief as she walked back to the kitchen to take the plates from Haley. She delivered them to a table of four before bringing his loaded plate to him.

"I'll be right back with your biscuits." Crossing back to the kitchen, she snatched up the extra plate.

"What's this?" he asked, poking his fork at the plate.

"It's gravy. We put it on almost everything in the south. It's best on biscuits, though, trust me."

Using his fork, he cut a small piece and put it in his mouth. When she turned to check her other tables, he reached out, grabbing her wrist. With a gasp, she spun back to him.

"You make gravy?" She managed to gently pull her hand away from him.

"I can," she answered, trying to make light of the incident. "But not as good as Haley."

"Hey, Tani. Everything okay?" one of the old farmers asked her. She noticed most of the easy conversation in the diner had stopped.

"Oh, yes, I'm good. We were just discussing the gravy prowess of Haley." With an unsteady smile, she returned to the kitchen and busied herself with making a fresh pot of coffee.

She managed to be in the walk-in cooler when he paid out. She stuck her head out just in time to see him bump into Dane coming through the door. She watched as the two men sized each other up briefly before the big man continued on.

"Hey, Dane. What's your pop up to?" one of the men greeted him as he stopped at the larger table to say hello.

"Same as always," he answered. He glanced around the diner until his eyes landed on her. His gentle smile warmed her all the way from her hair to her toes. "Hi," he said, taking a seat at the bar. "I have to run to Hugo for parts, so I thought I would stop for some of Haley's biscuits on the way."

"Well, you, sir, have come to the right place. Coffee?" Tani asked.

"Please," he said. She could feel him watching her as she turned to pour his coffee. Unlike the man earlier, it sent a shiver of thrill down her spine. "How late do you work today?"

Setting his coffee down in front of him, she leaned on the bar.

"I'm supposed to be done at two. Donna told me that Karla's kid wasn't feeling well this morning, though. I'm waiting to see if I need to cover her shift too. I don't mind, it gives me an extra day off."

"Let me know, and I'll come help you fill shakers again. I have the dubious honor of bringing Thyra to practice today. Thanks for giving her that idea, by the way." Dane scowled at her. "It's fine. It'll just give me a chance to hunt down the little shit talking her up."

"Dane, leave her alone. She's not a little girl anymore."

Haley set his breakfast in front of him.

"I know. That's why no man comes near my sister until she's at least thirty." He popped a bite of biscuit into his mouth. She listened to a deep growl bubble up from somewhere deep inside him. "These are really good, Haley."

"Thank you?" Haley said.

"How about you text me either way," he continued. "If you get off at two, I'll take you for a slushie after dropping Thyra at practice. You still drink slushies? The sketchy convenience store north of town got a machine."

Dane finished slopping up the remaining gravy with his last bite of biscuit. She watched in fascination as his Adam's apple bobbed with each swallow. How was it possible to even swallow sexy?

"I still drink slushies," she answered.

"Then it's a non-date date." Tossing a couple of dollars

on the counter, Dane stood. He placed his cap back on his head. "I'll see you tonight."

Turning, all three women watched him walk out the door. Truth be told, Tani was pretty sure everyone in the diner took a moment to watch that poetry in motion.

"What the heck was that?" Haley exclaimed, staring at Tani.

"What do you mean?"

"Tani, I've been working here since he came home from college. That was more than I've heard him say in the entire three years he's been back."

"I've known him his whole life, and I don't think I've heard him talk that much," Donna chipped in. "Even when Arne is with him, he just grunts a response while Arne talks. That crush he's had on you for so long must be back with a vengeance." Donna shook her head and turned to get more tomatoes from the cooler.

"Oh," was all Tani could think to say. Thinking back, she did remember that he had always been quiet. He would share something he thought was funny from school occasionally, but he had never been one of those kids who rambled on. Usually he was content to just sip on his Coke and wait for Roar to come pick him up after practice.

"Tani, if we're done with the Hallmark moment, can we get a refill?"

She felt the red creep up her neck as she carried the coffee pot toward the table of old farmers.

"Sorry," she mumbled, making her way to the rest of her tables. She couldn't seem to hide the smile that crossed her face though. It didn't matter, she had an evening with Dane to look forward to again tonight.

When two o'clock rolled around with Karla showing up as scheduled, Tani couldn't get out of there fast enough.

She texted Dane after clocking out telling him she was off the rest of the day. He texted back a few minutes later telling her he would be by later to pick her up.

She walked out of the diner. With her hands on her back, she stretched to work the kinks out. She was relieved to see there wasn't a seven-foot giant waiting to scare her in the parking lot. She wished she could figure out what exactly made her so wary around the stranger. It was just this feeling at the base of her spine telling her something wasn't right.

It took her a little longer to walk home, but she was too excited to feel tired. She took a long shower to wash the diner smell off. She wrapped her long hair in a towel to let it dry while she dressed.

What does one wear to a slushie invite with a friend? A ball gown seemed too formal, but her fuzzy pajamas seemed a little too casual.

With a laugh, she settled on a pair of modest shorts and a long-sleeve checked shirt. It was still a little cool in the evenings. If she was going to the trouble of shaving her legs, she fully intended to show them off. Her tennis shoes would have to do, though. She needed a full pedicure before she was sandal ready. She slid on a necklace before checking herself in the mirror. Good enough.

She had naturally thick wavy hair, so she decided to go with what nature gave her tonight. Taking it out of the towel, she scrunched it with her hands. Pulling it back when it was dry, she clipped it in place with a simple clip she picked up at one of the festivals. A little makeup and the addition of a few bangles on her arm made her ready when Dane arrived.

Walking into the living room, she met her dad coming in the front door. He took one look at her before letting out a low whistle. Feeling truly pretty for the first time in a long time, she indulged herself by turning in a circle for him.

"Where are you going looking so cute?" Only her dad would think being called 'cute' was a compliment.

"I'm just grabbing a slushie with Dane. He has to bring his sister to softball practice. We thought we would have a slushie while he was waiting for her. Just as friends, Dad." Roy looked at her with a raised eyebrow. She was saved from hearing another lecture, though, by a knock at the door. "Be nice, he's here."

"Hey, he minds his manners, I'll mind mine." With a kiss on his cheek, Tani turned toward the door.

CHAPTER

SEVEN

Dane stood at her door, positive he was suffering from a heart attack. His heart was racing, his palms were sweaty, and he had absolutely no spit left in his mouth. Why was he capable of having a perfectly civilized conversation with Tani at the diner, but was about to completely lose his shit picking her up for a fucking slushie?

Of course, just the thought of her had him growing hard. He wasn't ever going to make it out of the house with her in this state if her father was home. How often could a father be expected to allow his daughter to be in the presence of a man with a perpetual hard-on? If it was his daughter, the answer would be never.

"Hi," Tani said, opening the door. Dane took a long look from her shining dark hair to her Keds that matched her shirt perfectly. Christ, those legs should be outlawed.

"Wow," he whispered. "You look too beautiful for a slushie." The moment the words left his mouth, he knew he sounded like an idiot. It was the truth. She was stunning.

"Thank you," she answered with the most perfect smile

he had ever witnessed. How was she still single? A throat being loudly cleared behind her broke them out of their reverie. "Please, come in while I grab my purse."

Stepping into her house, he was met again by her father. This time Dane was hell-bent on keeping his eyes above her shoulders at all times. He reached out to shake the man's hand.

"Tani tells me you're going for slushies."

"Yes, sir. I just dropped my sister at practice. Figured we could get something to drink, then watch practice for a while. Thyra will be excited to see Tani there. I'll bring her back around nine after practice." He wasn't sure why he was describing their plans like he was in high school. The man did seem to relax a little, though.

"That sounds like a nice evening," Roy said. "I think I'm going to sit right here and catch the game tonight. You played baseball, didn't you?"

"Yes, sir. We all did through college except for my youngest brother. He could have gone either way or with basketball even, but the football coaches were drooling over him."

If Tani didn't find her purse soon, he would explode. He didn't do small talk with anyone, much less the father of someone he had fallen in love with years ago. Yes, he knew it was stupid to love someone he couldn't even get a date with. He couldn't help how he felt.

"Sorry," Tani said, walking out of the back. "I decided I didn't like how my other purse looked with this blouse, so I changed it out. This one goes much better."

"I'm sure whatever you carry will still look stunning next to you." Holy fuck, where had that sentence come from? It actually sounded civil. "We should go. It was nice seeing you again, Mr. Johnston. Enjoy your game." Placing his hand on Tani's back, he fought the shiver touching her always produced. He held the door open so she could go out first.

"Son," he heard her dad say as he started to follow her out the door.

"Yes, sir."

"Keep it PG."

With a nod, Dane ducked out. He guessed a warning was better than a shotgun blast to the face. Though they weren't fifteen anymore.

"What did he say?" Tani asked as they walked to his truck.

"Nothing. Come on, you look like you need a slushie." Taking her hand in his, Dane couldn't stop the shiver this time. At least her father's warning had done something to help tame his erection. He opened her door and helped her inside. Reaching over, he hooked her seat belt before closing the door. He stopped when he saw her grinning at him.

"What? What did I do?"

"You hooked my seat belt. We're going like two miles away. No one hooks their seat belt here."

"Well, I want you to be safe," he said with a scowl. Starting the truck, he pulled away from her house. "Have I told you how nice you look?"

"You've mentioned it, yes. But thank you again. You look very nice too."

"I couldn't exactly show up in clothes covered in grease."

"I'm willing to wager you did more than just change your clothes. Let's see," she said, leveling him with an appraising look. "You shaved your beard."

"It was getting a little scraggly for my taste."

"You washed your hair." Leaning toward him, she sniffed at his shirt. "Mmm, you smell like soap and deodorant. Old Spice? How many shirts did you try before settling on that one?"

He rolled his eyes. "That's a thing women do." When she remained silent, he finally relented. "Four. Arne gave me hell."

"I like this one. The color makes your eyes stand out even more than they already do." When he bought the button-down shirt in navy, he simply liked the color. Now he guessed it was elevated to the top of his wear list.

"I've had people tell me they make me look cold. My eyes, I mean." What would he do if she agreed? He knew he wasn't the warmest person around. That was fine for everyone else. He couldn't bear for Tani to see him as uncaring.

"I don't think so. I think it's the opposite. They're so full of power and strength. When you look at me, I feel as if nothing bad could ever touch me."

They pulled up outside the convenience store, and Dane turned off the truck. He looked at her. God, he loved her. But she said no, so he would learn how to shove those feelings down where she would never see them. He closed his eyes for a moment to refocus. Opening them again, he smiled at her.

"Let's get that slushie." Stepping out of the truck, Dane took a minute just to breathe. This was fucking torture. Why did he keep doing this? Meeting Tani at the front of his truck, he scowled down at her. "I was coming to open your door."

"If it's not a date, you're not obligated to open my door," she answered.

With a growl, he took her hand and led her into the

store. "I'm paying for your slushie," he said as he walked past the register toward the back. She laughed letting him pull her grumpily to the slushie machine. "It looks like our choices are Coke or Big Red."

"Wow, ooh this is a tough one. So many, many choices." He rolled his eyes at her teasing. He crossed his arms to wait while she did some eenie-meenie-miney-mo thing. "Fine, Big Red."

Crowding her as he reached around her for a cup, he gave her his best smirk. He wasn't ready, however, for the small gasp she made as he brushed against her. He took a quick step back. Facing the machine, he filled her cup with the frozen bright red drink to the top.

"Here you go. Do you want a snack?" he asked, filling his own cup with the Coke flavor.

"How about a bag of popcorn to share?"

"Perfect." He grabbed a bag of popcorn and followed her to the counter. Setting his drink down next to hers, he reached into his pocket to pull out his wallet.

"Hey, Tani," the punk behind the counter said with a leer.

Raising up to his full height behind her, Dane glared at the kid with a snarl. The punkass took one look at him before quickly ringing up their purchase. After picking up the money Dane tossed on the counter, the kid took one more quick look before he took a step back, his eyes wide.

"Oh, good Jesus, Dane," Tani said, turning around suddenly. "Come on. Bye, Chad." She took Dane's hand and pulled him out of the store. "That poor kid looked like he was about to be eviscerated. It's a wonder you didn't make him wet his pants."

"If he leers at you again, I will eviscerate him." Closing

her door, he scowled once more into the store before climbing into the truck.

"Dane, he wasn't leering. He said hello. Are you going to threaten anyone who says hello? I'm twice his age."

"He was staring at your tits." He flinched as the words came out knowing immediately that was the wrong thing to say. He looked over at her slowly. Her eyes were on fire as she glared at him.

"So you can stare at my tits, but God forbid anyone else do it? You don't have that right either."

"Then don't put them on parade." Yeah, that made it much better. Why couldn't someone just come along with a bat and knock him out? Maybe her father should have shot him in the face. Fuck knew he deserved it. Tani stared at the side of his head as she slowly picked up her cup taking a long pull of the slushie.

"Can we start over?" he asked.

"Nope."

"Can I apologize?"

"That would be a start," she answered, taking another pull.

"Okay." Turning, he leveled his most sincere gaze on her. "I'm sorry your tits are so perfect that just a glimpse of your hard nipples through your tank top is like watching a miracle happen. I apologize for not wanting any other guy to jack off tonight to that vision the way I will. Most men can't come back from that experience."

"Oh my god, Dane," Tani said with a snort of laughter. "You almost made Big Red come out my nose. What kind of apology is that?"

"An honest one?" he answered.

"Where did that mouth come from?"

He watched as she tried hard not to laugh. "It showed

up about the time you did. The jacking off, though, that's been around since junior high."

"Oh my god," she said again, turning a deep shade of red. Where *did* his mouth come from? Never, in a million years, should he be saying that to a woman. Especially not to Tani. "Go. Drive. I need some fresh air." Tani waved at the front windshield as she rolled down her window.

Starting the truck, he shifted into drive and pulled away from the store. Arriving a few minutes later at the softball fields, he backed the truck up against the fence. Shutting off the truck, he reached over, catching her arm before she could get out.

"I need to apologize now for my apology," he said.

"Nope. Don't you dare. That one I'll remember the rest of my life. You should work for Hallmark." With a laugh, she hopped out. Meeting him at the back of the truck, she handed him the popcorn.

"This is always the most awkward part. I'm too short to just glide onto the back of a tailgate." Stepping in front of her, Dane wrapped his hands around her hips.

"On the count of three, jump. One. Two. Three." Dane gently lifted her onto the tailgate when she jumped. He had to consciously release her hips when all he wanted to do was lever himself closer between her legs. "Good?" he asked, stepping back instead.

"Good. Thanks." Hopping up next to her, he handed her the popcorn. "Which one is Thyra? By the way, did I tell you she asked me if I thought you were gay?" Scooping up a hand full of popcorn, she tossed it into her mouth.

"Seriously?" Dane said, shaking his head. "Why would you want to be anywhere near any of us?"

Tani laughed around her mouth of popcorn.

"Don't worry, I told her you definitely aren't gay. Can I tell you something, and you not make fun of me?"

"I think after that, I don't have any right to make fun of you."

"Don't get me wrong, I love my dad. But it was always just the two of us. Being around your family is this fun cacophony. You're all so full of life."

"We're full of something for sure. You're always welcome at our house." His eyebrows knit together in concern when he saw her look of sadness at his last statement.

"Thank you," she said, looking away. Why did she suddenly seem sad? It was almost a feeling of longing. Putting on a smile, the sadness was gone as quickly as it had come. "Now, which one out there is your sister?"

Pointing Thyra out, their conversation turned to lighter things. She laughed at his stories of growing up in a house full of siblings, and he listened raptly as she shared the local gossip. To have started out so rocky, it had turned into the perfect evening.

When the air turned cool with the setting sun, he pulled out a small blanket he had shoved behind his seat earlier, just in case. He wrapped it around her legs. She pulled one side out, insisting he share it. As hard as he tried to control it, he shivered when she brushed against him. It was like a bolt of electricity hit him every time.

"Tani!" He heard Thyra blast out as she jogged out of the dugout.

Dropping her bag in front of Dane, she pulled Tani into a massive bear hug. Dane managed to shake his head and roll his eyes. It was a feat of multitasking even he was impressed with.

It wasn't lost on Tani either. She smiled over Thyra's

shoulder at him. Every time her face lit up like that, he wanted to drop to his knees and beg her for a chance to prove he was worth her time. Instead, he reached over to thump his sister on the head.

"Oww, Dane," she squealed, spinning around to shove him in the chest. He took a step back, laughing. "Oh my god, are you okay? Did you have a stroke? You're laughing." Pulling her over in a headlock, he rubbed a noogie on the top of her head. "Dane, stop."

He caught Tani laughing so hard tears were forming in her eyes. He loved her like this. He vowed whatever he had to do to keep her laughing, he would do. Even if it meant he had to open up to do it.

"Come on, brat, let's get you home." He turned his sister loose. He tossed her bag in the back. Closing the tailgate, he helped them both into his truck before climbing into the driver's seat. "How was practice?" Thyra was almost vibrating on the seat next to the door.

"He asked me out," she squealed. Oh, fuck no.

"No dating until you're sixteen. You know that's Mom's rule."

"Dane," she moaned, drawing his name out into at least three syllables.

"Let me think about it," Dane said. "No."

"Dane," she whined again. Reaching over Tani, she punched him in the arm. The truck swerved.

"Thyra," he growled, straightening the truck back out. The fact they were only driving about twenty-five miles an hour helped. Still, he had no urge to spend tomorrow morning replacing someone's mailbox. He had left the shredder in pieces all over the shop to get ready in time for his 'date.' He needed to be hunched over working on it first thing in the morning to avoid a lecture on trashing the shop.

Pulling up in front of Tani's house, he climbed out of his seat. He helped her slide out on his side. Taking her hand, he fought to keep the shiver barely noticeable this time.

"I had a really good time tonight," she said when they reached the front porch. "Thanks for the slushie." They stood still for a moment as if waiting for something to happen.

"Kiss her already so she can go inside," Thyra shouted from the truck.

"Thyra," he yelled back. That seemed to be his go to anytime she was around. With a shake of his head, he turned Tani's hand loose. "Good night. I'd better get her home before the neighbors start reporting a disturbance." He walked down her steps.

"I'm closing tomorrow night, if you feel like filling some salt shakers."

With a smile, he turned around. "It's a date," he said with a wink.

"It's not a date," he heard her call behind him with a laugh. Yep, he was going to just keep biding his time until she finally said yes. Climbing back into the truck, they returned Tani's wave before she disappeared inside.

"I like her so much, Dane," Thyra said as he pulled away from the curb.

"I do too, but she's just not interested in me."

Thyra shook her head with a laugh.

"Oh, Dane. She's totally into you. There's just something holding her back from climbing you like a tree."

"Thyra." He didn't disagree, though. He just couldn't figure out what.

EIGHT

After dropping Thyra at his parents' house, Dane drove home. He was met by Arne in the living room as soon as he walked in. He was sprawled on the couch watching a baseball game.

"How was your date?" Arne asked, turning down the game.

Dane ignored the question. Grabbing two beers out of the fridge, he handed one to Arne before flopping down on the other end of the couch.

"Think you could follow me around and hit me in the fucking face every time I open my mouth around her?" he asked.

"Gladly, but what did you say?"

Dane sat in silence, debating how much to share with his younger brother. Was it worth the ribbing he'd have to suffer for the next couple of weeks? Brothers were great for some things, but sharing feelings wasn't one of them. Still, he needed advice, and this was the least of the terrible options.

"I said something about stroking off to thoughts of her tits every night," he mumbled.

"God, that's priceless." Arne laughed, setting his beer down. "It's not like that's a surprise to anyone, though."

"Was to her."

Arne laughed a few more minutes until Dane finally punched him in the arm.

"It's not fucking funny," he growled. "I'm going to bed." Standing, he tossed his bottle in the trash on the way by.

"Try not to be too loud jacking off. I'm trying to finish the game."

"Fuck you," he said over his shoulder. Stripping off his clothes, he quickly brushed his teeth and fell into bed. Rolling over, he checked his phone. No messages. He wouldn't be surprised if Tani blocked his number now. Sure, she had been good-natured about the whole thing. But, in the end, he was worse than most of the other guys around here.

With a sigh, he rolled over and pulled the covers up to his waist. He'd think about it tomorrow. Right now, he needed to lose himself in his dreams for a while. Closing his eyes, he settled in. Now if he could just keep her out of his dreams.

～

"Dude, wake up."

Dane opened his eyes. The clock read two in the morning. Arne crouched next to his bed.

"What are you doing?" he asked.

"Shh, just listen."

Sitting up, Dane tilted his head, trying to hear whatever

had spooked Arne. After a few minutes, he heard it. It sounded like something sniffing around under his window.

"It's probably just a raccoon hunting for something to eat," he groaned, rolling back over in bed. Suddenly a roar loud enough to rattle his window echoed through the room.

Dane jumped up and jerked on his sweatpants. He caught the shotgun Arne tossed him at the door. Snatching up a flashlight, he followed Arne outside. They slid to a stop at the corner of the house. Dane looked around the corner toward his window. Nothing was there.

"Fuck," Arne said from behind him. "You heard that, right? That wasn't just my imagination, was it?"

"No, there was definitely something out here." Dane walked to the window. It had dig marks scored around it larger than he had ever seen. Spinning around, he shut off the flashlight and looked out into the night. His eyesight was better with just the moon illuminating the trees around them. He spotted several large paw prints heading through the trees.

"Come on. The ground is still soft enough for us to track him," he said.

They should take the time to grab more shells for the gun. Going back would lose too much time though. Pushing through the undergrowth, Dane started his slide down the hill to the bottom. Feeling Arne right behind him, he started running as soon as he made it to the bottom of the hill. If they were lucky, they could catch the bear before he made it to the river.

"Dane, look," Arne shouted, pointing past him as they slid to a stop.

Ahead in the moonlight was a large lumbering shape.

Taking aim, Dane squeezed out a shot. It went slightly wide, just missing the beast.

"Fuck," he didn't dare try again without getting closer. He was a good shot, but in the dark from this far, he questioned if the round could even penetrate a bear that size.

They both took back after it. Dane soon pulled ahead of Arne. He had always been the faster brother. Sliding to a stop at the river, he searched the side of the bank for where the bear might have entered the water.

"Over here," he heard Arne yell from down the bank. He started toward him when he saw Arne running across the field. "Dane!" he screamed as he sprinted.

Close on his heels was a massive wild sow. Taking a deep breath, Dane took aim, squeezing the trigger. The sow dropped right as she caught up to Arne. He lowered the gun, looking where he had shot. He knew the sow had gone down, but so apparently had his brother.

"Arne," he yelled, running toward where he had last seen them. Arne made it to his feet about the time Dane reached him. He slung mud from his arms.

"I'm good," Arne said. "I fell in one of those fucking pig holes full of mud."

Dane breathed a sigh of relief. Holding a hand out, he helped Arne out of the hole.

"I'm just glad you're a good shot. I thought she had me for sure. Didn't even see the bitch until she was heading for me."

Taking Arne's mud-covered gun, Dane broke it open. It would need a good cleaning before anyone used it again. He took the live rounds out to reload his gun.

"Clean this before you take it back out. Come on, let's go see if we can pick back up on his trail. Stay with me." He helped Arne brush some more of the mud off before leading the way back to the river.

Carefully approaching the river bank to avoid any more wild hog encounters, he searched until he found where the bear had gone in. After a half hour, both soaking wet, they found where it emerged on the other side. At least Arne wasn't as muddy anymore.

"He's long gone, Dane," Arne said.

They stood on a small hill on the other side of the river looking around. As far as Dane could see, there was no movement other than an occasional cow grazing in the moonlight.

"Yeah. Let's head back."

Dawn was just making itself known when they finally made it to their house. After a quick shower, Dane fell into bed. They would explain to their father why they were late for work later. He was positive it would all still be waiting for them.

He was in a dead sleep when he heard banging on the front door. Rolling over, he tried to ignore it, but it didn't stop.

"What the shit," he growled, rolling out of bed. Finding a fresh pair of sweatpants, he pulled them on as he stumbled toward the door. "Hold the fuck on," he yelled as the pounding started back up. He hoped it wasn't his mom. "What!" he growled, jerking the door open.

Tani felt all the air leave her lungs the second the door was jerked open. She had known who it was by the way he growled about her 'holding the fuck on.' Nothing, however, had prepared her for what now stood in the open doorway.

Dane had on nothing but a pair of sweatpants barely pulled over his hips. His hair was still damp and stuck up in all directions. He was rubbing his eyes like he had just climbed out of bed. In short, he looked like every woman's fantasy.

"Tani?" he asked, staring down at her. His eyebrows creased in confusion. "What are you doing here?" His hand moved down, rubbing his stomach as he squinted at her.

She shivered just thinking of what that stomach would look like under her as she rode him.

"Fuck, I'm sorry. It's cold out here. Come in."

Sure, that's what made her nipples point painfully, the cold.

"I got a text saying to meet here. That it was important. Aren't you usually at work by now?" she asked.

He grunted at her as he walked toward the kitchen.

"What's going on?" Arne asked, yawning from the hallway in his underwear.

"Pants," Dane answered. Placing his hand on Arne's face, he shoved him back into his room. There were a series of thumps that sounded like someone hitting the floor.

"You're a dick," he yelled.

"Why won't this work?" Dane asked.

Tani turned her attention back to Dane. He stood in the kitchen glaring at the coffee machine as if that alone would make it spit out coffee. With a roll of her eyes, she walked into the kitchen. They must have really tied one on to be this wiped out this morning.

Pushing Dane out of the way, she took the pot and filled the machine with water. Arne came staggering back out of his room, in a pair of jeans this time.

"So I have to put on pants, but you can parade around with a full tent?"

All three looked at Dane's crotch. Dane included. Arne was right, those gray sweatpants left nothing to the imagination. She didn't need Arne pointing it out though. She was enjoying the show.

"I'll be back," Dane said, walking toward his bedroom.

Tani wanted to scream "no" at the top of her lungs but decided that would do nothing to help.

"Tani?" Arne asked like she had just materialized in front of him. Handing him a fresh cup of coffee, she pointed to one of the stools at the bar.

"Arne, what did y'all do last night?" Leaning over the bar, she sniffed him for alcohol.

"Are you smelling Arne?" Dane asked with a growl at his brother.

"Dude, don't get pissed at me. I was just sitting here," Arne answered.

Tani took in Dane's new look. He had slipped on a pair of jeans, not bothering to button the top. He hadn't bothered with anything else either. She took a few minutes trying to determine if there was underwear under the jeans.

"My eyes are up here," he said.

Tani shook herself from her daydream. She could feel her face grow hot as the men chuckled at each other. Straightening her shoulders, she looked up to find a soft smile on Dane's face. He truly was beautiful when he let his guard down.

"Thyra sent me a text saying I was to meet her here this morning about an urgent matter. I was afraid something had happened to you."

She handed Dane a cup of coffee and followed both men to the couch. They groaned at the mention of their sister.

"Now, I think she might have been right," she added.

She was about to ask what they had been doing when Thyra burst through the door.

"Oh, good. You're all here," Thyra said, flopping down in a chair next to the couch. "I have the answer to the problem of how Thyra gets to date the hot new baseball player."

With a moan worthy of an Oscar, Dane set his cup down. He rolled over on the couch until he was lying with his head on Tani's leg. Looking down at him, she had a sudden panic attack. What the hell did she do with her hand? Did it go on the back of the couch? She didn't think she was tall enough to pull that off comfortably. Did she place it on his shoulder or side?

She could hear Thrya droning on about the cute kid at school while she wrestled with what could be one of the greatest decisions of all womankind. Out of the corner of her eye, she saw Arne stretch out on the floor.

Finally, she decided she would just kind of rest her arm on his side nonchalantly. Like it was no big deal. She watched as his big body shivered as her arm settled on him. His hair looked so soft. Would it be weird if she ran her hands through it?

"Tani, are you listening?" Thyra asked.

"Absolutely. Cute guy, date, got it. Go on."

She heard a soft growl. Without realizing it, she was playing with Dane's hair. It was hard to fake interest in Thyra's plan with him so close.

They all turned to look at Arne when an impressive snore rumbled out of his chest.

"Damn, I needed him to take me to school," Thyra complained.

"I tell you what," Tani offered. "You find a blanket for

Arne. I'll cover Dane, and we can discuss this while I drive you to school. Deal?"

She wished she could sit here all day. With a sigh, she thought about how life would have been if she had connected with Dane when he was in college. She might be doing this every evening while they watched TV together in their home. But it was no use wishing for things that could never be. He snarled when she tried to ease out from under him.

"I just dragged Arne's blanket off his bed." Throwing it over him, Thyra turned expectantly at Tani. She tried to work herself out from under Dane's head again, getting the same result. Thyra just shook her head slowly.

"Dane, be nice," Tani said, managing to free herself this time. Pulling the blanket off the couch, she tucked it in around him. His breathing evened back out.

"What do you think they did last night? Dane was fine when he dropped me off," Thyra asked.

"No idea. Come on." Quietly leaving the house, they climbed into Tani's car. "So tell me your plan."

Thyra did, talking non-stop the entire way into town. She laid out a plan of going on a date at the diner where Dane could sit at the bar. That way, if asked, they could claim she was there with Dane. Tani, of course, would be there too. If it went well, Dane could convince her mother that she was old enough to date. Tani couldn't wait to hear what Dane thought of this plan.

"So, you'll run it by Dane?" Thyra asked when they pulled up to her school.

"Why? Dane's your brother."

"Yeah, but he'll do anything you want him to do." Tani laughed. She was positive Dane didn't do what anybody wanted. "Please?" Thyra whined as she climbed out of the car.

"Fine," Tani said, laughing. "But I'm not responsible if he says no."

"Like he would ever say no to you," Thyra answered with a grin. "This is a done deal. Thanks, Tani." She slammed the door and jogged away to catch up with a group of giggling girls.

Checking her watch, Tani decided she had time for a nap before heading to work. She'd find out from Dane later what they had been up to last night. She closed her eyes for a moment. Her mind conjured up the image of Dane opening the door this morning.

Jerking upright when there was a polite honk from behind her, Tani gave an apology wave before driving away from the school.

She found her father had already left for work when she arrived home. He hadn't said a word when she explained she was heading to Dane's house that morning.

He had always liked the Ulvmands. If anyone else had openly gawked at her half-clothed body like Dane had, she knew without a doubt her dad would have decked him. But Dane had always been respectful of her father. Sure, Roy had threatened him. But she heard him chuckling about it later when he thought she had gone to bed.

Slipping off her jeans, she crawled into bed in her T-shirt. Trying to get comfortable, she wiggled around until she finally realized the problem. Sitting up, she worked her bra out from under her shirt flinging it across the room. Ahh, that was much better.

She drifted off with images of Dane racing through her mind. How his hair felt as she ran her hands through it.

How his big body settled under her hands. How it felt like she had tamed a beast; raw power hers to control.

She was woken up several hours later by her phone. She groped for it on her nightstand, knocking it on to the floor. Trying not to fall, she leaned over the edge until she snagged it. Staring at the screen, she pulled up the message with a grin.

Dane: Did you come to the house this morning?

Tani: I did. Thyra asked me to meet her there.

Dane: Did I answer the door?

Tani: Yes.

Dane: Did I have on pants? The reason I ask is that Arne remembers someone with no pants, and he's arguing it was me.

Tani: No such luck. It was Arne.

Dane: Thanks. I just made us some slushie money.

Tani: You were just sporting a tent.

Tani burst out laughing when Dane sent back an emoji face with big eyes and red cheeks. Throwing caution to the wind, she answered him with the eggplant, eyes and thumbs up. She started to worry when he didn't respond. Finally, she heard her phone ping.

Dane: Sorry. Arne grabbed my phone so he could read it. I had to chase him down.

Tani: Is he okay?

Dane: He'll mend. I'm sitting on him in the drive-way. I've got to go, Dad just spotted us. I'll see you tonight.

Tani: Have a good day at work.

With a laugh, she rolled onto her back. This wasn't the same Dane that growled at kids behind the counter. Could everyone be right? Was she really the only one that Dane opened up to?

It made her keeping the pregnancy from him even more cowardly. Tonight, she would simply have to tell him. It would hurt to watch him walk away, but it had to be done. She got out of bed. It was time to get ready for what she assumed would be a long shift.

"You smell nice. Do you have a date tonight?" Dane's mother asked. She stepped around him to finish the salad for dinner. He had finished work, ran home to clean up, and happened to show up in time for dinner ostensibly picking up Thyra for practice. Arne finished in time to show up also. He snorted at their mother's question.

"Like Dane dates." He snatched a piece of carrot from her on the way by. "He just stalks."

"Arne, be nice to your brother," she said, slapping his hand the second time he reached into the bowl. She had made a pot of chicken and dumplings they had both smelled from the yard earlier.

They had debated texting Roar. It was his favorite. They quickly vetoed the idea, worried there wouldn't be enough. Sure, they were brothers, but when it came to their mom's cooking it was every man for himself.

"Did you have any luck picking back up the bear's trail this afternoon?" Sten asked when they sat at the table. Arne went back out when they got to work to see if he could track where it went. "I'm worried it's found a den somewhere. How much damage did it do to the house?"

"It's not too bad, just some minor damage I think we can fix," Arne answered. "I don't know where that bear went. According to Cody, there should be scat or something we can track. He said there haven't been any other reports in the county."

"Which means he's probably staying around here," Sten said.

"Afraid so."

They ate most of their meal in conversation about the bear until it was almost time for Dane and Thyra to leave.

"Arne, do you have a shiner?" his father asked.

"Yes," Arne growled, looking over at Dane. Dane rolled his eyes. He hadn't thumped him that hard. He actually got it when he was tackled in the driveway wrestling over the phone. Scowling, Sten looked at Dane.

"Dane, why does your brother have a shiner?" Sten asked.

"Maybe because he's a douchebag?" When his dad growled, Dane quickly stood. "I know, I'm going. Come on, Thyra. Thanks for dinner, Mom." He noticed she was trying to hide a smile behind her napkin.

"Cocksucker," he mumbled at his brother, slapping the back of his head. "Go, Thyra," he said, pushing her toward the door. They laughed as they ran outside. Jumping in the front seat of Dane's truck, they slung gravel as he pushed on the accelerator.

"Oh my god, Dane. Dad's going to kill you," Thyra said, wiping the tears from her face from laughing so hard.

"So worth it."

"You're just lucky you're Mom's favorite." He grinned at

her as they pulled onto the main road. She studied him with a smile.

"What?" he finally asked.

"I like you like this. I think Tani's good for you."

He thought about it for a moment before looking back over at her with a smile.

"You know what? I think you're right."

Half an hour later they pulled up to the softball fields. "I'll be back to get you. Stay away from the boys." She rolled her eyes at him.

Backing out, he headed over to the diner. He sat watching Tani through the window in front. She worked around the tables of customers smiling as she chatted. He could watch her all night. She saw him and waved him inside.

"Come on, I saved you something," she said when he walked through the door. Taking his hand, she pulled him toward the counter. She disappeared inside the cooler. When she returned shortly she presented him with a piece of chocolate pie. "Last piece. I had to hide it behind the butter."

Taking a bite, he moaned. Donna always made homemade pies when she had time. Usually it was impossible to get a piece if you didn't come for lunch.

"You're amazing. I got kicked out of the house before dessert tonight," he said between bites.

"What did you do?" Tani asked.

"I called Arne a douchebag." He lowered his voice so he didn't offend anybody enjoying their meal. Freya had drummed manners into all of her children from an early age. Dane tried not to offend anyone most of the time. It was certainly more than could be said for a lot of the men who came in here. The women, too, for that matter.

"In front of your mom? Tell me you didn't." When he just nodded, she swatted at his arm with the towel she was holding. "I'm going to wash your mouth out with soap myself."

"Or you could just spank me," he said with a wink. They both looked behind her to the kitchen when they heard a metal bowl hit the ground. Donna was standing next to the grill with her mouth open. "Just kidding," he said, louder this time.

"Dane, behave. You'll give Donna a heart attack. I have to get back to work." He watched her fill his coffee before walking back toward the remaining tables.

He noticed she patted on shoulders, laughed at jokes, and caught up with the regulars. Until she approached the table in the back with the large man he had run into earlier. The man watched her move through the tables also, but like a predator. Tani reached over to refill his cup. The man leveled his gaze on Dane like he was establishing his territory.

"Hey, Donna. What's the story there?" Dane asked.

"I don't know, some drifter I guess. He hasn't done anything for me to ban him from coming in, but he gives me the creeps just the same."

Dane continued to watch him even after Tani moved on to another table. Finishing his pie, he waited until the man came to the register to pay his bill.

"Haven't seen you before. You from around here?" Dane asked. The man ignored him at first waiting for Donna to walk to the register. He had to be even larger than Erik. That was saying a lot. Erik topped out at six foot six inches.

"No," the man finally growled.

"What brings you to town?" The man paid his bill and

left a nice tip for Tani. Turning slowly, he scowled at Dane for a moment before walking toward the door.

"None of your business." Dane didn't think his accent was Russian, but then he wasn't a linguistics expert. Ducking through the door, the man walked off into the evening with no apparent direction in mind.

"Dane," Tani said softly, standing next to him.

"What?" he asked.

"You're growling." Shit, this growling thing had grown completely out of control. Had he always done it, or had it started when she moved back to town? He made a mental note to ask Arne later.

"Come on, Donna said I could take off a little early." With a smile, she tugged him off the stool. "She's going to close up for me. Let's go catch the end of Thyra's practice." He let her pull him through the diner until they were at his truck.

It took less than five minutes to reach the softball fields. After backing up in his favorite spot by the fence, Dane lifted Tani back onto the tailgate to watch. They only had about half an hour left until practice would finish for the night.

"What do you know about the big guy at the diner tonight?" Dane asked, staring out at the field.

"Not much. I don't think he speaks enough English to chat. He doesn't seem like the type to shoot the bull anyway."

"I don't like him."

"No kidding. I swear you came close to bearing your fangs at him. I don't remember you growling all the time as a kid." Dane scowled, thinking about their small run-in. "So what did you and Arne do last night to be so out of it this morning?" Tani asked, changing the subject.

"Yeah, so about this morning. Sorry about that. We usually have better manners. We were out half the night chasing the bear I told you about. He came sniffing around the house last night."

Dane smiled, watching Thyra's second swing fly into the outfield. The team was spending the end of practice focusing on batting. At this rate, he was positive she would follow in her brothers' footsteps as a college athlete.

"Did you find him?"

"What?" he asked, turning back to Tani. "Oh, no." He told her about hunting the giant bear across the ranch, downplaying how much danger they had been in.

Instead, he focused on Arne's escape from the pig. When he was done, he watched as she threw her head back in laughter. He would never get enough of watching her. Her laugh became contagious, raising a chuckle out of him. She was just so damn gorgeous.

Before Dane could stop himself, he leaned over and pressed his lips to hers. She should have slapped him. Instead, he felt her wrap her hand in the material of his shirt. She pulled him closer.

His hand raked into her long, lush hair. He angled her head slightly to the side as his tongue asked permission to taste her. When her mouth opened, he felt more than heard his growl as he devoured it.

He was losing himself in her. It was everything he dreamed about staring at her for years over the diner counter. He could stay like this forever, needed to. He felt like his body was on fire even though a shiver racked through him.

Then he was falling. Not figuratively; he was literally falling off the side of the tailgate. He tried to catch himself on the way down, but missed. He hit the ground with a thud. Looking up, he found Tani staring down at him. She had climbed off the tailgate and looked angry.

"Why would you do that?" she asked.

He scrambled off the ground, but she was gone. Panicking, he looked around. He caught her back as she quickly crossed the street toward her house.

"Tani, wait." Limping to the front of the truck, he called after her until she was gone. He knew he would have to wait for his sister before he could go after her. With practice letting out, it wouldn't take long for the parking lot to clear out, and he couldn't leave Thyra here by herself.

He stared back down the street where Tani had disappeared. What happened? Sure, he was in the wrong for kissing her. She made it plain she wasn't interested in anything more than friendship. But she'd pulled him to her like she wanted to be kissed by him as much as he wanted to kiss her. All she had to do was pull away, and he would have stopped.

"What happened?" Thyra asked, throwing her bag into the back of the truck. She watched him limp to the driver's door.

"Get in," he growled.

Thyra was smart enough to know not to argue. He glared out the front windshield until she was settled in the cab. Damn, his hip hurt. He assumed the rumors about the scene he caused were already circulating around town. He didn't care, he just needed to make sure Tani was okay.

"Wait here," he said when they pulled up outside the Johnstons' home. Climbing gingerly out of the cab, Dane walked to the front door. He knocked three times before her father pulled open the door.

"She's gone to bed," he said before Dane could speak.

"Maybe wait until tomorrow to talk to her." With that he closed the door again. Dane limped back to the truck.

They were halfway home before Thyra spoke. "What happened?"

"Just let it go," He really didn't need to air his sex life or, more accurately, lack of sex life, to his little sister. This was something he would have to figure out on his own.

She must have sensed something was going on though. She didn't say another word the rest of the ride. She did take his hand where it was laying on the center console however. The little punk still got to him. He knew without a doubt that the first guy who tried to force a move on her like he had tonight, would die a bloody death.

"Good night, Dane," she said when they pulled up outside the main house.

"Night, Queen." He never missed getting an eye roll when he called her that, and this time was no different. She was named after the first queen of Denmark. Queen Thyra had her praises immortalized on the Jelling Stones in 965. A fact her brothers never let her forget.

She walked in the door, and he turned toward his house. Pulling up outside, he sighed. Chances were good Thyra had already texted Arne.

This time it was Arne who got up to get the beer when Dane dropped down on the couch. There was another baseball game on mute on the television.

He and Arne had played baseball together one year when Dane had been a senior in high school then again in college at Oklahoma State. Dane had loved winging a grounder from his position at shortstop to Arne at first base knowing his brother could catch anything sent his way.

"We should join an adult league this summer," Arne said, handing him his beer. "Think about it. Erik will be home. If we can get Roar to sign on, we won't need that many more for our own team."

"Arne, when would we have time to play baseball? If I don't get something put in the ground pretty soon, it's going to be a slim fall." Dane knew between planting, haying, and harvesting, his days from spring until fall were a blur of exhaustion. Still, it would be nice to play again.

"Just think about it. We have time before sign-ups."

Dane shrugged, twisting the top off his beer. Maybe it would give him something to do rather than obsess about Tani for a while. Pulling his phone out of his pocket, he fired off an apology. He still hadn't heard back by the end of the game. He hadn't really expected to.

"Did Thyra text you?" he finally asked.

"Yeah." They watched the weather on the news in silence. Dane was trying to decide if this was going to go in the record books as the first time Arne had not given him crap about Tani. "What did you do?" No, he guessed not. It was his fault. He should have kept his mouth shut. Except, he really needed some advice.

"I kissed her."

"No shit? And?"

Dane could see in his peripheral vision that Arne had turned in his chair to stare at him.

"And, it was fucking amazing. Right up until she pushed me off the truck. I think she pushed me anyway. I hit the ground either way."

"Shit." Arne turned back to watch the sports section of the news. "What are you going to do?"

"I don't know. I was hoping you could tell me."

"Dude, I don't know what to do. I mean, do you see a woman waiting for me somewhere in this house? I can't remember the last time I even went on a date. Roar won't be any help either. He had that hot girlfriend in college who dumped him at graduation. He hasn't been the same since." They watched the news for a few more minutes before Arne laughed. "She pushed you off the truck?"

"Like a bulldozer." With a sigh, Dane hoisted himself off the couch. Quickly finishing in the bathroom, he flopped onto his bed to stare at the ceiling. There was nothing more he could do about it tonight. Tomorrow he would begin fixing this.

TEN

Tani was still trying to wrap her head around what had happened when she walked in the door to her house. One moment they were laughing about Arne being chased into the mud by an angry sow, the next he was kissing her.

She could still taste him on her tongue. He was a combination of chocolate pie and a peppermint he must have had after the pie. She knew better. She knew she needed to walk away from him while there was still time. But she messed that up. Dane was too close.

"Hey, Dad," she greeted him. He sat in his chair in front of the baseball game. "I'm going to head to bed, it was a long day. Do me a favor? If anyone comes looking for me, tell them I'm already asleep." Setting her purse on the kitchen counter, she headed to the bathroom to get ready for bed.

It wasn't a complete lie. She really was tired. She also needed time to get some perspective on the situation before she saw Dane tomorrow. There was no doubt he would show up at some point. He was persistent if he was anything. He wouldn't give up easily.

She walked out of the bathroom and heard a knock on the door. Her dad ignored it until it became obvious it wasn't going to stop. She hid around the corner while he opened it. She listened to him mumble a few words she couldn't quite make out and close it again.

"Was that him?" she asked, walking into the living room.

"That was him." Roy resettled in his chair to finish the game.

Moving to the couch, she curled her feet under her to watch the game for a few minutes.

"Did he act hurt? Was he injured?" she asked.

"He was limping."

"He kissed me. I pushed him off the tailgate of his truck." With a sigh, her dad muted the game. He turned to face the couch, his dark eyes settling on her. She knew he could wait in silence forever until she confessed. This time, however, he didn't wait.

"The boy likes you," he said. "What's the problem?"

"Dad, you know what the problem is. The Ulvmands are not going to want their golden boy to take up with a woman carrying some other man's baby."

"Tani, I told you to tell him and let him make up his own mind. It's not fair what you're doing." Roy rarely scolded her. He usually left her to make her own way through to a decision. But he liked Dane. He was also right, it wasn't fair. She had to clean this mess up.

"I know. I'll take care of everything tomorrow." Standing, she kissed him on the cheek. "I promise."

"Look at me." Roy reached out, taking her hand before she could leave. She turned to look down at him. "Whatever happens, no matter what anybody says or what that boy does, I will always be here. I love you no matter what happens."

Tani cleared her throat, willing the tears burning in her eyes not to fall.

"I know, Dad. I love you too." With a squeeze, he dropped her hand. He returned to his game.

She walked back down the hall to her bedroom. Flopping onto her bed, she closed her eyes. With any luck she would fall asleep quickly. She couldn't handle any more heartache today.

THE NEXT MORNING didn't promise to be any better. Her alarm didn't wake her. By the time her dad shook her awake, she was already running late for work. She had to skip breakfast.

Jumping in her car, she raced to the diner only to find a hulking man waiting by the door. It wasn't the man who made her heart stop. It was the one that set her on edge.

"Good morning," he said as she reached the door.

"Good morning. We'll be open in fifteen minutes."

"Good. I wait."

She smiled and unlocked the door to slip inside. She didn't want to seem rude. She just wished he would drift onto the next town.

"So sorry I'm late," she called to Donna as she set about getting ready. She started the coffee and helped pull out the food from the cooler. Too soon it was time to unlock the door.

The first customer was the big man. He smiled when he

ducked through the door. A group of loggers on the way to one of the ranches followed close behind.

She moved through the tables as she took orders. She almost missed Dane leaning on the front of his truck watching her through the window. He was standing stock still with his arms crossed over his chest, a scowl on his face. She held up a finger to let him know she would come out in a moment.

"Donna, I need to pop outside. I'll be back in five."

"Take your time, honey."

"Dane," she started when she walked outside. He was now standing at his full height, his arms at his side.

"You haven't taken any of my calls." He tried calling last night, then again this morning twice. "I thought..." he ran his hand through his hair. "I don't know what I thought. I guess I misread the signals."

"No, I'm sorry. It should have never gotten that far." Tani could see the frustration building in his face. "Whatever this is between us..." She waggled her hand between them. "Well, there's nothing between us. There can't be."

"I don't understand why." He looked around before his icy gaze speared her. "You're breaking up with me, and we're not even together yet. I guess I just don't get it."

Tani felt her heart shatter at her feet in that dirt parking lot. She stepped closer to him.

"You are the best man I've ever known," she whispered, "but our paths are going in two different directions."

"How can you say that? We're both right here."

"Because I'm pregnant." Dane stared at her in disbelief.

"Whose?" he ground out with a snarl.

"I don't know, I can't remember." His eyes turned into a blue flame in front of her. She couldn't remember ever seeing Dane truly angry before now. "You need to let me go, Dane. You don't deserve to be stuck with me."

He was silent as she turned and walked back toward the restaurant. She slipped through the backdoor and made it to the bathroom before anyone could see her. She splashed water on her face.

"Hey, sweetie. Are you okay?" Donna asked, knocking on the bathroom door.

"Yeah, sorry. I'm good." She wasn't good. This was her life now, though. The sooner she faced it, the better everyone would be. Most of all, Dane.

She returned to the counter in time to deliver her orders. She walked back into the dining area plastering a smile she didn't feel on her face. Dane wasn't outside when she chanced a glance through the front window. Just as well. Grabbing the coffee pot, she refilled cups until she came to the big man in the corner.

"You are better without him. He was...what do you call... asshole. You better with Jakub," he said, patting his chest. At least she had a name for him now.

"I think I'm better off on my own for now. Men are too complicated." He scowled at her. It wasn't the same scowl as Dane. This one felt almost dangerous. Why did he think she would date some drifter anyway?

He obviously had money since he was dressed well and ate his meals out, but still. With a small shudder, she walked back to the kitchen, busying herself in the cooler until she knew he was gone.

"What was that? He was looking around for you before he finally stomped out," Donna asked when she emerged again.

"I think he was trying to ask me out. He apparently

watched the whole thing with Dane this morning out the window. Must have decided he would throw his hat in the ring. I don't know what it is, but he gives me the creeps."

"Yeah, hopefully he'll move on soon. Come on, the breakfast rush is almost over."

Tani walked out to sit at the counter. The diner had cleared out except for the old guys at their table. Donna set a coffee pot in the middle of them so they were good. Handing her a cup of decaf coffee and a biscuit, Donna sat down next to her on one of the stools.

"So what happened with Dane this morning?" she asked. "I swear, if I didn't know him, I'd think he'd lost his mind since you came back to town."

"Yeah, well, I took care of that. I don't think we'll see much of him now. I should have shut him down from the beginning. I was blindsided by the fact that he's now this gorgeous, funny, kind, attentive man."

"So what's the problem?"

"You know why it's a problem. He's too good of a man to deal with all of this." Tani made a circular motion over her stomach.

"I don't know. I think you underestimate him. He's a determined guy. If he's set his sights on you, I'm not sure that's going to stop him," Donna said, nodding at her stomach.

Tani shrugged, popping a piece of biscuit into her mouth.

"I don't see what the big deal is anyway," Donna continued. "Half the kids in this town don't have the dad they started with."

It was true, these small towns had a large percentage of teenage pregnancies. But never had she heard a rumor that any of the kids were Ulvmands, at least not Dane's. Arne's maybe. Or Erik's. Never Dane's.

"It doesn't matter. I told him not to come around anymore," she said.

"You know this is a very small town with only two diners, right? You're going to run into him again." When she sighed, Donna threw her arm around her shoulders. She gave her a quick hug. "We'd better get ready. I see the early lunch crew heading in."

Tani snagged her order pad, walking toward the door to welcome the next shift of diners. Most were locals that she'd known all her life. Donna's was known for having one of the best burgers in the area. The room quickly filled up.

After an hour, there still didn't seem to be any relief in sight. Haley was flipping burgers as fast as she could. Karla showed up at the peak of the rush to help. She would stay after lunch to work the evening shift so Tani could go home.

Tani was visiting with one of the local preachers and his family when she heard the front door crash open behind her. Spinning around to see what had happened, she felt her heart slam into her throat.

Standing in the doorway, his eyes blazing, was Dane. He looked like an avenging angel. His blond hair fell to his shoulders, and his chest heaved from exertion.

All the air left her lungs when he stomped toward her. "Damn it, Tani," he growled. He wrapped his fist in her hair. With a tug, he pulled her head back until she looked up at him. Time seemed to stand still as he stared down at her. Then his mouth crashed onto hers.

He devoured her mouth in a way that made her forget everything she said to him. There was raw passion coursing from him. If she had been delivering food, the plates would have crashed to the floor. Instead, only her order pad was sacrificed as she clung to his shirt.

Then he stepped back, and she felt the loss deep in her soul.

"We're not done yet," he growled. "I'll pick you up at six tomorrow night for our date. If it takes the next fifty years, I'll prove to you I'm a better fucking man than you think I am, Tani Johnston." He turned around and stomped back out the way he had come.

"I swear, I thought we were just getting some lunch," Arne said from the doorway. He spun around when he heard Dane start up the truck. "Yeah, so I guess no lunch today."

The entire diner sat in shocked silence. They watched as Arne barely made it into the truck before Dane roared out of the parking lot.

"Is it just me, or is it suddenly hot in here?" the preacher's wife asked. The room burst into a dull roar. Some of the locals were appalled by Dane's actions. Most cheered him on.

Of course it was hot. Dane had just set her on fire. Tani turned slowly with her mouth still open to look at Donna. The older woman gave her a wink before breaking into a grin.

Dane had just announced to the whole town that they were together. Did he not realize he would be blamed for her pregnancy? Everyone would just assume they had a past based on his performance today. She couldn't even wrap her head around what had possessed him to do that.

Looking back out the window where his truck had just been, she caught angry eyes looking back at her. Jakub was staring in the window. Rage was plain on his face.

The heat she had been enveloped in evaporated

instantly. It was replaced with the cold mantle of fear. She pulled her eyes away to answer a question about the special. When she chanced another glance outside, he was gone. Chills broke out over her arms as she wondered what he had planned. Hopefully, he would move on.

ELEVEN

"What the holy fuck was that?" Arne yelled at Dane as they came close to drifting the corner back onto the road leading to the ranch. "Have you lost your mind?"

Dane was almost positive Arne screamed when he slid the truck to a stop in the middle of the road. He didn't worry too much about getting run into. It was one of the least traveled roads in the county. If anyone came along, they would just go around.

"I'm done," he yelled back. If it was going to turn into a yelling match, he sure as hell was going to be heard. "I'm fucking done with being pushed away. She doesn't get to decide I'm too good for her. She's mine, I'm claiming her. I'm not playing the nice guy or the supportive friend anymore. I'm going to marry that woman."

"Dude, you have to calm down before you stroke out." Arne chuckled.

Dane felt his heart pounding in his chest. His breath was coming in shallow pants, and he was positive he had soaked through the work shirt he had on. Maybe Arne was right; he was having a stroke.

He had been thinking about the bomb Tani dropped on him all morning. Could he love another man's child the way it deserved? The simple answer was yes.

He had loved Tani for so long he couldn't remember a time before her. Even after they left for college, she was all he thought about. Fate had placed her back in his path. He wouldn't let her get away again.

She and her child would be the center of his universe as long as he drew breath. No, not her child. Their child. He didn't care about the whispers by others behind his back. Tani was too important. Dane began to build his family in his head as he sat in his truck in the middle of the road.

"Arne, can I trust you to keep something to yourself for a little while?" He looked over at his brother. Arne was watching him in silence. He nodded. "Tani's pregnant."

"Shit, you've only been together for what, a couple of days? How could she even know that fast?" Arne was still yelling. "I swear to God, if you hurt her…"

"It's not mine," Dane said. "You know me better than that. I swear on my life, I would never hurt her. I need someone to help me figure this shit out."

"You're ready to be a dad just like that?" Arne asked. His voice had calmed finally.

"I don't know. But it's Tani, I'll do anything for her." He stared out the windshield for a moment in silence. "Yes. I can be a dad."

Arne contemplated him for a few minutes more, his face drawn in concern.

"Okay," he finally answered. "Okay. What do I need to do?"

"I don't know. There's not much you can do, I guess. Just listening to me when I'm completely in over my head. Can you do that?"

"I can do that."

"Okay. Good." Dane shifting back into drive. Accelerating back down the road, he sighed. "I'll take Thyra to practice tonight. It'll give me a chance to apologize for today's display of crazy. That seems to have become a recurring theme with me lately. I can't seem to keep from fucking up on a regular basis." They pulled in at the house they shared. "Oh, and sorry about lunch."

THE REST of the day Dane worked at cutting hay. It was still early in the season, but they had had an unusually warm winter. Spring had made an early appearance.

If he could at least get it all laid down today, his father would help by raking it up. Then he'd just have to roll it into bales. It would have to dry on the ground tonight before it could be raked.

With any luck, by the time he headed to Thyra's game tomorrow night, he would have at least one barn full. It would be one more thing marked off his list.

It was almost time for supper when Dane pulled the windrower back onto the gravel pad next to the shop. Climbing down, he was met by his sister as she ambled over from the main house.

"Arne said you're taking me tonight," she greeted him. "Mom sent me to get you for supper. She was pulling out the waffle iron."

"Mmm, breakfast for supper. Always a good choice." He locked up the machine. They walked to the house together.

"So, I heard you made a big splash in town today," she said. "It was all over school by fifth period."

"Thyra, can we wait to dissect my life until we head for town? Right now all I want to do is clean up and get something in my stomach."

"Fine. I can't believe Arne didn't text me all the details. I heard he had a front row seat to the fireworks."

Dane smiled. Arne had stuck to his promise to keep everything to himself until Dane could figure it out.

Arne was trying to get all of the bulls put out this afternoon with the help of their dad. If he had mentioned anything to their parents, his dad would have shown up at the windrower to pull him out by his hair and whip some sense into him.

He decided Arne had ratted him out afterall when he was met by his father's stern stare as soon as he walked into the mudroom. Crossing to the sink, he washed the grime off his hands. He turned around to face Sten.

"Do you need to get whatever tirade you have planned for tonight's meal over with now so we can eat in peace?" Sten asked. If his father hadn't had such a scowl on his face, Dane would have laughed.

"No, sir. I believe I'm all done with tirades for today. You won't hear a single curse word out of me." Dane started to reach for the door that led into the main part of the house when Sten placed a hand on his chest stopping him.

"You know I've known Royal Johnston since we were kids. I know you've had a hard-on for his daughter for a long time," Sten said with a scowl still firmly fixed on his face.

"Dad."

"Shut it and listen. I like that girl. You thinking you can stomp into town to pitch a fit in the middle of where she works isn't doing you any favors. Next time think before you act. You know, we expect this out of your brother, not you."

"Did Arne say something?" Dane asked. He was about to beat his little brother into a bloody pulp.

"He didn't have to. The preacher's wife, who apparently had a front row seat, damn near burnt up the phone lines calling your mother. I know I raised you better than that. Pull your head out of your ass."

Sten opened the door and walked into the kitchen ending any argument Dane might have attempted. He had just been dressed down like he was fifteen again. He couldn't argue he didn't deserve it. His dad also made a valid point. He did need to pull his head out of his ass for a change.

"There you are, honey," his mom greeted him when he followed his father inside a moment later. She tilted her head so he could give her a kiss on the cheek. He knew she heard every word that Sten had said, the walls weren't that thick in this house.

She also had an amazing ability to pretend to be deaf. Dane appreciated that more than ever right now. He noticed she had chased Thyra into the living room where she couldn't hear.

"Hey, Mom." Dane crossed to the stove where he picked a piece of freshly cooked bacon off the plate.

"Hungry?" she asked, sliding a fresh waffle on a plate. "Tell your sister to come get one when you head to the table." He loaded his plate with more bacon before walking into where his dad was already eating.

"Thyra, go get your plate," he called.

"Did you get all of the south bottom done today?" His

father never harped. He said what he thought needed to be said then moved on.

"Yes, sir. It should be ready to bale tomorrow. The dew should be burned off by ten if you can rake for me."

"Not a problem. I'll help Arne get the bulls pushed into the pens tomorrow, then head your way."

"That works. By the time I get everything over there, you shouldn't be far behind me. I'll start until you get there." Dane felt himself relax as the discussion centered around spring planting when his mother and sister joined them.

It moved on to spring calf weaning when Arne finally arrived. Arne announced that Roar had the next day off and was coming to help with the bulls. That freed up Sten to help Dane get the hay finished.

Most of the hay would be fed to their cattle through the winter. But if he was lucky, he would have extra to sell this year. It would give them each extra profit when the dividends were split at the end of the year.

They didn't earn a salary like everyone else who worked at a normal job. Instead they got a percentage of the profits. It was why Dane was willing to crack his head on the windrower instead of calling a mechanic for the simple repair jobs.

He picked up his last piece of bacon as Thyra scooped up both of their plates to carry to the kitchen. He could hear her quickly rinse them off before sliding them into the dishwasher. She snagged her bag from near the stairs. When the back door opened, Dane stood from the table.

"I guess that's my hint she's ready to go. We shouldn't be back too late since tomorrow they have a game." With another kiss on his mom's cheek, Dane followed Thyra outside.

She was already sitting in the cab of his truck waiting on him. He climbed in on the driver's side and started up the engine. He made it all the way to the front gate before she spun in her seat to face him.

"So spill. By the time it made the rounds around the school, the whole thing had reached legendary status. The girls were all swooning over you, and the guys were convinced you have balls made of gold."

Dane laughed. His sister never did filter her words.

"It wasn't quite that epic. Unfortunately, the diner was full at the time I had my moment of insanity. I don't know what it is, she just makes me crazy whenever I see her. I start out with a perfectly reasonable argument. Then I just lose my mind."

"You know you're in love with her, right?" she asked. "I mean, not just the lust kind but the whole 'put a ring on it' kind. You don't get to fuck this up, Dane Ulvmand. Tani would be the coolest sister-in-law ever. Get your shit together." Thyra nodded her head with determination at him.

He couldn't stop the grin that broke out on his face. That could possibly be the best ass chewing he had ever received.

"I'll try my best," he growled.

"See that you do."

"You're a brat, know that?" Reaching over, he pushed her shoulder making her rock in her seat.

"Yeah, but I'm a lovable brat."

Dropping Thyra off at the ballfields, he promised to return to get her in an hour. He needed to apologize to Tani for his outburst in the diner today. He wasn't sorry for what he said. He meant every word of it. His delivery could have been better though.

He pulled up across the street from her house. What was he going to say to make it past her father? The fact that man hadn't gutted him yet with a Bowie knife was a miracle. When he was ready, he opened the door and stepped out. He took a deep breath as he headed toward her door.

Something wasn't right. Taking the steps two at a time, he stopped on the porch. The screen door was hanging from the bottom hinge only. The heavy front door was sitting ajar where it had been kicked in.

Opening the door carefully he called her name into the gloom inside. Hearing nothing, he stepped inside.

The living room looked like there had been a struggle. The lamp that sat next to Roy's chair lay broken on the floor. The stools at the bar were on their sides. Several pictures from the walls were laying in shattered glass on the carpet.

"Tani!" Dane called, stepping farther into the house. Hearing a moan, he quickly rounded the couch, finding Roy lying on the floor. He had a gash on his forehead, and at least one of his eyes was going to sport a nasty shiner tomorrow. "

Mr. Johnston. What happened?" Dane said, dropping to his knees next to the man. Ripping off the T-shirt he had on, he pressed it to Roy's head to try to staunch the bleeding. Dane could see what looked like a broken arm also.

"He kicked in the door. Took Tani," Roy wheezed.

"Who did? Where did he take Tani?" Dane's blood turned cold. He was trying to be gentle with the man, but he was starting to panic at the thought of someone hurting Tani.

"Big guy. Went out the back."

Dane lifted his head looking toward the sliding door that led from the kitchen into the backyard. It was wrenched from the track. He pulled out his phone and called Arne.

"Someone broke into Tani's house. I'm going to go see if I can track her. Mr. Johnston needs an ambulance," he yelled into the phone.

"Go. I'll take care of it," Arne answered.

"Will you be okay until the ambulance can get here?" He helped Roy use his good hand to press against the head wound. It could be a little while until help made it.

The ambulance was manned by volunteers that had to come from their houses to emergencies. They did a good job, but it always took a little longer after work hours.

"Go. Find her." It was all Dane needed to hear. He was on his feet tearing out the back door. Shoving out the back gate, he searched around trying to pick up their trail.

Who would have had a reason to take her? Her home sat in front of a series of empty lots overgrown with trees and scrub. The woods ended somewhere near an old farm that looked abandoned now. If they went out the back, chances were whoever took her didn't have a vehicle near.

It wasn't much, but he finally found a slight trail through the trees. Fighting into the undergrowth, Dane kept a close eye out for broken branches or smashed-down grass. Soon he left the sound of town behind as he continued to fight his way through the bramble.

He made it as far as the old abandoned farm before he caught a glimpse of something ahead. Moving faster, he caught up to the large man from the diner. Tani was struggling futilely as he dragged her down the trail. Her hands were tied in front of her with a piece of rough rope.

"Hey," Dane called out to catch his attention. Grabbing Tani by the hair, the man swung around putting her between them. "What are you doing? Just let her go. I promise there are plenty of women in this town that would be happy to go with you."

It was starting to get dark. Dane knew he needed to get her away from the man soon while he still had time. He held his hands out in mock surrender as he slowly approached them.

CHAPTER

TWELVE

Tani was carrying their empty bowls into the kitchen when it felt like the house exploded. Running into the living room to see what had happened, she found Jakub standing next to her father. She screamed when he stepped forward, grabbing her arm.

Her father tried valiantly to fight him off. Jakub rained several blows down on him before he slumped unconscious to the floor. She rushed to help him, but was lifted off the floor before she could reach him.

She tried everything to get him to put her down. She kicked, bit, and even tried to hit him in the face with her head. The harder she tried, the more he laughed at her struggles.

"Hold still, or I kill your father," he growled.

All of the fight drained out of her. She couldn't risk her father. Jakub pulled a piece of rope out of his pocket. He tied her hands in front of her and pushed her toward the back door.

"Jakub, stop. Let's just go back inside where we can talk," she tried as he pushed them further into the bramble behind her house. Her eyes searched for a way to distract him long enough to get away.

She didn't know where he was taking her, but she had no doubt it wouldn't end well. If she just didn't have her hands tied. She had been on the track team in high school. She might be able to outrun him. But she had a hard enough time trying to stay on her feet as it was. She wouldn't make it five feet running like this.

"Jakub, please," she begged. She was beginning to give up hope of getting away.

"Hey," she heard a voice shout out behind them. Jakub grabbed her hair and spun her around to face the voice. Staring back were the most beautiful blue eyes she had ever seen. She felt her heart pounding in her chest. Dane had come for her. He would save her.

"There's no need for this," Dane said, taking a step forward. "I'm sure we can work something out. Just let her go."

She heard a deep rumble begin in Jakub's chest. He let go of her hair just long enough to pull her to his chest. His strong arm wrapped around her neck.

Dane stopped moving forward. His gaze met hers for a moment before returning to the man over her shoulder. His eyes grew wide as the rumble from Jakub grew until it became an ear-splitting roar in her ear.

"Dane!" she screamed as the thing behind her morphed into something unnatural. Her feet left the ground as whatever now had her towered above it. She wanted to scream at Dane to run, to save himself but she couldn't find the breath.

"I'm sorry," Dane whispered. Then Dane was no longer standing on the path. A wolf had taken his place.

Tani couldn't understand what she was looking at. It

was as if she had dropped down some rabbit hole, waking in another universe. Her struggle to understand what she was seeing ended when she was tossed away. She fought not to cave into the darkness surrounding her when her head hit the base of a tree.

Glacial eyes looked at her in concern before turning back to what she recognized was a giant bear standing on its back legs. The great white wolf looked back at it with a snarl. The only thing recognizable about Dane was the blue eyes. She searched around for him not believing he was standing in front of her. How could he be? Nothing in this world made sense.

The wolf bared its teeth in a growl, saliva dripping from its long canine teeth. Tani shrank against the tree. If she believed her legs would hold her, she would run. But she must have a bad enough head injury to hallucinate that Dane was a wolf. Jumping up would only make her faint.

The wolf gleamed a brilliant white in the waning twilight. He snarled and snapped as he danced near the bear. The bear lunged at the wolf. The wolf jumped out of its way. He snapped, driving the bear back a little at a time. The bear finally managed to catch the wolf on the shoulder rolling him across the path. The wolf raised back onto his feet with a snarl.

The bear turned and tore through the trees to escape. The wolf glanced quickly at her before tearing through the trees in pursuit.

"Tani," she heard, calling from the trees. Arne burst through the underbrush and slid to a stop on his knees in front of her. "Are you hurt?" He took her arms in his strong hands. "Are? You? Hurt?" Arne asked slowly this time before feeling her head for cuts. She slowly came out of shock at what she had just witnessed.

"Arne?" Thyra crashed through the trees next to them. "What's going on?" She knelt down next to her brother still wearing her cleats from practice. "Is Tani alright?"

"How did you get here?" he asked Thyra. Leaning Tani forward slightly, he checked her back.

"I saw you slide around the corner toward Tani's house, so I just took off running. Where's Dane?"

"Arne," Tani suddenly gasped, grabbing at his shirt. "The wolf chased him farther into the trees." She watched Arne and Thyra exchange glances. "The wolf was hurt." She could feel herself start to shake but couldn't seem to stop. "There was a bear." She couldn't focus on anything but where the wolf had come from and how Jakub had turned into something otherworldly.

"Hey, sweetie, easy," Arne said. He hugged her against him. "Take some deep breaths. We don't want anything to hurt the baby. Don't worry, I'll find Dane."

"Dane," she whispered. Was the wolf really Dane? Was she not in some dream?

"Listen to me, Thyra," Arne said over her head. She still clung to him. "Can you get Tani back to Dane's truck? The keys are in it. There's a blanket behind the seat you can wrap her in. Drive the both of you to the house.

"If the cops are already there and stop you, tell them just the facts you know. Roar was on his way to make sure Mr. Johnston was taken care of at the hospital. Can you do that? I'll find Dane and meet you at home."

Arne eased Tani off the ground. He cut the rope that held her hands together and Thyra looped an arm around her waist. She nodded nervously at him before turning them back toward the house.

It seemed to take years before they made it to the edge of the trees. Thyra eased carefully out of the undergrowth down from Tani's house. They slipped unnoticed across the street. It was already full of sheriff's officers and EMTs. They skirted the neighbors' houses until they stood next to the passenger door of Dane's truck.

"Roar is already inside with the EMTs," Thyra said, settling Tani in Arne's truck. She pulled out the blanket from behind the seat. "He must have broken a land speed record. He'll take care of everything, he always does."

Thyra turned the engine over and slowly pulled away from the curb.

"Don't worry," she continued. "It'll be fine. Dane will be fine. No one will know." Tani watched her talking. Nothing she said made sense though. Thyra looked like she was trying to reassure herself as much as her. It matched the death grip she had on the steering wheel.

Pulling through the front gate of the Ulvmands, Tani saw Dane's mother standing in the yard watching for them. Thyra managed to drive without causing a wreck. She only swiped her tears away a couple of times.

Tani felt too overwhelmed to cry. What had she seen in the trees? Rolling to a stop, Thyra threw the truck in park. She jumped out to meet her mother. With a quick hug, Freja sent Thyra into the house. Freja calmly opened Tani's door.

"Come on, honey, let's get you inside. You've had a very bad evening." Dane's mother wrapped an arm around her and led her into the house. In the kitchen, Thyra was working on making tea.

Freja pulled Tani into the living room. She sat her down on the couch where she wrapped another blanket around her shoulders. Handing her a mug of tea, Thyra sat down next to her on the couch.

"I think we could all use a shot of whiskey to calm our nerves," Freja said, pulling a bottle out of a cabinet.

"Mom, Arne said something about a baby," Thyra said, cutting her eyes to Tani.

Freja seemed to take the news in stride.

"I guess Dane didn't wait around. Here, a little whiskey never hurts. It's more important that she not go into shock. Drink, Tani." Freja splashed a small bit of whiskey in her cup before doing the same to both hers and Thyra's.

"My dad. I have to get to him," Tani burst out in panic looking wildly around the living room. How could she forget him lying on the floor of their house?

"Easy," Freja said, stopping her from standing up. She sat down on the coffee table in front of Tani. "Relax, child. Your dad is on his way to the hospital. Sten is with him. He called to let you know your dad is awake. Roy's going to stay the night there, then go to stay with your aunt for a couple of days. Sten will call the feed store tomorrow to arrange for the time off."

"Thank you," Tani whispered. She managed to get two sips of tea down her before she began to shake again. A sob escaped her throat prompting a floodgate of tears to open.

Freja took her mug, setting it on the coffee table. Tani felt Thyra's arms wrap around her. She clung to Thyra as her body was racked with sobs. Finally, exhaustion overtook her.

She had only been asleep for what felt like a few minutes when she was woken by a commotion in the kitchen.

"I need to see her," a voice growled.

"She's fine. You need to sit down before you pass out again."

She sat up slowly listening to the argument. A small wave of dizziness swept over her but quickly passed. She stood and walked to the door of the kitchen. Dane sat in a chair. His face was pale, and there were three long jagged slices across his shoulder. His icy gaze met hers.

He was wearing nothing but a pair of sweatpants and the charms around his neck. His eyes had a wild look in them. There was blood smeared down his chest onto his lap. He closed his eyes. Was it from pain or her reaction to seeing him? He looked away before she had a chance to ask.

"Okay," Roar said, walking in the door. "I think I have everything settled down at the Johnston's house tonight. You'll both have to give a statement tomorrow though. I got the door fixed at least. Damn." He bent to study Dane's shoulder.

Freja pushed him out of the way. She held a towel under Dane's arm as she poured antiseptic into the wound. Dane hissed when it hit his shoulder.

"I think I have everything," Arne announced, carrying an armload of stuff into the kitchen. He laid everything in his hands on the counter. "I don't have anything to numb it. I brought some Dex to stop any infection though. I also brought the smallest sewing needle I had."

Tani looked at the stuff in horror. They intended to treat Dane right here instead of taking him to the emergency room.

"Dane, are you sure you don't want us to take you to the hospital?" Freja asked.

"No, they'll have too many questions I can't explain. Just do it here." Tani stared as his gaze flitted for only a second to hers before refocusing on the floor in front of him.

Freja used the iodine Arne brought to clean Dane's shoulder. Arne knelt on the floor next to the chair to help hold him. His mother had to sew three gaping wounds closed without any numbing agent.

Tani knew at that moment she had a decision to make. She could remain here cowering at the periphery of the room while her best friend endured the pain. Or she could push her fear to the side and help. He risked death to save her. Taking a deep breath, she stepped into the room. She knelt in front of him and took his hand in hers.

Dane's gaze met hers. He dropped her hands quickly. His strong arm wrapped around her waist. He pulled her to him until her head rested against his chest. She listened to his heart pound for a moment. Then she slid her hand across him to help hold him in place before nodding to Freja.

Freja pierced his skin with the needle to close it where the bear had slashed it open. Dane squeezed her to him. She felt a warm hand close over her shoulder in encouragement as the thread was tugged through his skin. Looking over her shoulder, she found Roar's soft green gaze.

"Ahhh," Dane moaned.

"Hold on to him," Arne encouraged. He helped Freja as she continued to work the thread through Dane's shoulder.

Roar helped Tani hold Dane in the chair when he finally lost consciousness and slumped forward. Freja worked quickly on the remaining gashes and injected him with a dose of antibiotics. She broke open a vial of smelling salts from the medicine cabinet.

"Thyra, you and Tani come over here," Freya said. "Dane is liable to wake up swinging. I don't want either of you to get hurt."

Tani moved to the counter next to Thyra. Roar wrapped his big arms around Dane from the back of the chair. Arne pressed his shoulder against Dane's chest. Freja broke the smelling salts in front of Dane's face.

"Tani!" he roared, jerking upright.

"I'm right here, Dane," she said, moving to him quickly. He was covered in a sheen of sweat, and his hands shook. He slowly lifted one to her face.

"I thought you were gone."

"He didn't take me. You saved me. You came for me, Dane."

He pulled her to him. His arms crushed her in his embrace, but she didn't mind. They were both still alive. That was all that mattered. The rest they could figure out later.

"Come on, buddy," Roar said. "Let's move you to the couch so none of us have to try to hold your big body up when you pass out again."

With Roar on one side and Arne on the other, they hefted Dane to his feet. Slowly they helped him into the living room. Tani sat down next to him. He tucked her into his good side. She felt his arm go slack when he fell asleep. They all sat in silence until Sten walked in the back door.

"Your father was resting when I left," he assured her. "They set his arm and cleaned up his head. They wanted him to stay overnight for observation. I convinced him to go home with your aunt tomorrow when he's released. You'll stay with us for now. We can protect you until we get to the bottom of what this is." He took a seat next to Freja.

"What can anyone tell me about tonight?" he asked no one in particular.

"Dane said it was that big guy who's been coming into the diner," Arne said. "He broke in, took Tani, and roughed up Mr. Johnston when he tried to stop him." Arne waited until his father was looking at him to continue. "Dane said he shifted into a brown bear while he was holding Tani. He had no choice but to shift also."

Tani watched in silence as they exchanged a look similar to the one he and Thyra had in the woods.

"Can someone please tell me what happened? Unless I'm going crazy, I know I saw the bear fighting with a large white wolf. I think I have a right to know what I'm involved in." Tani looked around at the Ulvmands. Not one of them would meet her eyes.

"She's right," Dane said from next to her. His eyes were still closed, but he had obviously not missed a word.

"It's best if Freja tells it. But Tani, if anyone finds out..." Sten answered. He turned to his wife. Freja took Sten's hand before she looked at them each in turn. When her gaze finally fell on Tani, she began her tale.

THIRTEEN

In the days before the Vikings, before Gorm the Old unified the country, before Harald Bluetooth brought Christianity to the Scandinavians, there was the time of the Drott.

During peacetime, the people were governed by a leader who saw to their needs. But in times of strife, the people would choose a warrior called the Drott. It was his job to lead the chieftain's soldiers into battle. His council was made up of an elder warrior, a younger warrior, and the captain of the chiefly vessel who in turn controlled the chieftain's soldiers.

It was during one of these conflicts, perhaps a dispute with another tribe over trading with the Romans, that a fight broke out. The people elected a battle-proven man to be the Drott as tensions rose between the two tribes.

He quickly set about calling in his warrior council. It included a young man who was working on one of the farms left by his father. His father had died under the Drott in the last skirmish, proving himself a man of great courage. He passed onto Valhalla in battle. The current Drott surmised that courage that great would be passed down to his sons.

Leaving the farm to his younger brother to tend, the young warrior picked up his crude knives and homemade shield to answer the call. He was given a group of men to lead south on a frontal assault. The elder warrior's men would flank from the north.

After three days of walking, they finally found themselves ambushed in a pass between two rock faces. The scouts sent earlier failed to report back making it impossible to know where the enemy was.

His men fought bravely. But knowing they had no chance to overcome the enemy, he called for retreat. If he could get his men reformed in safety, they could find another way to attack.

He watched as his men disappeared into the hills before narrowly fleeing from a barrage of arrows himself. He ran from his pursuers for hours until he stopped beside a waterfall to rest.

The young man squatted down on his hands and knees, scooping water out of the pool made by the surrounding rocks to get a drink. When he was finally full, he rocked back on his heels, listening for the approach of an enemy. He had made it this far unscathed. He didn't want to be snuck up on while resting.

Hearing nothing, he sat back against a tree by the water's edge to rest before trying to find his men. As he fought the fatigue that threatened to claim him, he suddenly saw an apparition appear from behind the waterfall.

Peering cautiously from behind the curtain of water was a young woman. Even from a distance, the man could tell she was beautiful with long golden hair. As she approached, he slowly rose from his perch near the tree. He stepped out into the light and raised his hands to his side when she looked up in fear.

"Don't be afraid. I won't hurt you," he said. He took a step toward her, expecting her to run. Instead, she stared him down, daring him to come closer. "I have become separated from my men. Have you seen anyone pass this way earlier?"

She remained glaring at him in stony silence.

"I just need to rest then I'll be on my way." He would get no information from this woman.

Without warning, she suddenly lunged at him, pressing her hand over his mouth. She took his hand and pulled him toward the waterfall. He barely managed to get his shield on the way.

She pulled him behind the waterfall. Rushing to a small fire just inside a cave, she kicked dirt on the flames, dousing any light that had existed. She led him deeper into the dark cave as if she could see without light.

Taking his shield, she shoved it aside and pushed him after it. He found his back flat against a piece of rock. He was wedged into a small cutout in the cave.

Opening his mouth to protest, he quickly found her hand covering it again. Her body flattened against his. He could feel her breath, warm against his neck. She began to whisper something in a language he couldn't understand.

Soon, he could hear the voices of men searching inside the cave. They had found the opening behind the waterfall. They were looking for him and his men.

Offering a quick prayer to the gods, he wrapped his arms around the woman. He moved her slightly so they wouldn't be able to see her around him. If he was to be caught, he could at least try to spare her. He eased one of his knives out and prepared himself to die an honorable death.

Her whispering grew louder as the men moved with their torches closer to the crevice where they hid. He should try to silence her murmurings, but he knew they were not well hidden enough not to be discovered.

He prepared to jump out at the man who walked up to their hiding spot. But an odd thing happened. It was as if the men could not see them. Even the man who stood staring at them, his knife ready.

The beautiful woman slid her arms around him, holding him in place as she continued to murmur at his back. The men filed back out of the cave to continue their pursuit.

They stood together in the dark as they listened to the sounds of the men grow fainter until they faded into the distance. The warrior spun around tripping over a rock. He landed on his backside in the dark cave.

"What are you?" he whispered into the darkness. "Where did you come from?"

His heart pounded as he stared into the blackness. Softly, he felt a hand brush up his chest as if trying to calm him. She gently helped him off the ground and pulled him to the front of the cave.

Turning him loose, she began busying herself rebuilding the fire. He watched her in amazement for several minutes.

"I'll go get more wood," he said, walking out from under the water.

Gathering up the dry wood he could find near the waterfall, the warrior noticed a rabbit emerge from a hole to get a drink. His stomach rumbled. He tried to remember seeing any food in the cave.

Leaving the pile of wood, he crept close to the opening of the warren to wait in the undergrowth. He speared the rabbit with one of his knives when it returned.

He was proud of his speed. He was fast enough to add what he could to her food stores. He turned around to collect his pile of sticks. The woman was standing at the edge of the waterfall, watching him.

Holding the rabbit in the air, he smiled back at her. She held up a basket containing hazelnuts, raspberries, and wild apples with a laugh. Tonight, they would have full bellies to sleep on.

They returned to the cave behind the waterfall. The warrior laid against the wall watching the woman slowly turn the spit he had constructed to cook the rabbit on. The reflection of the fire made her pale skin glow and turned her fair hair into gold. He watched her in silence. His curiosity finally overwhelmed him.

"Is this where you live?" he asked, trying to learn something more about her.

She shook her head sadly.

"Is your home far?"

She shook her head again, motioning to the east and then showing him two fingers.

"It's two days to the east?"

When she nodded again, he sat silently in thought until the rabbit was ready.

"Why did you leave your home?" he asked between bites.

She looked at him with sadness before patting his chest.

"Raiders took your home? What about your family?"

A tear stole its way down her cheek making him want to kill whoever hurt her.

"I'm sorry."

She shrugged.

"I have to find my men soon. We are at war with another tribe. I was to lead my men against them."

She watched him closely as he explained what had happened to bring him to her cave. He told her he would leave at first light to search for his men. She became agitated, motioning to him wildly.

"I don't understand what you're trying to tell me."

Picking up one of the sticks of kindling, she drew in the dirt on the cave floor.

The warrior paid close attention as she showed him a story of other warriors hunting for him. It would be too dangerous to leave until they went back through. He would then be behind them and could easily kill them as he gathered his men.

"I must stay two more nights to let them get ahead of me. You will protect me until then?"

She nodded vigorously.

"How will a woman protect me from the enemy?"

With a scowl, she began to whisper something before pointing at the fire. He scooted back quickly as it exploded in flames almost to the ceiling.

"You're a sorceress," he said, his eyes wide.

Sorceresses were to be feared. They could ruin crops, kill stock, and inflict horrible plagues. He should kill her before she could curse him.

But when she smiled, he knew he could no more kill her than he could defeat the other army single-handed. Her eyes turned soft as she eased toward him. She ran her hand up his chest again like she did earlier in the dark.

"Why would you help me?" he asked.

She grabbed the stick again using it to explain how a vision came to her telling her about a young warrior who was to lose his way. The vision told her she must protect him until he could return to his men. The battle he would win would bring great honor to his tribe and change the course of the world.

"How am I to believe you won't slit my throat in my sleep?"

She grabbed the knife he used for her portion of rabbit and handed it back to him. He laughed at her enthusiasm.

"I guess I will have to trust you then."

She gave him a brilliant smile before pulling two grass mats out from behind one of the large stones.

"You must have had time to plan." Rolling his mat out near the fire, he settled onto it. He fell asleep almost instantly.

When he woke the next morning, he felt more rested than he had in weeks. He sent a small prayer to the gods asking that his men had found shelter.

Sitting up, he had a rough-hewn mug pressed into his hands. He took a sip. It was mulled wine made out of the nuts and berries she had been gathering.

"Is there a stream nearby? I can catch us fish for tonight."

The woman nodded, handing him a pot that contained a gruel she had cooked. Sitting next to him, they took turns eating the breakfast until it was gone.

She gathered her basket and motioned for him to follow her outside. He followed her through the trees until they came to a stream teaming with trout.

He used one of his knives to make a rough spear. Taking off his tunic and shoes, the warrior climbed into the icy stream to patiently wait for a fish.

The woman, having finished her scavenging, sat on a rock overlooking the stream to watch him. He stood perfectly still for fifteen minutes. He stabbed at the water bringing a fish out. She cheered when he held it over his head in triumph. He tossed it on the bank to her. She jumped off her perch to add it to her basket.

When he speared the second fish, he tossed his spear on the bank. He took out another knife as he waded toward her on the bank. He sat down next to her. She was wiggling her toes in the cold water.

He cleaned the fish before trading her for the first one. Quickly cleaning the second fish, he handed it to her. He lay back in the grass on the bank. Setting her basket aside, she flopped next to him and stared up at the clouds.

He must have fallen asleep for a moment. He was woken when he felt soft lips brush over his. Opening his eyes, he looked up at two laughing pools of cerulean blue.

She jumped up quickly and ran toward the trees with a laugh. He raced to slide back into his clothes before chasing after her through the trees. Catching up to her at the edge of the pool by her cave, she put an arm up to stop him. He waited until she nodded it was safe to return.

That night, they once again filled their bellies. He helped her grind the hazelnuts into flour using a large flat rock. She made a flat type of bread they shared with the fish he cooked on the spit.

After dinner, he built up the fire as he told her stories about life where he was from. She sat with her knees pulled up to her chest in rapt attention as he explained how he had been chosen to serve as a warrior.

As he fell asleep that night, he felt her drag her mat next to him. He pulled her against him before falling into a deep slumber. He woke the next morning as refreshed as the day before.

A part of him felt sad knowing this would be the last

day he would see the woman. Tomorrow he must return to battle. Sitting up, he again found her ready with his breakfast.

They spent their last day shoring up her food supply. He taught her how to trap rabbits and spear fish; though that simply had them both shivering from a fall in the stream.

He made sure the wood supply inside the cave was stocked and sharpened one of his knives to leave behind for her. She only rushed him into the cave to hide once when the other warriors crossed through on their way back to the battle.

By afternoon, he had decided he could use a bath before leaving again. He slipped off his clothes and waded into the pool. It was cold but had benefited from a series of warm days, unlike the stream. He was floating with his eyes closed when he heard a splash on the other side of the pool. He watched as the woman swam toward him.

She wrapped her arms around his neck and pressed her naked breasts against him. He was pulled into a chaste kiss. It wasn't enough. He wanted to taste her more than he had ever wanted anything.

He moaned when she opened her mouth to him letting him taste his fill. It only took him a moment to grow impossibly hard as he devoured her mouth at the edge of the clear pool. He hesitated only a minute before sliding inside of the most beautiful woman he had ever seen.

She gasped as he thrusted into her. She moaned at his release, her muscles clamping down on him. He held her to him as he stood in the water whispering how beautiful she was.

He finally softened, and they swam back to the other side. Dressing in silence, he followed her into the cave to help begin their dinner. Soon it would be dark, and he would have to rest for tomorrow.

They ate a small pig he caught out hunting. She prepared more bread. They drank wine she made out of what she could find. He helped her clean up before they retired for the night. She laid out the mats together. Then she waited for him.

He slid her tunic over her head. Naked, he laid her down on his fur cloak covering their mats. He kneeled between her legs as she looked up at him. Lowering himself, he entered her slowly.

He closed his eyes as she wrapped her legs around his hips, pulling him deeper. They made love until they both fell asleep from exhaustion wrapped in each other's arms.

The next morning he woke up from a strange dream. He had been a great wolf pursuing his enemies through the forest. Shaking himself awake, he looked around in confusion.

He was lying completely nude outside the cave in the grass. There was a string with pieces of smooth stone on it around his neck. Taking a closer look, he saw they had strange drawings on them. The woman watched him from behind a boulder.

"What have you done to me?" he growled.

She ducked back behind the rock. Standing, he swayed for a moment feeling dizzy. It passed quickly as she fled. He chased her. Wrestling her to the ground, he straddled her hips.

"Tell me what you've done." He felt himself losing control as he snarled down at her.

She struggled against him until she freed a hand. Calmly she ran it down his chest as she began to whisper.

Something about the motion made him feel calmer. He

rolled off her. She reached for a stick, grunting at him to pay attention as she drew in the dirt.

He struggled to make sense of her story. She had cast a spell on him to make him into one of the greatest warriors this land would ever know. He had been given the ability to turn into a wolf. He could now flank his enemies in silence. The wolf would have greater strength, faster reflexes, and would be able to see in the dark.

She had also enchanted four stones he must always wear. One was for protection from harm. The next was to help him control his new power. The third was for courage. She wouldn't tell him what the fourth stone held but that it would guarantee his safe return to her.

When she finished her story, he stood silently. Without looking back, he walked into the cave to dress. She chased after him begging him with her actions to look at her.

Gathering up his things, he shook her off and walked out of the cave. Behind him, she sank to her knees.

He was cursed to a life as a creature roaming the earth. How could she let him into her body then do something so abominable? Climbing back through the trees, he vowed to forget her.

FOURTEEN

Freja paused her story when they heard a truck pull up outside. Sten walked into the kitchen to see who it was.

Tani turned to Dane, checking to see if he was still awake. She found his glacial gaze focused on her. He pulled her forward and kissed her on the temple. She felt guilty for becoming so enthralled by the story Freja was telling. He needed to rest more than she needed answers.

"Hey," Erik said, walking into the living room.

Thyra jumped up, throwing her arms around him as he pulled her into a hug.

"Hey, brat."

She slapped him on the stomach, drawing a small oomph from his lips.

"Dude, that looks like it sucks." He walked over to get a better look at Dane's shoulder. "Roar didn't say you just wanted to get out of working." He laughed when Dane made a marginal attempt to hit him with his injured arm.

"Leave your brother alone," Freja said, reappearing with a tray of mugs filled with coffee. Tani wondered how many times that phrase had been used in this house. Taking the cup she was offered, she waited for Freja to finish the story.

"You're in luck, Erik. Mom was just finishing her fairy tale," Roar grumbled.

"Roar," Thyra said indignantly. "It's not a fairy tale. Right, Mom?" She took a swipe at Roar who dodged it easily.

"It's as good an explanation as any," Arne added, walking out of the kitchen carrying a carton of cream. Leaning over the coffee table, he added some to both Tani's and Thyra's coffees before mixing it in his own cup.

"Pussy," Dane growled at Arne. "Real men drink their coffee black."

"Real men don't like the taste of tar," Arne followed up.

"Dane," Sten growled a warning. Though he wasn't as harsh as he normally would have been. "You kids shut it so your mother can finish the story."

"Well, let me think. Where was I?" Freja said, looking at the ceiling as if the answer were somehow floating above her.

"The warrior had just ridden off," Tani offered.

"Like a dick," Thyra mumbled. She drew a growl from her father but a chuckle from Dane.

"That's right, okay, here we go."

IT DIDN'T TAKE the young warrior long to learn the benefits of turning into a wolf at will. As long as he stripped his clothes off first so he didn't destroy them, it was easy to shift.

He soon found his men hiding throughout the forest and amassed them back into an army. Though scared at first, his men learned quickly to accept the white wolf that slipped through the forest in silence picking off their enemy.

When they reached the battlefield, they found the other force starting to sag after days of continuous fighting. Rallying around their leader, the men flanked the enemy, quickly overpowering them.

The men received a hero's welcome home that lasted five days. The large party included plenty of food, drink, and conquered women to be passed around.

But try as he might, the young warrior could not get the beautiful sorceress out of his head. He continued to wear the amulets she had enchanted, fearing that taking them off would cause him great harm.

After five days, the chieftain called his warriors forward, bestowing on them large grants of the conquered land. He divided the pillaged valuables among them.

The young warrior was now a wealthy man. Returning to his farm, he announced his brother would be in charge of the farming on his new holdings. Within six months of returning home, he made a good marriage for his brother. He threw them a wedding feast that was talked about for years after. The warrior, however, could not find any interest in the eligible young maidens.

Finally, after a year, he chose five of his best manservants and went in search of the waterfall. They spent weeks hunting for it. As he was giving up hope, one of his men stumbled into a clearing with a pool being fed by a waterfall. Reporting back to his master, the servant led the warrior to the spot.

Climbing through the trees, he stepped out at the edge of the pool. Looking around, he noticed it looked much the same as when he left.

Motioning for his men to wait for him, he entered the cave. He held out his hand near the fire ring and felt the warmth coming off of it. She was here somewhere. He remembered well how she had hidden him when the enemy was near.

He had one of his servants bring him a torch. Walking deeper inside, he began to look for the crevice they hid in. Finally finding the small slit in the rock, he saw nothing unusual. He heard the barest whisper coming from the rocks.

"Wife," he said. "I've come to take you home." He watched carefully as the rock turned into a shimmer then into the beautiful woman he now knew he couldn't live without. His eyes traveled down to the small bundle she had firmly wrapped against her breast. He pulled her into an embrace, careful to not crush the baby between them.

She kissed him. He had come back for her. She knew he would come for both her and their son if she was patient. Without another word, he helped her out of the cave and onto his steed. Sitting proudly, with their son secured against her, she looked down into the glacial eyes of the man she knew could not live without her.

For when she cast a spell turning him into one of the greatest leaders his tribe would ever know, she also turned herself into the female he would need by his side. Much like the wolf chooses his mate for life, so would each generation of men from their family line, starting with her warrior.

～

BY THE END of the story, Tani found herself clutching Thrya's hand as they sat listening. It was one of the most beautiful stories she had ever been told. They both sighed in unison as they sat back on the couch.

"Oh, Christ." Arne rolled his eyes at them. "Bought right into the fairy tale."

"Say what you want, Arne Ulvmand, but that story got your father laid about ten minutes after your grandmother told it to me," Freja retorted.

"Well that's something I can't unhear now," Roar said.

Dane stood with a grunt. Reaching behind him, he pulled Tani to her feet.

"We need to get to a bed," he said. "I need to sleep." He started toward the stairs. "We're taking my old room."

"Let me grab you something to sleep in, Tani." Thyra ran up the stairs. By the time they reached the top, she had a pair of shorts and a T-shirt. Giving Tani a bear hug, she whispered into her ear, "I'm so glad you're okay."

"Thank you, Thyra." They almost made it through the bedroom door when they were stopped by Arne.

"I have something to put on the stitches to keep them from pulling as bad," he said. He held up his hands full of gauze, tape, and some kind of ointment. "Also, Mom said to give Tani the room next to yours." Arne smirked as he followed Dane into the room.

He quickly smeared the salve on Dane's shoulder while he sat on the bed. After expertly wrapping it to protect it while he slept, Arne hugged Tani good night and left the room. He closed the door firmly behind him.

"Do you need help with anything before I go?" Tani asked.

"You're staying in here," Dane growled.

"Dane," she started.

"Until he's stopped, you will be with me." Standing, he crossed into the bathroom.

Tani stood staring indignantly after him. She stomped out of his bedroom to the one next door. Dane was not in control of her, no matter what he thought. She determined where she slept.

She had just finished brushing her teeth when the bedroom door crashed open. She let out a small scream. Had Jakub waited until now to come back for her? But it wasn't Jakub. Dane stood in the door. His face transformed from anger to concern in a heartbeat.

"I'm sorry," he said. "I guess after everything, you have reason to be afraid of me." He closed the bedroom door. "Are you? Afraid of me?" He stepped closer to her.

She took him in, thinking carefully about his question. He looked like the warrior from the story with his long hair, tattoos, and necklace of silver. She let her eyes drift to his torn shoulder, the one he had sacrificed to keep her safe. Was she afraid of him? He was still the same Dane she had known most of her life. No, she wasn't afraid of him. She was in love with him.

"No, I could never be afraid of you," she answered.

"Then let me protect you," he said quietly.

His hand reached for hers. He waited to see if she'd take it. She watched the shiver roll through his body when she slid her hand inside his. He led her back to his childhood bedroom. She helped him get settled in bed before sliding in next to him. Using his good arm to pull her against his chest, he fell asleep.

Tani listened to him breathing for a long time. Even in sleep, he wore a scowl on his face as if ready to fight. She shifted slightly feeling his hold on her tighten immediately. She let out a deep sigh. Not only would she never be afraid of him, but in his arms was where she felt truly safe.

THE NEXT MORNING, Tani woke to the sensation of sleeping in a furnace. She quickly remembered why it was so hot. She had a six-foot-four-inch rock-hard heater pressed against her.

She was lying on her side with her head propped on Dane's bicep. Her back was pressed firmly against his chest. He had his arm wrapped around her, his hand spread on her lower stomach. The hand on the injured arm was holding her hip.

She tried easing out from under him only to be met by the growl she was now so familiar with. Settling back against him, she looked around the room, trying to guess what time it was. Sunlight peeked from around the curtains. She reached for her phone sitting on the dresser next to the bed.

"Woman, lie still," Dane snarled. Since when did he decide it was okay to just call her woman? It made her sound like his possession. Tani decided to think about that later.

"Are you hurting? What do you need me to do?" She turned slightly to look over her shoulder. Out of the corner of her eye, she could see the centipede of black thread sticking out of the edge of his bandage. He must have rubbed some of it off in his sleep. She slid her hand down him to ease his big arm off her side.

"Fuck," he groaned with a slight thrust of his hips. As if a brick had finally knocked some sense into her, Tani realized with a start what was rubbing between the cheeks of her ass. She had a decision to make. Knowing she could do nothing to help the ache in his shoulder, she smiled, thinking about how she could at least help him with this ache.

She worked her hand between them. His growl turned into a moan when it found its way inside his boxer briefs.

There had always been rumors in school about the size of the Ulvmand brothers' endowments equaling their body sizes. She had never heard of anyone who had actually witnessed it firsthand though. Finding that her hand couldn't close fully around his girth made her wonder what it would feel like to have it thrust inside her.

Tani began to run her hand up his erection, using the precum leaking out of the head to lubricate her hand. She listened to his labored pants behind her, hoping she wasn't putting too much stress on his stitches.

His hand made a slow journey under her shirt until his fingers grazed her nipple. She gasped. Her sensitive nipples begged him for attention, and he was happy to give them some.

She quickly forgot about his shoulder when he slid his other hand under the waistband of her shorts. He muttered a curse as his finger started a lazy circle against her clit. She bucked against his hand. He slipped one of his long fingers inside her, then a second one.

"Dane," she moaned.

"Fuck, yes. Say my name when I make you come," he growled as she rocked against his hand. Dane pinched her nipple with his strong fingers and her mind fractured. She spiraled and tossed on waves of ecstasy.

He brought her down slowly like he had done this a thousand times. Or, maybe, he was meant for her in ways she couldn't understand yet.

"Dane?" She wasn't sure what she was asking. Everything seemed to be happening so fast. She was getting so swept up in Dane that she worried she'd make a mistake. Or he would. Like tying himself to her and the child she carried.

"Shhh, it's okay," he whispered against her ear. "Nothing's set in stone yet."

"Yes. Right." She started to ease out of the bed. "I should get ready for work."

"You might want to wait a while. You screamed my name loud enough for the next county to hear."

"Oh no," she said, placing her head in her hands. "This is worse than high school."

"Did you do that a lot in high school?" he asked teasingly.

"No. I mean, it just feels like we're sneaking around trying not to get caught. Why? Did you?" She turned to face him. He was even more beautiful in the morning light. His eyes sparkled as he watched her.

"No," he said. "You're my first."

"That can't be possible. You were too popular and too good at that for it to be your first time."

"I think you're thinking of Arne." Dane grinned at her. He gave them out so sparingly that they felt like a gift when they happened. Everything inside her settled. "Or maybe Erik." She returned his smile. He could try to pass it off, but she knew he was always the hottest of the brothers.

"We probably should dress anyway. I imagine there are a million things that need to be taken care of today. We have to give our statements to the sheriff."

"I guess." His face transformed back into his regular scowl.

She climbed off the bed and crossed into the bathroom.

Turning on the water, she stepped into the shower. A groan escaped her lips as the water hit her sore body. Her body felt battered from being dragged through the undergrowth behind her house.

Her mind was still struggling to wrap itself around what happened in those trees. Tani had to hold on to the story Dane's mother told or risk being overwhelmed by everything.

She had heard the stories of men who could turn into animals in her own culture growing up. She never believed them until now. Why did Jakub want her? He almost killed her father to take her. What would keep him from trying again?

She sank in the shower until she was sitting against the wall. Bringing her knees up to her chest, she wrapped her arms around them. Hot tears rolled down her face.

She felt more than heard Dane step into the shower. He sat next to her and pulled her onto his lap. His strong arms embraced her. Rocking gently, he held her until her eyes ran dry.

"Let's get you dressed and fed," he said finally. "We'll stop by the sheriff's office first, then go see your dad. Does that sound like a plan?" He helped her off the shower floor. Taking a towel from the cabinet, he wrapped her in it.

"Roar took Thyra to your house this morning to gather up some of your stuff. There's a bag with clothes and other stuff in it in the other bedroom." Tani nodded her head, too tired to respond. He walked her back into the bedroom and sat her on the bed.

"I think we should have you checked out while we're at the hospital too. Make sure everything is okay with the baby." He walked to the bedroom door. "Sit here until you're ready to get dressed. I'll get dressed in the other room."

He left her alone to regroup. He knew she needed some time to herself. How he always seemed to know just what she needed still baffled her. It was just one more thing she loved about him.

FIFTEEN

Dane walked into his brother's old bedroom to scavenge for clothes. He knew Tani needed time to breathe without him hovering over her. Finding her in the bottom of the shower had crushed him, but he understood how overwhelming it was for her.

He had been turning into a very large white wolf since puberty, and it still freaked him out sometimes. To see two shifts in one night would render most people catatonic. But Tani was too strong to shrink from the unbelievable.

Pulling one of Erik's T-shirts out of a drawer, he pulled it over his head. It would be huge on him, and he debated where he could find a pair of jeans that fit him. He wasn't rolling a pair of Erik's up like a toddler wearing his older brother's clothes. He could probably get some from his dad, but that meant he would have to blow off underwear. Um, no thanks. Sliding Arne's sweatpants back on, he headed downstairs.

"Hey, sweetie. How are you feeling?" Freja said from the stove as he entered the kitchen. Walking over, he kissed her on the temple.

"Like I've been rolled by a bear," he answered. Pulling the orange juice out of the refrigerator, he poured himself and Tani a glass.

"Let me have a look." Wrestling the big shirt back over his head, he waited while she studied the sutures. "It doesn't look too bad. Arne left another shot of antibiotics to give you."

Crossing back to the sink, she picked up a syringe off the drainboard. He sank into one of the chairs at the small kitchen table. He tried his best not to flinch too badly as she slowly fed the medicine into his body.

"Where's Tani?" she asked, turning back to the stove.

"Upstairs dressing. I thought she could use some space." She nodded her head as she dipped two large slices of bread into egg batter before laying them on the griddle.

Dane's stomach growled. He loved his mother's french toast almost as much as he loved her. As hard as he tried, he could never quite duplicate it.

"So how far along is she?" Freja asked.

Dane sat in silence. He sometimes forgot that his mother was every bit as powerful as any of them. It just manifested itself differently. Of course, she knew Tani was pregnant.

"I don't know."

"Is it yours?"

"No, ma'am."

"How do you feel about that?"

He sat in thought for a few minutes. She would demand an honest answer, not just the same knee-jerk reaction he had been using lately.

"Honestly? I'm still trying to wrap my head around it. But I've loved her since I can remember. If it means embracing this baby so Tani is in my life, then I'll be the best fucking father that baby could ever have."

Scooping the toast off the grill, Freja added two pieces of sausage to a plate before turning to slide it in front of him. Fortunately, his mom had a better sense of humor than his dad. He wasn't in too much danger of losing his breakfast over his cussing before he could eat it.

"Son, look at me." Dane put his fork down so he could focus his whole attention on her. "If you truly mean that. That you'll love this baby as your own. Then you do whatever you have to do to keep them safe. Do you understand me?"

"Yes, ma'am."

"I'm serious, Dane. No matter what it takes. I'm going to start this afternoon making her a protection amulet. I might add one for good health and love too. Do you think she'll wear them?"

"I will," Tani answered from the doorway. Dane jumped up from the table in a panic at the tears rolling down her cheeks.

"What's wrong?" he asked, rushing to her. He looked over her body, making sure she wasn't bleeding or otherwise hurt. Finding nothing he could see, he pulled her against his chest. "What happened?"

"Dane," she whispered. "Why couldn't I see it before?"

"See what?"

"How good it could be? Between us?"

"Probably because I was in junior high." He squeezed her tighter.

She gave a watery laugh. That was better. He didn't know how many more tears he could handle. He squeezed her to him one more time before leading her to a chair. His mother quickly sat a plate full of breakfast in front of her.

Taking her first bite, Tani moaned. She grabbed his forearm where it sat on the table.

"My god, that's so good." A shiver raced through his body before he could control it. "Why do you do that?" she asked.

"What?" he asked, embarrassed that she noticed the uncontrollable impulse. He wasn't fooling himself. He was positive she had noticed it years ago. But he hated that he wasn't able to overcome the reaction.

"The shiver. Why do you shiver every time I touch you?"

"Oh, your dad used to do that before we finally..." His mother blessedly let the thought drift away before he had to learn any more about his parents' sex life. Obviously, it was a healthy one. There were five of them. That didn't mean he wanted to hear about it though. "Well, I guess it's obvious that all the moaning and screaming this morning wasn't from that."

"Mom. Please stop before I'm irreparably scarred for life."

His mother rolled her eyes as she joined them at the table. "Your father put out some feelers to see if he can find out anything about this man. He has to come from somewhere, there has to be family looking for him."

"Let me know if he hears anything. We need to head to town." Dane took his plate to the sink. The sooner this day got underway, the sooner it would be over. All he wanted was to wrap himself back around Tani. Taking her plate, he added it to the sink.

"Thank you so much, Mrs. Ulvmand. For everything," Tani said.

Freja pulled her into a hug. They stood locked in an embrace until Dane finally let out a sigh. He could hear Tani starting to sniffle again and didn't want her upset again. It couldn't be good for the baby. Freja placed a quick kiss on her cheek before releasing her. Sliding her hand into Dane's outstretched one, they headed out the door to his truck.

"Dane?" Tani asked.

"Yes?" he responded, turning the key in the ignition. The truck roared to life, and he pulled away from the house.

"Tell me what to say to the sheriff. We only have twenty minutes to come up with an official story. I don't want to slip. They don't need to find out about your...gift."

Dane glanced over at her with a relieved smile on his face. He knew she had a million questions swirling around in her head. But for right now they needed to present a united front if they were going to survive this.

FREJA WATCHED out the window as Dane and Tani drove out the gate. She had a few more things to do around the house then she planned to head to the small shed out back.

The men laughingly joked that it was her "she-shed." They knew it was where she kept her supplies to craft the charms they wore around their necks. The story she had told last night, regardless of what the men said, was not just some romantic dribble passed down through the generations. It was very much real.

She knew without a doubt that the charms she made protected the ones she loved. She had seen proof of it on more than one occasion.

When a woman was brought into the family, either through birth or marriage, it was the duty of the older generation to teach them how to weave magic through different items. They included protection spells, binding spells, love spells, and any other charm needed at the time.

She hung protection charms on her children from the moment they were born.

When she married Sten, her mother-in-law spent countless hours teaching her the old ways. Freja had already started teaching Thyra the art. Now she would begin Tani's instruction. There was no doubt the young woman would be joining their family soon. It would be her job to keep her family protected, including Dane.

Freja smiled as she slid the last plate into the dishwasher. She had always liked Tani. Her mother had been a mess, but Royal raised a nice daughter despite that fact.

"Was that Dane and Tani I saw heading out the gate?" Sten asked, walking into the kitchen.

"Yes. Dane said they had to give their statements to the sheriff, and then he was taking Tani to see Roy." Freja picked up the coffee pot, automatically pouring Sten a fresh cup when he sat at the small kitchen table.

"Roar and Erik are putting up hay. I told Erik to head back to school, but he said he would be fine staying today. Arne is sorting bulls." Freja joined Sten at the table with her coffee. She agreed with Arne, it was better with a helping of cream.

"I emailed my cousin back in Denmark first thing this morning," Sten continued. "He answered just now when I was walking to the house." He took another sip of coffee. Freja knew he liked to build suspense before imparting what he had learned. It was a habit both enduring and frustrating.

"Do I have to guess?" she asked.

"Cool your heels, woman. I'm getting to it." He grinned at her before taking another sip.

Freja had met Sten when she signed up for a course on Norse history as a freshman in college. Sten had been a junior looking for something to fulfill his history require-ment. Somehow he convinced her to go out at the end of a disastrous date with his friend. They were madly in love by their second date and married that summer. Roar had made his appearance soon after she graduated.

"As I was getting to," Sten said, "Malthe responded with some interesting news. He said he heard there was a group of bear shifters from eastern Europe that settled some-where south of Dallas."

"Well, that doesn't help us much."

"He said he would have to ask around but should have something by next week. Always expecting miracles," he mumbled at her. He broke into a grin when she swatted her hand at him. Freja returned his smile.

Even in his early fifties, he was just as handsome as the day she met him. Most of their children had gotten their height and blue eyes from him. Dane, Arne, and Erik had also inherited his blond hair. Roar had her darker hair and green eyes, and Thyra fell somewhere in the middle. It was no wonder they had five children when the man sitting next to her could still make her melt into a puddle with just a touch.

"What does that mean for Tani and Dane?" she asked.

"It means we keep her with us at all times. She's not safe until something can be done to catch him. She can stay here at night, and Dane will just have to watch her at work. We can manage for a little while without him."

"But Roar has work, and Erik needs to go back to school," Freja began to protest.

"Have I not taken care of this family in the past?" Sten asked, his eyebrow raised in challenge.

"You have taken very good care of this family."

"Then let me do my job. It won't be long before Tani is a

member of this family if Dane has his way. Nothing will touch her again on my watch."

Freja felt the gooseflesh rise on her skin. When Sten became this protective of their family, it made her want to clear the table off and have her wicked way with him. Unfortunately, she had other things she needed to do. Tonight would be soon enough. Leaning over for a quick kiss, she stood.

"I should get to work then. Tani will need a protection charm."

Rinsing their cups, she placed them in the dishwasher. She followed Sten out the back door. After one more kiss, she entered her workshop. She knew her husband would do everything in his power to protect them. She also knew he couldn't do it without her help.

SIXTEEN

Dane sat in a chair next to Tani in front of the sheriff's desk. They had known Sheriff Barton since they were kids. That still didn't dispel the feeling they had been called to the principal's office.

Tani insisted they go over their story on the way into town so she didn't say anything that could hurt him. A simple version of what happened was crafted that came as close to the facts as possible. There was less chance they would be caught in a lie if they weren't lying, just omitting some of the facts.

"So, Dane," Sheriff Barton said, "you said you went to Tani's house and discovered this Jakub character had broken in. Why were you at Tani's house?"

"I needed to apologize for something I did earlier," he answered.

"What did you do earlier?" Sheriff Barton asked with a smirk. Dane had no doubt he knew what had happened at the diner. Ever since Dane had made varsity baseball as a freshman and his son had not, the sheriff hadn't missed a chance to bust his balls.

"I made an ass out of myself as I'm sure you've already heard."

"Um-hmm. And Tani, you say you were being forced toward an undisclosed location when Dane happened to find you?"

"Yes, sir."

"A fight ensued, and this man ran off?"

"That's right."

"Then how did Roar just happen to show up not five minutes after we did?"

"I called Arne when I found the door kicked open. He must have called Roar on the way into town," Dane said.

They had been over this for the last hour. Tani looked exhausted, and his shoulder felt like it was on fire. If they didn't get out of here soon, there was a real possibility he would turn into a wolf again. If for no other reason than so he could eat the sheriff and take some painkillers. Breakfast had long worn off.

"We're not done here," Barton said when Dane stood.

"We are," he answered, pulling Tani up beside him. "We didn't do anything wrong, and we're late to the hospital. If you have any more questions, you know where to find us." He took Tani's hand and pulled her out of the office.

"Blowhard," he mumbled when they were at the truck.

"He hasn't liked me since I turned his son down as my prom date my senior year," Tani said.

"He was in the same grade I was," Dane answered.

"I know. He kept pestering me. As if I would go to prom with a freshman." She cocked her head at him. "Well, maybe there was one, but he didn't ask."

"Like I had the guts to ask you to prom," Dane said, opening her door.

"Can you imagine Roar if that had happened?" she

continued when he climbed into the seat next to her. "He would have insisted we dance three feet apart. No grinding there."

"I doubt I would have been able to handle you grinding against me. I would have either panicked and fled or been dragged home by my ear for coming in my tux pants."

Tani laughed as he started the engine.

"I do have a confession," he continued.

"Do tell."

"I talked Mom into parking outside the high school that night so I could see what you wore."

"Dane, that's so sweet." Her smile lit up her face.

"Yeah, I beat off like a fucking beast that night."

"Dane." She smacked his chest with a laugh.

It was good to hear her laugh again. He was worried after what she saw last night she wouldn't be able to get away from him fast enough. Surprisingly, she seemed to take it in stride. Well, at least she was putting up a good front.

"Can we get something to eat at Donna's?" she asked, breaking into his thoughts. "They have been calling all morning. It will help put their minds at ease if we make an appearance, and they can see I'm okay."

"Of course." He pulled into the parking lot. He made it around the truck to open Tani's door when Donna came flying outside.

"Let me see if you're okay," she said, doing a quick scan. "You scared me."

"I'm fine," Tani said.

"How's Roy and the—" Donna stopped mid-sentence.

"It's called a baby, and Dane knows," she answered. "Do you think we could have a couple of burgers?"

"Yes, come inside. I'll go put them on the grill."

"We'll be there in a minute," Tani called, holding Dane back. When Donna returned inside, she turned to him. "Dane," she started before faltering.

"What?"

"You know everyone will assume this baby is yours?"

"Okay."

"It's not fair to you. They'll drag your name through the mud with mine."

"I don't care what they say," he said.

"But, Dane," she began again.

"Tani, can we please eat before having this conversation? I can't fight properly with my stomach growling."

They ate quickly before hitting the road again. He had to answer questions about what happened throughout most of his lunch. They gave everyone a condensed version of what they told the sheriff. No doubt, the story would be blown all out of proportion by the time they got home. He didn't care.

The nearest hospital was an hour away. Their small town had a clinic that was fine for the occasional scratchy throat or sprained ankle. For bigger problems like broken bones, babies, or heart attacks, you had to travel.

They got to the hospital only to find out Roy had been checked out an hour earlier. Dane inwardly groaned, knowing he was going to drive the extra half hour to Paris and then back around to the ranch.

"Let's just go home. I can call Dad later," Tani said.

Dane could see how disappointed she was at having missed him. It was his fault. He should have insisted on coming here first. The sheriff would have been pissed, but he could have waited to take their statements.

"No, we're going to see your dad. I think we should have the baby checked while we're here, though."

"I have an appointment next week. It can wait until then."

Dane raked his hands through his hair.

"Can you just humor me, please?" he asked.

She nodded. He took her hand and headed toward the maternity ward. It didn't take him long to find someone willing to check her over. He helped her settle onto a rolling bed. She laid back so an intern could run a fetal Doppler over her lower abdomen. The man jumped when Dane growled at him pulling her pants down slightly.

"I have to get to the baby," he said.

Dane stood on the other side with his arms folded over his chest, one eyebrow raised. He dared the man to make a wrong move. The intern rolled the doppler over her lower abdomen until a loud thudding began.

"Is that it?" Dane asked. It sounded like the poor little thing was running a marathon. "Why is it so fast?" Had everything that happened last night hurt the baby? He would kill that fucker Jakub when he found him. No one hurt his family and got away with it.

"Dane," Tani said, laying her hand on his arm. "Calm down. It's supposed to be that fast." Looking up at the intern, he found the man frozen in place. Had he been growling again? "The baby's fine," she said, taking his hand.

"Is it?" he asked the intern.

"Yes, yes. Everything sounds normal." Quickly putting his doppler wand back in his pocket, the intern patted Tani on the shoulder. "You can follow up with your regular doctor at your next appointment. Excuse me." He quickly walked out of the room.

"That wasn't very nice, Dane," Tani said.

Dane grunted. He listened to his footsteps disappear

down the hall. His hand grazed over where the heartbeat had come from.

"Can I go with you?" he asked quietly.

"Go where?"

He removed his hand and helped her sit up.

"To your next doctor's appointment."

"Why?"

She didn't understand that something in him had changed when he heard the heartbeat. This was the start of his family. This was the child he would raise. He would be the one to make sure they were fed, clothed, and had a roof over their heads. It was now his responsibility to provide for their happiness.

"You might not realize it yet," he said, stepping between her legs. "But I'm a part of this. You're stuck with me whether you like it or not. I'm not letting you go."

He placed his finger under her chin and tilted her head back. Her gaze met his. His lips brushed hers with a sigh. Her hand wrapped in his shirt before pulling him closer.

He pulled back to study her face. Her eyes were closed. Slowly, they opened. Lust swam in the deep chocolate pools. He felt the growl swell from his chest. His mate. His mouth found hers again. His tongue asked permission to taste more. When she opened to him, he took what was his.

She was as sweet as she was in his dreams. He wanted to lay her back on the bed and taste her everywhere. He wanted to mark her as his. If he lived a hundred years, he would never get enough of her.

He angled her head slightly to the side so he could reach every inch of her mouth. Her hands eased under his shirt. The feel of her hands running over his body was pure bliss.

"Excuse me," someone said from behind him. "I hate to interrupt, but we need this room."

Dane straightened up. Turning around, he found the same intern who saw Tani. His responding snarl was cut off by her hopping from the exam table.

"I'm so sorry. Come on, Dane." Taking his hand, she pulled him toward the door to check out. He managed to get at least a sneer in before she jerked him down the hallway. "What did that poor guy do to you?"

"He stuck his hands in your pants."

"He barely pulled down the waistband so he could get the doppler where it needed to be. What are you going to do when the doctor gets to digging around down there?"

Dane pulled her to a stop near the doors to the hospital.

"I'll rip him apart," he said seriously.

"You're not helping your case."

He scowled at her as they entered the parking lot. Climbing into the truck, they sat in silence.

"I'd prefer you have a female doctor," he finally said.

"Dane, there are only so many obstetricians to go around here. I have a very nice man who came highly recommended."

"Is he at least someone's grandpa, great-grandpa would be even better?"

"He's a little older than I am. He's very professional. I promise you'll like him."

It wasn't lost on Dane that she was trying to hide her smile. The man could be a damn angel sent from heaven to deliver her baby. That didn't mean he wanted the man's hands on her. Turning, he gave her his most serious frown.

"You're killing me," he said.

Tani burst into laughter. Leaning over, she grabbed his hair, pulling him toward her for a quick kiss. He couldn't stay irritated when she did that.

She leaned back in her seat. He turned to look at her.

She was still smiling as she looked out the front windshield. The sun was shining through her window playing with the gold in her hair. As if in slow motion, she turned her gaze on him. The laughter in her deep-brown eyes made his heart skip a beat.

"What?" she asked.

"You know I love you, right?"

"I don't think you're supposed to tell someone that after just two kisses and a little mild fooling around," she said with a chuckle.

"Tani, I've loved you since the first time I saw you in second grade at your elementary school graduation. I'm just stating the obvious."

"Dane," she said, shaking her head.

"What?" he responded. "You think it's too soon? I'd be happy to lay you on your back and prove it." Her face turned a deep red. "Just name the place and time."

He waited for her to say something. When she didn't, he started the truck.

"That got you thinking, huh?" He smirked. She opened her mouth to say something but then shut it again without uttering a sound. "Nothing?"

"Just shut up and drive," she said.

With a laugh, he pulled out of the parking lot.

CHAPTER

SEVENTEEN

It was dark by the time they made it back to Dane's house. Tani had talked him into stopping by her house so she could gather a few more things she needed before leaving again. He helped her straighten up the living room. Roar had done a good job of ensuring the mobile home was secure, but he couldn't be expected to do it all.

It was late when they finally pulled up to the front of his house. Dane let out a sigh, glad to be back home again. His shoulder ached more than he was willing to admit, and he needed some sleep.

He walked around to the passenger side and took her bag. Following her, they climbed the steps to the door.

He needed to put together some plan to watch her at work until they could find Jakub. The man had become unhinged. If they couldn't find any relatives soon to deal with him, Dane would have to take care of the problem himself. But that could wait for tomorrow.

They found Arne and Roar sitting in the living room watching a game.

"Hey, we were starting to worry about you," Roar said. He pulled Tani into a hug. "You doing okay?" he asked.

"Just tired," she answered. Dane carried her bag into his bedroom before rejoining them. She sat at the table while Arne heated them something to eat.

"Let's take a look at your shoulder," Arne said when Dane sat down. Carefully, he pulled the shirt off over his head. It was raw where the stitches held the skin together. "I think I'll give you another shot of antibiotics just to make sure."

Returning to the kitchen, Arne returned with a syringe and a large bottle of penicillin. Dane ground his teeth when Arne stuck the needle into his hip. It felt like fire being forced into his body. He sat back down at the table while Arne replaced his bandage.

"What did the sheriff say?" Roar asked.

Arne began setting supper on the table. Tonight he made some skillet mixture using hamburger meat and potatoes. Dane was hungry enough it could have been anything, and he would devour it.

"He knows we're not telling him everything, but he can't figure out what he's missing," Dane answered.

"How's the baby?" Roar added quietly. "Mom told us. But I promise no one will hear it from us. It's your decision who knows and when. She's just worried."

"It's fine," she said. "It won't remain a secret much longer. Everything looked good at the hospital. I have an appointment next week to have a better look."

"Good." Roar nodded. "You know we're here if you need us." He squeezed her hand. "What's the plan regarding this Jakub person?" he asked, effectively ending the subject of the baby.

"What I can't figure out is why he's so obsessed with

her. You said he's always at the restaurant waiting in the morning?" Arne said, filling Roar's plate.

"Yeah, and I've had a couple of minor run-ins with him. Nothing too extreme before last night. Enough to know he didn't like me hanging around," Dane answered. "The sheriff said they had all law enforcement in the surrounding area keeping an eye out for him. I'm not sure how much luck they'll have. If he can shift into a bear, he can live hidden for years, and no one will find him."

"Dad is still hunting for where this guy came from, but he hasn't had any luck yet," Roar said. Scooping up a forkful of Arne's concoction, he chewed thoughtfully for a few minutes. "Arne said he has a Russian-sounding accent, is that right?"

"I think it's more Eastern European than Russian. I know there's not much difference. I had a colleague from Serbia. He sounds more like that," Tani answered.

"How old would you say he is?"

"Maybe around thirty or thirty-five."

"So, probably not a student."

Tani shook her head. She didn't think that was the case either.

"It just doesn't make any sense why he would show up here. It's not like this area is the melting pot for new immigrants or even on the top ten places to visit when in America. I'll ask around campus anyway. See if I can find anything. Maybe someone knows him."

"I guess that's all we can do until he shows himself again," Dane said.

"But how long do I have to hide before that happens? I can't live like this forever. I have to work." Tani looked at each one of the men in turn receiving nothing more than shrugs.

They finished the rest of the meal in relative silence, only broken by the occasional comment from Arne. He had always been the most talkative of the brothers.

"What are you smiling at?" Dane asked.

"I was thinking about when y'all would come to the diner as a family," she answered. "You would sit and scowl. Arne would talk my ear off."

"Sounds about right," Roar said.

"Never in a million years would I have believed I'd be sitting here now discussing a man who can shift into a bear."

"Welcome to our world," Arne said.

"But it shouldn't have to be your world. I feel like I've dragged you into this."

"That's not how I see it," Roar said. "I see it as divine providence that you happen to fall under the protection of the one family who can handle this. Like it or not, Tani, you're one of us now."

She opened her mouth to protest but closed it again. Dane knew she saw the same serious look on Roar's face mirrored on both his and Arne's. Roar was right. They would die before anyone laid another hand on her.

"I think we've had enough excitement for one day. We're going to turn in. Thanks for dinner, Arne," he said, pushing back from the table.

"I'm sleeping on the couch tonight if either of you need anything," Roar said.

"And you know where I'll be," Arne added.

"Thank you," she whispered. Turning to Roar, she threw herself at him in a fierce hug. He stroked her back, telling her everything would be okay. Next, she circled the table, pulling Arne into a hug. Finally, she reached out for the hand Dane extended to her. She let him pull her against his chest.

"It's going to be okay," he said. "You've got us now."

DANE WAS DRAGGED out of the most amazing dream. In it, Tani was curled up in his arms, her soft snores like a lullaby to his ears. Something woke him. Something that sounded like a dog sniffing. It was odd since he didn't have a dog.

Prying his eyes open, he was startled when he realized it wasn't a dream. Tani was truly snuggled against him with her ass firmly pressed against his cock. A slow smile crept over his face as his thoughts turned to ideas of every dirty thing he wanted to do with her.

Before he could begin to act, a noise brought him fully awake. There was definitely something outside the window sniffing. As realization dawned on what it could be, there was a massive roar.

Something crashed against the bedroom wall hard enough to rattle the window. Dane was out of bed, dragging Tani with him in one move. He heard her scream when the wall shook with another crash.

"What the fuck," Arne yelled, throwing the bedroom door open. Roar stood behind him as the bear let out another mighty roar.

"Arne, get Tani to safety," Dane yelled, pushing her into Arne's arms.

He wasted no time running through the house with Roar close on his heels. Unlocking the door, they barreled outside. They came to a sliding stop when the same bear Dane had fought only yesterday let out a terrifying roar.

THE WHITE WOLF SNARLED, his fangs dripping with saliva. His red brother joined in his warning. The creature was threatening his mate and child. A roar ripped from the creature's mouth. The white wolf lunged toward it.

With one more warning bellow, the creature turned into the night. The white wolf followed in pursuit, the red wolf at his side. They ran for miles, the creature just out of reach. It was faster than he thought possible.

How had he found her? His need to take her had grown beyond just obsession. The white wolf knew it was up to him to end this. Spurred on by the thought of the danger it posed to his mate, the white wolf pushed faster trying to close the gap. Soon he heard the rasping pants of the red wolf on his flank.

They topped the crest of the hill and dropped down toward the bottom. His shoulder burned from the exertion. There was red blood mixing in his white. No amount of pain, though, could make him slow down. He saw the creature grow larger as he closed the distance between them.

The red wolf started to lag behind. He should have brought the other one, the fast one. This brother was stronger, however. In a fight, the red wolf would make a better warrior.

The white wolf had almost closed the distance to the bear when they reached the river. They had him trapped. He stopped a few feet away snarling. The creature raised back up before lunging at the white wolf with a spine-chilling bellow.

The red wolf came to a sliding stop, baring his teeth. He slowly flanked the bear to the right. The white wolf snapped with a growl, trying to keep the creature's attention on him. If the red wolf could get close enough, they could bring him down.

Without warning, the creature plunged over the ledge into the river and began paddling downstream. The white wolf knew it was a better swimmer than him. It could swim longer than he could. He worked through the underbrush trying to follow on land.

With the red wolf following in his tracks, he pushed through the bramble. He barely felt the scratches left on his face and legs. Knowing how the river cut through the land, he pushed out of the undergrowth. They cut across the country to get ahead of the creature. They could attack at one of the bends. Nearing one of the cutbacks, he crashed back into the undergrowth along the bank.

Reaching the bend, the white wolf jumped into the river. He surfaced with a sputter kicking with his legs. As hard as he kicked, the creature pulled too far ahead of him.

The pain in his shoulder was slowing him down. He could feel fatigue set in from his efforts to follow. He finally had to give up. Dragging his body out on the far side, he collapsed on the bank to catch his breath.

The red wolf crashed through the undergrowth near him. His brother nuzzled him until the white wolf rose to his haunches. With a howl, the red wolf expressed the frustration they both felt over losing their quarry.

The white wolf finally caught his breath and rose. He shook the water from his coat. His brother rubbed his head over him, checking for injuries and assuring him that he had done all he could.

The white wolf turned to stare at the river for a long time. If he couldn't catch the creature, what chance did they have? He would have to reassess his plan when he returned to his home.

The red wolf shoved him toward home with his head. The red wolf was tired of waiting for him to give up for tonight. Without looking back, the white wolf started to trot down the riverbank.

They soon found a crossing that led them to the other side of the river. Leaving the river behind, they headed back up the hill. They stopped at their parent's house to check everything was okay. They found no sign the creature was there. Quietly, they continued down the road.

Fifteen minutes later, they were standing outside the white wolf's home. Looking over at the red wolf, he watched as he turned back into his human form. The white wolf followed.

"Do you see my pants?" Roar asked, looking around. "I took them off first, so they should be in one piece."

Dane was impressed Roar thought that far ahead. Hunting around, he spied Roar's pants. He also found his shorts, though they were a little worse for the wear. They would at least hold together until he could change.

Dane slowly pushed the front door open. He was met by the shotgun Arne had pointed at his chest. Tani was standing behind Arne. Dane knew without a doubt his younger brother would defend her with his life if necessary.

"Jesus." Arne quickly dropped the barrel of the gun to point at the floor.

Tani pushed around him to throw herself into Dane's arms. He heard her sob. Lifting her to his waist, he carried her to the bedroom.

"Hey," he said softly, sitting Tani on his dresser when they reached his room. "You're okay."

"Oh Dane, your shoulder."

"It'll be fine. Arne can stitch it back together."

"What happened?"

"Let me change, then I'll tell you while we get something hot to drink." He reached between her legs and pulled out some sweats. "Look at me," he said, pulling them on. "We're going to stop this. You trust me when I tell you I'll protect you?"

She nodded.

"Then let's go get something hot to drink," he said. Pulling her to him, he pressed his lips to hers. "I think we could all use a little something extra in it."

EIGHTEEN

After a long restless night, Dane left Tani curled up asleep in his bed when he heard movement in the living room. He found Roar pouring coffee into a travel mug in the kitchen. He motioned for Dane to take a seat at the bar and poured him a cup.

Dane dropped wearily onto one of the barstools. He noticed his brother looked just as exhausted as he felt. It seemed no one got more than a few hours of sleep last night. Arne dropped into the seat next to him. Another cup of coffee was shoved into his hands.

"I have to leave for work," Roar said. "But I'll be back this evening. You both need to be careful today. He could be anywhere." Roar walked toward the door, grabbing his bag on the way.

"Hey, Roar," Dane said, swinging around to face his oldest brother. Roar stopped with his hand on the doorknob. "Thanks."

"You'd do the same for me," he answered. Without saying more, he left for work.

"You too, Arne. I mean it. Thanks," Dane said.

"Don't even have to say it. We're just protecting what's ours, right?" Arne said with a grin. "So, I don't know about you, but I could eat a horse." He stood and walked to the refrigerator. "Eggs okay?"

Without waiting for an answer, he pulled out a large carton of eggs, milk, cheese, and sliced ham. Dane wasn't sure when his brother learned how to cook. But thank God he had.

He sat in silence, sipping his coffee as he watched Arne. Ham was tossed into a pan. Eggs, some onion, and a little pepper were added. Using a spatula, he worked the egg to the bottom until it was almost done. He melted cheese on top before folding it over to form an omelet. Half was placed on a plate next to a buttered English muffin and slid across to Dane. How had he missed the muffin in the toaster?

"Your talents might be wasted on cows," Dane mumbled around a mouthful of perfection.

"Nah. I don't mind cooking for you. I just don't want to make a profession out of it. There she is," Arne said. A very sleepy Tani walked toward the kitchen. "You're just in time." He slid the plate he made for himself in front of her as she sat down. Dane smiled at him. They really did take care of their own. Arne poured Tani a glass of milk before tossing more ham into the skillet. "How did you sleep, sweetheart?"

"Not bad for a short nap," she answered. "I called Donna. She doesn't have me scheduled again until after the weekend."

"That's good. You could use some extra rest," Dane said.

"I could. I don't know how I'll survive today."

"You'll be safe at my parents' house while I catch up on some work." He was being a little heavy-handed, but he refused to even consider her being alone. He would get everything done today. Then he could take the weekend off. "I've got to spray the hay fields if I hope to get another cutting done before the heat sets in."

"You'll be alone?" she asked.

"Don't worry. Arne and I both carry guns, and I'll be in the spray tractor," he said, reaching over to squeeze her hand. "Arne, you need to be careful. Are you feeding today?"

"Yeah. I need to start moving the cattle closer to the pens for spring work in a couple of weeks. I'm waiting a little late this year, but I could use Erik's help. He gets done with finals next week." Arne finished his breakfast. "Well, I've got to go."

"Leave everything," Dane said. "I'll clean up. We'll see you for lunch."

"Thank you, Arne," Tani called after him as he headed to the door.

"Anytime." With a wink, Arne headed out the door.

"He's such a flirt," she said, laughing.

"Always has been, but I'm glad you aren't swayed by it," Dane answered.

"I don't know, he is kind of cute." She laughed again at his scowl. "But I do have a thing for grumpy and demanding."

Pulling her off the stool onto his lap, he kissed her neck where it met her shoulder. He could feel the shiver run through his body even stronger than before.

"Hmm, you came to the right place then," he said. He nipped and kissed his way up her neck.

"Is that right?" she moaned, tipping her head to the side to give him better access.

"That's right."

His tongue plunged into her mouth and slid over hers.

His hand swept under her shirt to find her nipple straining for his touch. One stroke had his cock fighting angrily against the zipper of his jeans. The moan she released into his mouth almost had him coming in his pants. He should take this to the bedroom instead of balancing precariously on a bar chair.

"Stop," Tani said. She slid off of his lap. He helped her find her balance and then held up his hands. "Just, stop."

"I did stop." What did he do? Everything had been perfect. They had the house to themselves, and he didn't have to head to work just yet.

"How many women have you been with?" she asked.

"What?"

"It's a simple question. How many women have you had sex with?"

"None, you know that." Was she trying to tell him he was a shitty lover before he even got started?

"Not even in college?"

"No. I mean, there were opportunities. It just never got that far."

"Why?"

"What do you mean why?" He stood and paced across the room. "What does it matter?"

"Do you believe the story about being cursed to only love one woman for all eternity that your mother told?" she asked.

"Jesus," he snarled. "Is this about what you saw in the woods? Because you've been acting a little too calm about it all." He stomped back to her. "We should talk about it."

"I'm trying, but you're being impossible."

"I'm not being impossible." He blew out a breath. He was being impossible. But it was an impossible thing to talk about. "Okay. No. No sex. I don't know if I buy into the fairy tale. I just never wanted to tempt fate either." He blew out another breath, this one of resignation. "Our sons would be cursed, though. I know that for a fact."

"Our sons would be blessed to have you for their father. It's not that you shift into a wolf. It is otherworldly, but I know there's more to this universe than what we can explain."

"What is it then?"

"It's you." He searched her warm gaze, trying to understand. "If the tale is true, you only have one chance. You won't get to change your mind and walk away. How is it fair of me to ask that of you? How is it fair to trap you in a curse?"

"Tani." He ran his hand through his hair. He desperately wanted to reach for her, but he hesitated. "I've had other chances to tie myself to someone. But I've never been able to get you out of my mind." He gave up fighting his impulses. His hands cupped her face. "I've loved you forever. I think I loved you before we even were. How do I not keep that forever?"

"I love you too, Dane," she whispered. Her hands pressed against his. "I just want us to make sure."

"Then we'll make sure," he said. "But my mind won't change. You are my family now. I won't give up on us."

"And neither will I," she whispered. "When it's time, there will be no doubts."

"In that case, you should get dressed. The sooner we push through time, the sooner we can be together." He smiled down at her. His lips swept over hers before turning her loose.

She walked back down the hallway to his bedroom. He watched as her hips swayed. She was going to kill him. But he had waited most of his life for her. A little while longer was all she was asking. He would never change his mind. She was all he wanted in life; it was just taking her a little longer to see it.

He walked into the kitchen to load the dishes into the dishwasher. His mind ran through the list of everything he needed to do today. Tani's safety didn't worry him. She would be safe at the house. His father would be there to watch over her. And, if he was being honest, his mother was as big of a badass as anyone. She once killed a murderer in their kitchen. Not that he remembered, he was a baby at the time.

"Are you ready?" she asked, breaking into his thoughts.

"Yeah. Do you have everything you need?" He turned off the water and put the last dish in the dishwasher.

"I don't have much." She followed him out the door and waited for him to lock up. They drove toward his parents' house. It wouldn't be long before he had to leave her again.

"Are we good?" he asked.

"Of course we're good. Why?"

"I don't like when we argue."

"It didn't seem to bother you when we discussed my obstetrician."

"Mmm," he snorted.

She laughed. "Dane Ulvmand, you're a good man. You know that, right? Hard-headed, but good."

"Only because I'm in love with a good woman."

"I think I could get very used to having you around," she said with a smile.

"Then my fiendish plan is working."

She laughed loudly this time. His heart missed a beat. He didn't mind; she owned it anyway.

They pulled up in front of the house. He helped her from the truck, and they walked inside together. His mother was in the kitchen working on something for lunch.

"Are you still good if Tani spends the day here? I don't want her to be alone while I'm spraying."

"Of course," Freja answered. "I'm looking forward to getting to know her better." She took Tani's hand and squeezed it. "Maybe we'll go tinker in the shed. I haven't been out there in a long time," she added with a wink at Dane.

"Don't wear her out," he said. "And no heavy lifting."

"Women have been having babies long before Dane Ulvmand arrived to bark orders," Freja said. "Now, go before the wind picks up."

FREJA STUDIED Tani as she slumped into one of the chairs at the kitchen table. Dane didn't have to worry. The exhaustion on her face backed up everything Arne told them about what happened last night.

Sten closed himself in his office to see if he could hunt for anyone even remotely related to this Jakub. It was apparent they would need help bringing him in. What no one could understand was what he wanted with Tani.

Dane had set his sights on Tani a long time ago. Before he even understood what it meant himself. But Freja saw the raw emotions on his face every time he looked at her. She also knew if Dane was determined to have something, he would do whatever it took until he got it. She assumed that applied to Tani more than anything.

She just hoped Tani felt the same way about Dane. She wasn't so sure. Fortunately, she had the whole day to get to the bottom of it. She had always adored how sweet Tani was. She would be a good choice for her son. They just had to convince her of that.

"Arne told us all about last night," Freja said. "Would you like to lie down for a while?"

"No, I'm fine." Freja could see that her mind was a million miles away. "Mrs. Ulvmand?"

"Freja," she answered. She placed the meat she was slicing into a marinade. Crossing to the refrigerator, she placed it inside. She poured herself another cup of coffee and sat at the table.

"Freja," Tani said, starting again. She chuckled quietly. "It seems so strange to call you that after so many years of referring to you as Mrs. Ulvmand."

"Yes, but you're a grown woman now. And if you're going to be with Dane, it's time we moved to first names." She handed Tani a bottle of water she had pulled out of the refrigerator. Tani laughed again when she saw it.

"Arne keeps giving me milk. I don't think I've ever consumed so much milk as I have in the last twenty-four hours."

"Knowing Arne, don't be surprised when he wants to discuss your birth plan so he can be prepared." Freja smiled. "He's the sweetest boy, but sometimes he forgets to engage his common sense. He and Thyra are my two impulsive children. Though I hear Dane is quickly catching up."

"So you heard about him storming into the diner?"

"Lord, everyone in the entire state heard about that."

They both laughed. Freja watched as Tani turned quiet again. There was definitely something bothering her. She would simply have to wait until the girl was ready to tell her. Freja knew she would eventually in her own time.

"Mrs. Ulvmand. Sorry, Freja," Tani corrected herself. "Have you ever regretted—" She broke off. With a deep breath, she began again, "I mean, did you ever think—" She stopped again.

"Are you trying to ask if I've ever regretted all of this?" Freja asked, waving her hand vaguely around.

"Yes. But I'm not trying to sound offensive." Tani pulled at the label on the water. "It's just that Dane is so sure, and I don't want him to rush into anything he'll regret later."

"You know, I think every woman has asked themselves that at one point in their life," she answered. "If I'm honest, I've asked myself that on more than one occasion. But the answer has always been the same."

Tani's soulful gaze met hers. She was truly struggling to decide what she wanted to do. Freja didn't want her to jump at anything she wasn't ready for. But she also wasn't about to mince words.

"I think marrying Sten was the best thing I ever did. Even after thirty-some years, I'd do it all again."

"Really?"

"Absolutely. But," Freja added with a wink. "That doesn't mean I didn't need some convincing."

"You did?"

"Of course. We can't just jump because some man thinks we should. No, I made Sten work for me. You see, he was a lot like Arne when I met him." She laughed when she saw the look of surprise on Tani's face. She knew everyone thought Dane took after his father, but they were wrong. "Hard to believe, huh?"

"A little."

"It's true. He was full of swagger and self-confidence. Sten waltzed into that classroom the first day, looked around, and plopped down at the desk next to mine. I looked over at him, and he winked at me. Winked. Of course, I thought he was possibly the most handsome man

I had ever seen. But I refused to turn into one of those women who followed just because he crooked his finger."

"What did you do?" Tani asked.

"I rolled my eyes and turned away from him."

"What did he do?"

"He asked me out. I said no. He asked me out every day after that."

"What made you change your mind?"

"First, he was charming. The more I got to know him, the more I realized the swagger was all for show. That under all of that was a good man. Second, did I mention he was beautiful with all of his floppy blonde hair, blue eyes, and dimples? Even a strong, independent woman can only hold up her defenses so long."

Tani laughed as Freja took another sip of coffee.

"How long was it before you learned what he could do?"

"Oh, you mean the shifting? It was when we got engaged. He asked me to marry him. Then he asked me to wait to answer. That there was something about him that might make me want to change my mind. I didn't understand until the first time I saw it, though. It can all be overwhelming."

"Dane is just so certain we should be together. I don't think he's thought it out. I can accept what he is, and I know he's a good man. But Freja, he doesn't understand what raising another man's baby will be like. He'll come to resent us, and he'll be trapped."

Freja took Tani's hands in hers.

"My son might be a lot of things–grumpy, obstinate, silent. But I do know when he loves someone, it's with his whole heart. Believe me when I say he's thought about the consequences of being with you. He's been in love with you for as long as I can remember. If loving you means loving your child, then he will with everything he has. If you want to be with Dane, then trust him to do what's best for all of you."

Freja hoped she was reaching Tani. She could see the girl loved her son. She was just terrified to admit it. What Tani didn't understand was she was stronger than she thought she was. With Dane by her side, there would be nothing she couldn't handle.

"Now, how do you feel about snapping some beans for lunch?" she asked. "You handle that. I'll make a pie."

"For the promise of pie, I'll do anything you want." Tani laughed.

Freja smiled and handed her the beans. Tani was a beautiful woman, inside and out. If Dane could just hold on, she would be well worth the fight.

NINETEEN

"Hey," Tani said, stepping through the shop door.

"Hey," Dane replied. He stepped out from behind the tractor he was replacing the hydraulic hose on.

"I brought you something to eat."

"Thanks." He wiped the grease off of his hands. Everything was progressing right on schedule until he blew the hose moving hay. He worked through lunch to catch back up. He took the plate and sat in one of the old chairs.

"I'm going back to work tomorrow," Tani said, sitting next to him. "I've already talked to Donna. She's short-staffed, and I still need the paycheck."

"I don't think that's a good idea."

"Hold on. Let me tell you what I came up with."

He waited, preparing mentally for the fight. It wasn't that he wanted to control her every move. Her self-sufficient nature was one of the things he loved about her. She didn't sit around whining, she went out and got it. But he also wasn't taking any chances. Until Jakub was dealt with, her safety was his only concern.

"I told her I would take the first shift when the diner is busiest. You can see me safely inside every morning and pick me up in the afternoons."

"How does that keep you safe if he eats breakfast there every morning?" he asked.

"I don't think he'll show his face at the diner again after what happened. If he does, Donna will call the sheriff."

"Mmmm," he rumbled. He didn't like the idea of that. The sheriff's office had already proved they were ineffectual. There had been no sign of Jakub, and they didn't seem very inclined to look for him.

"Dane, I need to work. This baby isn't going to pay for itself. And I don't want to live with Dad forever."

"You could move in with me," he pointed out.

"We barely know each other, and what would we do with Arne? Last I checked, y'all shared the house."

"He can live in his truck." He smiled at her. "I'd rather have you there. You smell better."

"Thanks?" she said with a laugh.

He pulled her chair to him. "Seriously, though," he said before pressing his lips to hers. Gently, he eased her over until she was straddling him. His tongue swept inside her mouth. If he could convince her to move in, they could do this whenever they wanted. His lips left hers to find the soft skin of her throat.

"Dane," she moaned.

"Mmm," he agreed as he kissed her collarbone.

"I thought we were taking this slow?"

"Much slower, and they'll just find our fossils."

Her heat rubbed over his cock as it strained to reach her. His mouth found hers again. Only this time, she met him halfway, their tongues tangling in a delicious slide. His scalp tingled where she gripped his hair. His body ached to feel her move over him. If this was foreplay, he wasn't sure he wouldn't explode when they finally made love.

He was beginning to understand why she wanted to go slow. It would never be just sex between them. Too much was at stake. He needed her gaze on him when he first entered her. She needed to see that he was choosing her because there was nothing else for him. That he wanted to be hers until the end of their time. It wasn't that she didn't want to be with him. It was because she loved him enough to make sure it was what he wanted.

"You know I love you, right?" he asked.

"I do."

"And you know I just want you safe?"

"I know that, too."

"And I'll respect your wishes to wait? Even if everything tells me to take you right here, right now."

She pulled him back into a bone-crushing kiss. Maybe he was wrong. Maybe now was the right time and place.

"Hey, Dane. Can you help—" Arne said, sticking his head inside the shop. "Oh, my bad." He stood staring around the shop like he was looking for someplace to hide.

"I guess this isn't the time or place after all," Dane mumbled.

Tani laughed, and he gently helped her off his lap.

"What do you want, Arne?" he asked.

"I was going to see if you'll help me push this bitch of a heifer into the trailer. I don't want to interrupt the shop sexcapades though," Arne said with a smirk. "Do you have a subscription service or are you strictly private only?"

"Keep it up," Dane answered. "And I'll spread the rumor you spent prom night with Mrs. Ratliff." Dane's old history teacher retired to Florida with her husband the year after Arne graduated. She had to be in her seventies now.

"Dude," Arne said. "That's just mean. But if it gets me some, why not? I'm not picky."

"Gets you some what?" his mother asked, walking through the door.

"Nothing," Dane muttered, trying not to laugh. He knew Arne talked a good game, but his brother had no more experience with women than he did. His reputation was just trashier.

"So, Tani, are you going to stay this afternoon?" Freja asked. The two women shared a knowing smile that was lost on Dane.

"Yes, I think I will stay for a while," Tani answered. Dane watched as, arm in arm, they walked together back to the house.

"That looks like trouble," Sten said, joining Dane and Arne. They watched until the women disappeared back inside. "I've heard back from cousin Malthe," he continued. "There's a family of bear shifters that live in the Czech Republic. He said a group of them immigrated years ago to Texas."

"Do they know anything about this Jakub?" Dane asked.

"I don't know yet. I tracked down a Viktor Medvēd. Talked earlier on the phone. He said they're driving up from West Texas this evening. They should be here sometime after supper. Maybe they can shed some light on this situation."

"Did he say why Jakub is so fixated on Tani?" Arne asked.

"He said he would rather discuss it in person. We'll meet here tonight and see what he has to say. We need to be very careful," Sten said, splitting a look between his sons. "The last thing we want to do is start a war between shifters."

～

STEN WAS HELPING Freja finish the supper dishes when there was a knock at the door. Noting her look of concern, he squeezed her on the shoulder. He was also worried about who stood outside. He knew in the past there were once a large number of shifters throughout the world. He assumed most were wiped out over the years. This would be the first time he would meet a shifter of another species.

"Sten Ulvmand?" a large man asked when he opened the door.

"Viktor Medvēd?" Sten asked, reaching out a hand. Viktor only hesitated a moment before clasping Sten's hand in his. Perhaps they were both concerned about meeting each other.

"Please come in," Sten said. He stood back to let Viktor and three younger men enter. "This is my wife, Freja." The men greeted her in turn. "If you follow us to the living room, we can make the other introductions." Sten led them to the living room making sure he was between Freja and their visitors.

"Let me introduce you to my family," he continued when they were in the living room. "My sons: Roar, Dane, and Arne. Erik is on his way down. He should be here soon." The men shook hands. "This is my daughter, Thyra, and my son's girlfriend, Tani."

"My sons: Felix, Leo, and Lucas," Viktor responded. They stepped forward to shake more hands. Sten cleared his throat when he noticed Lucas holding on a little too long to Thyra's hand. The boy didn't look much older than her. He didn't need any more headaches than the current one though.

When everyone was seated comfortably, Freja returned to the kitchen. She brought out coffee with Thyra's help. Sten noticed the boy watching his daughter the entire way into the kitchen. Then he watched a massive grin appear when she offered him a cup. Apparently so had Roar, based on his scowl.

"I made it," Erik said, bursting into the living room. "So sorry I'm late. Did I miss anything?" He worked down the row of men, introducing himself and shaking hands.

"We were waiting for your mother to return first," Sten said.

"I'll help so we can speed this process along," Erik replied, bouncing back toward the kitchen.

"I can too," Lucas said, quickly rising.

"Sit down," Viktor growled. "We all know it's not the coffee you're interested in." Lucas turned bright red. But it helped break the tension in the room as the rest of the men fought to hide their laughter.

"Dang it. I did miss something this time," Erik said, returning with a large tray containing a sugar bowl, cream pitcher, and a carafe of coffee.

"As I explained briefly on the phone, we have had several incidents with a man named Jakub," Sten began when Freja rejoined him.

"Incidents," Dane snorted angrily. Sten held up his hand to quiet Dane.

"He broke into Tani's home, attacked her father, and tried to kidnap her," Sten continued. "Dane pursued them into the woods. Jakub turned into a large bear. Larger than anything found in this area. Dane was injured in the fight that followed. Jakub has continued to harass Tani and this family."

"We believe it's a cousin from the Czech Republic. He was supposed to meet us in Dallas, but never showed up," Viktor said. "He's become too much for our family to handle. They believed some time with us would help."

"Have you been able to contact him?" Roar asked.

"We have tried repeatedly with no success. I'm sorry he's now causing problems here."

"Why do you think he's so obsessed with Tani?" Dane asked.

"He may be hunting a mate. Our cousins said he's been studying the old ways and has been slipping farther into madness," Viktor answered.

"We would truly like to help you, but I don't know how to bring him in. We would prefer for this to end peacefully. But we will not stand in your way if you have to take extreme measures. We only ask that you let us come collect his body ourselves, not the police. I have no wish for our people to be dragged into something we've spent centuries hiding."

They sat in silence for a minute before Dane spoke. "So we're on our own."

"Unfortunately, yes."

"Then this has been a waste of time," Dane answered, standing. Taking Tani's hand, he pulled her up next to him.

"Dane," Sten said in warning. He understood his son's frustration, but it would serve no purpose to make an enemy out of the Medvēds.

"What," Dane snarled. "They won't help us find him. They can't tell us anything that will help us find him. All he's saying is, if we do the dirty work, they'll come clean up the mess. We're going home. It's late. Tani has to be at work early. And I doubt either of us will get much sleep tonight."

Sten watched Dane tug Tani out of the room. Seconds later, the door closed.

"We had better follow them," Roar said. "I apologize for my brother's rudeness. I'm sure you can understand his frustration. Come on, Arne." With a nod, Roar walked out of the room followed by Arne.

"I understand his frustration perfectly," Viktor said when the door closed again. "I truly wish we could help you. You understand we can't go against our people. All we can do is hope this comes to a swift conclusion." Viktor stood, motioning for his sons to follow him. "Thank you for your hospitality, Mrs. Ulvmand. Sten, please keep us informed. Good night."

The Medvēds left with one last longing glance from Lucas at Thyra. It was hastily cut off, though, by Erik stepping in front of his sister. Sten showed their visitors out. He slumped back down on the couch when he returned to the living room.

"I don't know what that look was, but that's not happening," Erik said.

Thyra rolled her eyes at him.

"What do we do now?" Freja asked.

"I guess now we fight," Sten answered.

CHAPTER
TWENTY

Dane sped away from his parent's house. He knew he should wait for his brothers, but he was too frustrated. What kind of bullshit were they trying to pull? It was now squarely on his shoulders alone to finish this. Tani kept sneaking glances at him like she wanted to say something before changing her mind. She stared out the window.

"Say what you're thinking. I'm not pissed at you. I'm pissed at this situation," he said.

"I know. What do we do now?"

"Honestly? I don't know. I guess I'll wait until he shows up again and see what happens." They bounced along the dirt road in silence for a few more minutes. "Was it my imagination, or was that kid making eyes at Thyra?"

Tani laughed. "I thought I was the only one who noticed. It's a wonder she didn't burst into flames, he was staring at her so hard."

"Good thing he's heading home. I'm not good with it."

"She's going to grow up sooner or later. What happens when she brings someone home from college?"

"They'll never find his body."

"You know that's not the solution, right?" he growled, and she laughed. They bounced down the road another half mile in silence. Finally, they pulled up in front of his house.

"Stay in the truck," Dane said, opening his door. He climbed out and made a loop around the house, looking for anything that was out of place. His senses picked up nothing of the bear tonight. He opened her door and ushered her into the house.

"How can you tell if he's out there?" she asked when the door was securely locked.

"I see really well in the dark. I can also smell and hear better than most people."

"Because you're part wolf?"

"I assume."

"How else?"

"How else are we like wolves?"

Tani nodded.

"We're pretty fast, I guess. We're athletic and strong. We usually have good stamina which is why we all did well at cross-country in school."

"And that will be passed on to our children?"

Dane couldn't help but smile. He liked that she was already thinking about their children.

"The boys, yes. I think something else is passed down to the women in our family. Thyra is naturally athletic, but not supernaturally so. She's incredibly smart too. Much smarter than any of us, even Roar. He'll be the first to admit it."

"At what age can you begin to shift?"

"We can technically from birth from what I understand. But the impulse becomes almost uncontrollable starting around puberty. Dad began instructing us on how to curb the desire sometime in junior high. It's also part of why I wear this." He held up his necklace.

Tani's next question was interrupted by Dane's brothers coming through the door.

"Nice mic drop, bro," Arne said with a smirk at Dane.

"Yeah. I'm not sure about the delivery, but I agreed with the summation," Roar added. "Besides, if they hadn't left pretty soon, I was going to snap that little prick in half."

"So I wasn't the only one who saw him eyeing Thyra?" Arne asked.

"No, we all noticed. That's a fight for another day though. We're heading to bed. It's been a long day, and I have to have Tani at work early," Dane said, taking her hand.

"Cool," Arne said. "We promised to play one of Erik's online games with him. We'll have the headphones on. You know, in case it gets loud."

"Dude," Dane warned.

"You're such a prig," Roar said. He thumped the back of Arne's head.

"Really? A prig?" Arne asked. "You can't just say asshole like normal people?"

Dane left his brothers to argue. Tani looked exhausted. The meeting with the group from Texas had done nothing to allay her fears. He waited for her to get done in the bathroom before taking his turn.

The small house seemed palatial when he first moved in after college. It had been where his parents lived until Roar arrived and his grandparents moved to town. It was the perfect bachelor pad for three years. Then Arne moved in. It still hadn't seemed too bad. But with four of them crammed into the space, sharing one bathroom, it now felt minuscule.

He knew Roar would much rather be lounging at his own house in town instead of staying on the couch. He gave up his own comfort to help watch over Tani. He got up early every morning to drive the hour back to work with no promise of an end in sight.

Dane stood staring in the mirror in the tiny bathroom. There were shadows under his eyes from lack of sleep. His hair stuck up from constantly running his hands through it in frustration. He would never get caught up on work at this point. With a sigh, he opened the door.

A quick check on his brothers found them both bent toward the television with headphones on. He found Tani already tucked under the covers with her eyes closed when he returned to the bedroom. As tired as he was, he couldn't even fathom how exhausted she must be. He slid into the bed next to her.

With a soft moan, she snuggled closer to him. Her head rested on his shoulder. She wrapped an arm over his chest and a leg across his upper thighs. Dane pulled her closer. His hand ran down her body. He felt the shiver race through his veins.

"I'm going to miss that if it ever stops," Tani whispered. "How will I know you still want me if it's gone?"

"I'll just have to show you in other ways," Dane answered.

"How? Show me."

"You need to rest."

"I need you more."

Dane only hesitated for a moment before lowering his mouth to hers. He levered himself up on his good arm. His tongue traced the seam of her mouth. Her moan sent him moving down her throat to where it met her collarbone. His teeth nipped at the delicate skin. With her help, he pushed her T-shirt over her head.

"You're beautiful," he growled. His hand feathered the skin on her chest before gliding to her abdomen. "Stunning might be a better word."

He peppered kisses across the top of her breasts. His thumb ran over her hard nipple before he pulled it between his lips. Her back arched as he flicked the nub with his tongue. Every instinct told him to take her now. That she was his. But he fought those urges. She had asked to go slow, and that was what he intended to do.

"Dane," she begged when he moved to the other breast.

His senses took in everything about her. The smell of lavender on her skin. The sound of her gasps when he sucked her nipple between his teeth. Every inch of her golden skin as he moved lower. The feel of it against his calloused hand was imprinted on his brain.

"I've dreamed of this for years," he said. His fingers found the edge of her panties and slid them down her legs. "How you would taste has haunted me." He captured one of her legs under his torn arm. "The first time I stroked myself, this was what I saw when I closed my eyes." He dipped his head. His tongue took its time swiping through her folds. It was everything he had fantasized about.

"Dane."

Her hips bucked against his mouth. He growled as he buried himself in her taste. Time stood still as he learned her body. He discovered what made her pant and what made her moan. She ground against his face while he met each move she made with one of his own.

He thrust his tongue into her channel as her legs began to shake. He flattened it against her clit as she cried out. She took a fistful of his hair. He followed her silent instructions until she came down from her high.

With his mouth still wet from her orgasm, he picked his head up to watch her. She was even more beautiful than before. Her breasts rose and fell as she tried to catch her breath. Her skin was flushed from the waves of ecstasy he gave her. The eyes he had got lost in so many times were now glassy with lust. He kissed her lower belly before moving back up on the bed.

Her gaze met his, then she smiled. Her hand wiped his mouth. Before she could wipe it on the sheets, he caught her wrist. It cost him a shooting pain in his shoulder, but he would not deny himself even a small bit of her. He pulled her hand to his mouth and licked it clean.

"That's mine," he growled. She watched with wide eyes as he pulled each finger into his mouth.

"You've only succeeded in making me wetter." Her hand moved to grasp his hard cock. His hand closed around her wrist again.

"You need rest."

"You'll deny me returning the favor?" she asked.

"It wasn't a favor. It was a gift you gave me," he answered. "You are mine to pleasure and protect as I see fit. You need rest more than you need anything."

He watched as she opened her mouth in protest. It was a heavy-handed thing to say. It wasn't because he was trying to control her, though. It was because he was here to serve her. Her orgasms were his to give on her terms. Her safety was his to guard at all costs. She could barely keep her eyes open.

"Do as I ask, please," he said.

She studied him for a few more minutes before laying her head on the pillow. He gathered her in his arms as she fell asleep. His shoulder ached. Once he was certain she was settled, he eased out from under her. He had to talk to his brothers. With any luck, Arne had something stronger to deaden the pain.

He left the door ajar when he left the room. He wanted to hear if anything disturbed her sleep. Nothing would keep him from running back to hold her. After being sure her breathing had settled into a gentle rhythm, he walked back to the living room. Both Arne and Roar were sitting on the couch. The game had ended, but they spoke quietly.

"How is she?" Roar asked.

"She's sleeping."

"We were trying to figure out where we go from here," Arne said. "We can't just wait around for something to happen."

"I agree," Roar added. "We need to get on the offensive. This won't stop if we simply keep reacting. We have to get ahead of his next move."

"How do we know what his next move is?" Dane took a seat in one of the armchairs. It had been a long day. He needed sleep just as much as Tani did, but this couldn't wait. They were right. They needed an advantage somehow.

"Fuck if I know, but there has to be something," Arne said. "Can we bait him somehow?"

"Not with Tani. She seems to be what's motivating him."

"No, I wouldn't consider Tani. Jesus, Dane, I'm not an idiot."

"Are you sure?"

"Fuck you."

"Hey," Roar interrupted. "I should have banged your heads together more as kids. No one is suggesting Tani,

Dane. I don't think that's all he's thinking about, though. I think he wants you out of the picture permanently. You need to watch your back until we can come up with some kind of plan. I think everyone is on edge tonight. Let's plan to sit down tomorrow and come up with something."

"That's probably a good idea. I wouldn't want to have to pop you a good one while you're hurt." Arne grinned at Dane.

"Phht. In your dreams. Speaking of, do you have anything for my shoulder?"

"You're in luck." Arne took a syringe off the counter. He stuck it in Dane's shoulder and pushed the plunger. "You might want to hurry before it takes effect."

"Damn it, Arne. What was that?" Dane felt his head start to swim. "I'm kicking your ass tomorrow. Once I'm upright again." He staggered toward the bedroom. The shot probably had some kind of cow pain medication in it. Or worse, a horse tranquilizer. If he lived, he would kill his little brother.

"Good luck with that."

Dane made it into the bedroom just as his eyes were closing. Careful not to wake Tani, he sprawled on the bed. He was out before he could pull the blanket over him.

CHAPTER

TWENTY-ONE

ane was in the middle of the bed, snoring like a freight train, when it came time for Tani to get ready for work. He didn't even break rhythm when she climbed out of bed. She vaguely remembered him sneaking back out of the room last night. Whatever they did must have wiped him out.

She threw on a pair of pants and a sweatshirt. Her hair would go up in a tight ponytail when she got to town. How she was going to get to work was going to be a problem. There was no way she was going to insist Dane take her. Not sleeping that soundly. Quietly, she crept from the bedroom.

"Hey, sweetheart. Are you ready for work?" Roar asked when she stepped into the kitchen. He was fully dressed and hovering over the coffee pot.

"Are you taking me? Because I don't think Dane is coming to anytime soon."

"Yeah. I think Arne filled him full of horse tranquilizers."

"Should we be worried?" She looked back toward the bedroom.

"If he's still breathing, I'm sure he'll be fine. Come on. Donna has better coffee than whatever this crap Arne has anyway."

She snatched her purse on the way out. Roar followed her and locked up. He stopped her on the porch so he could look around. Nothing jumped at them out of the darkness. Nothing even sounded like it would. He finally led her to his truck. With both of them settled inside, he turned toward town.

"If I'm being honest, I'm a little nervous about today," she said.

"You don't have to be." Roar reached over and squeezed her hand. It was a simple gesture between friends, but it went a long way to reassure her. "I'll be there until I feel it's safe to go to work. Arne will be in for lunch. I'm sure Dane will be, too, if he's awake by then."

"I worry about leaving him in Arne's care."

"If those two haven't killed each other by now, they'll be fine. Trust me. Arne won't let anything happen to Dane. They squabble like cats in a bag, but they're as close as two siblings can be."

She smiled thinking about Arne tagging along behind Dane when they were kids. Dane would have a scowl on his face; his little brother would be happily chatting away as he followed. Some things never changed. They rode the rest of the way to the diner in silence. Roar turned off the engine of his truck. She took a few moments to gather her courage as he walked around the hood.

"I'm here, remember," he said, seeing her apprehension. "Nothing happens on my watch." He held out his hand. She took it and slid out of the truck. "I've got you."

She nodded. She truly believed him. Roar was the class-mate who watched over the smaller kids. He never toler-ated a bully. If he said he had her back, then she believed it.

"I'm so glad to see you," Donna said, pulling the front door open. Tani wasn't sure if she was speaking about her or Roar. "I've got the shotgun loaded under the register. Just in case there's a problem."

"Or you can just call the sheriff if he shows up," Roar said.

"Pssh, like they'll show up on time."

Roar raised an eyebrow at Tani. She would laugh if she wasn't so worried. It was easy to be brave with a man big enough to fell a tree with one blow next to you. But what about when he left for work? She hated feeling this vulnera-ble. It pissed her off. Would she ever feel safe in her own home again?

"Hey, Donna." Roar took one of the barstools at the counter. "Can I get some eggs?"

"Give me a minute to get the griddle hot."

Tani took the fresh pot of coffee from the machine. She placed a mug in front of Roar and filled it to the brim. No one in the Ulvmand family, except Arne, drank it anyway but black. She moved to the main dining area to finish getting ready to open. With a glance outside, she sighed in relief. No one was waiting outside the door.

The first of the customers arrived at six. She busied herself taking and delivering orders. Before she realized it, Roar was tapping on her shoulder.

"I'm going to head out," he said. "Are you okay?"

"Yeah. I'm fine. I don't think he'll have the nerve to show up here."

"I wouldn't think so. I'll see you tonight."

She watched through the window as Roar climbed into

his truck. He waved before pulling onto the highway. She had wanted to tell him she wasn't okay just so he'd stay. But he was the head accountant for the local college. He had an obligation to show up at work. She wouldn't want to get in the way of that. She was proud of how much he had accomplished since they were kids in school together.

He was one of her few classmates who made the effort to keep in touch. It wasn't a surprise when he went to college on a dual athletic and academic scholarship. She had even attended a couple of his games.

By the time they graduated, though, they had drifted apart. She had heard through the grapevine that he was devastated after his college girlfriend broke up with him. Why didn't she reach out? He might have needed a friend.

But Roar never seemed to hold a grudge. She might have turned into a crappy friend, but he was still right there making sure the bullies didn't get her. They all were. She took a deep breath. If she didn't stop thinking about the sacrifices they were all making for her, she would begin to cry again. That wouldn't serve any purpose.

"Good morning," she said, stepping up to a table with one of the local logging crews waiting to order. "What can I get you this morning?"

"Hey, Tani. Where's Dane?" the foreman asked. "I figured he'd be sitting here scowling at everyone after the break-in."

"I'm sure even the great Dane Ulvmand has to work sometimes," one of the other men chided.

"You know, if you ever get tired of all that pent-up cantankerousness, I'm available," a third said.

"I'll keep that in mind." She smiled and walked back to the kitchen. "Get tired of Dane?" she mumbled to herself. "Not in this lifetime."

"Tani!" Dane roared, sitting up in bed. He searched the bed to no avail. He fought through the fog surrounding his mind. Then he remembered. "You're dead, Arne. Tani?"

"Calm down," Arne said, sticking his head into the bedroom.

"I'm ending you." Dane attempted to get out of bed. The sheets were tangled around his legs. He hit the floor in a mass of covers.

"Yeah, I'm real scared. Here." Arne held a bottle of water out. Dane snatched it. Ripping the top off, he drank half before stopping for a breath.

"What did you give me? How long have I been asleep? What time is it? Where's Tani?" he slurred.

"A cocktail of sedatives, antibiotics, and anti-inflamma-tories. About twelve or so hours. It's noon, and she's at work. Roar took her; I'm about to go get her."

"You could have killed me."

"I'm offended," Arne said with a grin. "There's a reason I took those pre-vet classes. If I wanted you dead, you'd be dead." Dane glared at him which only served to ramp up his grin. "But how do you feel?"

Dane cautiously moved his arm in a circle. The shoulder felt pretty good. Near-death experience aside, Arne's concoction had done its job. He took his time getting up. His body still had bruises and stitches, but they didn't hurt as badly. Arne smirked at him.

"Fine," he growled. "It's better."

"Now was that so hard? Feel free to call me a genius."

"Asshole."

"Mmmm." Arne wagged his head back and forth. "Close

enough. Get dressed. We'll get lunch while Tani finishes her shift." He stalked back down the hallway.

Dane watched him go. His little brother wasn't an asshole. He was his best friend. In their world, calling each other an asshole was a term of endearment. Arne had certainly called him much worse. He never had to question, though, if his brother had his back. They all did. Arne was the kid who never passed a stray animal. It was no surprise to any of them when he moved back to care for the cattle.

They met in the kitchen so Dane could get his shoulder rebandaged. He let Arne climb behind the wheel of the truck for a change. There was no telling when the narcotics would wear off. He didn't need them to end up in the bar ditch. Donna's still had a few remaining lunch customers when they arrived. He slid out of the truck and followed Arne inside.

Tani stood with her back to the door taking an order. He drank her in. It felt like too long since he had her in his arms. Any time apart was too long. Slowly, she turned around. Her face lit up with a smile. His heart missed a beat. She was smiling at him. She was his.

"Hi," she said.

"Hi."

"Riveting," Arne mumbled. He wandered across the room to visit with a friend. Dane glared after him but was ignored.

"How are you feeling?" she asked.

"Better. My shoulder isn't as sore."

"That's good. You were sleeping so hard this morning, I don't think anything could have blasted you awake. I bet you're hungry."

"I could eat." She followed him to the counter. Arne showed up just in time to add his order. They were motoring through burgers when the door opened and Thyra walked in. She took the remaining barstool next to Dane.

"What are you doing here?" Dane asked. "I thought you had school and practice."

"Short day. Teacher in-service, so practice was canceled for some reason. Tani saved the last piece of pie for me."

"Hey, Tani," Arne whined. "I thought we had an understanding."

"Chicks before dicks," Thrya answered.

"Stop saying that," Dane said, glaring at his sister.

"Besties before testes."

"I will wash your mouth out with soap myself," he threatened.

"Ovaries before–"

"Stop." Dane placed his palm over Thyra's mouth.

"Anyway," Tani said, placing the pie in front of Thyra. "She called to check on me. I told her to let your mom know she can catch a ride back with us. I hope that's okay."

"We'll have to strap her to the top."

"We can squeeze."

"But it'll cost her," Dane said, scooping up a large bite of pie.

Arne reached his fork over to snag a bite also, but Thyra was faster this time. She knocked his fork away. A squabble broke out between the siblings, so Dane finished off most of the pie while they fought.

"Ready?" he asked.

Tani nodded. He took her hand and pulled her around the end of the counter. She waved at Donna as they walked to the door. He didn't bother to check if his brother and sister were following. They could find their own way home if not.

"You drive," he said, throwing the keys to Arne.

"Why?"

"Because there's not room for all of us, and Tani is not sitting on your lap."

"She can sit on mine," Thyra said with a smirk.

"She's definitely not sitting on your lap," he growled, shoving his sister into the middle of the truck cab. He helped Tani inside before sliding into the seat under her. "Are you alright?"

"No," Thyra complained. "You're hogging the whole seat."

"I wasn't asking you." He raised an eyebrow at Tani. She nodded before settling more firmly on his lap. "Let's go, and Arne–" His brother leaned forward to meet his gaze. "If you do anything to cause a wreck, I will kill you myself."

"Dramatic much?" Thyra rolled her eyes.

Dane wrapped his arms tighter around Tani feeling her shake with silent laughter. At least someone found his younger siblings amusing. Being tossed around by them shoving at each other, fighting for space, made him want to throttle them both.

Tani had the luxury of laughing. She never had to fight an older brother just to ride in the front seat of the car or put up with a younger one following you everywhere you went growing up.

By the same token, she didn't have a readily available army to have her back at a moment's notice. Growing up an only child seemed lonely. It didn't matter now, though, if she had siblings. His army was now hers. They would do what they had to to protect what was theirs. He only had to listen to Thyra and Tani discussing homecoming dresses to know they already believed she was family.

"What do y'all think about trying a new recipe for Asian

glazed short ribs tonight?" Arne asked as they turned onto the dirt road.

"That sounds amazing. Can I stay?" Thyra asked.

"Fine by me. Dane?"

"Let Mom know," he grunted.

"Where did you learn to cook, Arne?" Tani asked.

Dane felt his body relax as he listened to them chat about cooking. He rested his head against the headrest and let his eyes drift shut. Just a couple more miles until they would be home safe.

"Fuck!" Arne yelled.

In the space of a second, Dane felt his arms tighten around Tani as he pulled her against his chest. The truck slid sideways as it came to a stop in the middle of the road. Thyra grabbed onto his arm as his eyes flew open. Nothing could have prepared him for what he found.

TWENTY-TWO

Tani braced her hands on the dashboard of the truck a split second before Dane jerked her against his chest. The truck slid to a stop inches from the massive bear standing in the middle of the road. It had appeared out of nowhere as they sped around a corner. She watched in horror as it rose onto its back feet and crashed its front paws against the hood.

"Reverse, Arne," Dane shouted. The truck began to race backward down the dirt road. The bear simply chased after it. She couldn't look away as it gained on them. Soon he would be on top of them again.

"The truck won't reverse fast enough to get away," Arne yelled as the bear raced to catch up to them.

"I need to get the gun from under the seat. Can you buy me enough time to get out?"

"Depends on how attached to this truck you are." Arne had his arm braced on the seat as he stared out the rear window trying to stay on the dirt road.

"Just do what you have to."

"Hold on to Tani." Arne turned around to face the front

and dropped the truck in drive. The engine screamed as it caught. Launching forward, he steered directly for the bear. They crashed into the animal, and he quickly threw the truck back in reverse. "Go before he gets up."

Dane passed her to Thyra before diving from the truck. He pulled the gun case out from under the seat as the truck started backward again. He tossed the case aside and slammed the clip in.

The bear had risen from the ground, giving him just a fraction of a second to get off a round. But the bear didn't rush him as he expected. Instead, he ran into the undergrowth.

Arne slid the truck to a stop as they watched Dane crash into the undergrowth after the bear, his gun at his side. "No, Dane," Tani breathed as he disappeared from sight. She slid onto the still-warm seat where moments ago she sat happily on his lap. "Arne, what do we do?"

"Nothing," he answered. "If I went after him, he would kill me for leaving y'all alone. I also can't leave him here to take you home." His gaze met hers, and he shrugged. "We wait."

They all three jumped at the sound of a gunshot from somewhere on the other side of the tree line. It was closely followed by a second report. Tani tried to see through the trees. Even just a brief glimpse of Dane would help calm her. They sat in silence as the echo died. Just when she thought she couldn't stand it anymore, Dane walked out of the trees.

"Dane," she said, climbing from the seat. He met her with the gun in one hand and the other outstretched. "Are you hurt?"

"No. Maybe my pride is a little." He looked over at Arne. "He's faster than he should be. By the time I got a shot off, he was already in the trees. I don't think I even winged him." He drew her tight against him and placed a kiss on the top of her head. "Let's get out of here. I wouldn't be surprised if he circles back around for another try at us."

He helped her back into the truck. Five miles later, they pulled up outside his house. She and Thyra sat in the truck while the men searched around for any sign of Jakub. "I don't see anything," Dane said, returning for them. He held his hand out for her. She followed him inside.

"I'm going to get dinner started," Arne said. "Thyra, you want to help?"

"Sure." They walked into the kitchen.

"Are you okay?" Dane asked.

The sounds of pots and pans clanging reached Tani as she took a deep breath. Was she okay? That was a good question. She stared up at Dane's icy gaze. Would it ever be okay again? There was a bone-tired feeling settling so deep inside her that she wondered if she would ever survive it. She watched his brows crease.

"Tani?"

"I need to shower," she said.

"Oh, yeah." He stepped back, motioning down the hallway.

"Come with me." She held her hand out. His fingers twined in hers. She wondered if he understood what she really wanted. Or needed more accurately.

This was when she claimed Dane Ulvmand as her own. They had waited long enough—too long. When he ran into the trees after the bear, she realized that life was too fleeting. They needed to grab onto it now if they had any chance of a future.

In the bathroom, she slid her shirt off her shoulders. Dane watched with such a hunger in his eyes that she worried about him shifting just from the lust in his gaze. She pushed her pants down her legs. His gaze followed her, stopping on the baby bump that was now prevalent enough that rumors had begun spreading around town.

"People are starting to notice," she said.

"Let them notice," he answered. "It changes nothing."

It was what she had been waiting to hear. Stepping toward him, her hands caressed up his torso, taking his shirt off over his head. Her hands smoothed over the hard muscles of his torso as she mapped every inch. He moaned when they ran inside his waistband, hunting for the buttons. She popped each one open slowly before pushing his jeans down.

"Tani," he warned when she shoved his underwear to the bathroom floor.

Her hand wrapped around his shaft with a gentle slide. She marveled at how he was hard as iron yet velvet soft at the same time. He stepped out of his clothes, and then his mouth was on hers. He tasted sweet. She guessed he'd found another peppermint in the truck.

She pulled away from him and stepped into the shower. Water cascaded down her body as he watched her. There was a question in his eyes as he studied her. Finally, as if he had made up his mind, he joined her under the spray.

His hands found her wet hair as his lips pressed again to hers. His manhood pressed against her belly where their family grew. She still didn't know if he believed the legend, but she was beginning to. She wanted to anyway. It would mean Dane was about to become hers forever.

He growled when she cocked a leg around his hip, drawing him closer to where she needed him. Cupping her ass, he picked her up around his waist. "Are you sure?" he whispered against her lips.

"More than I've ever been," she answered.

His gaze fell on hers as he slowly slid inside her. She felt the tile of the shower wall at her back as he pressed her firmly against it. Her hands slid against his shoulders as the muscles worked to move her against him. When he pushed into her, she felt so full. But it was more than that. It was a feeling of claiming what they both wanted.

"I'm not going to last much longer, Tani," Dane breathed. "I want you with me." His eyes looked distressed at the thought of coming before her. She wouldn't let that happen. Sliding a hand between them, she found her clit. His gaze followed until he was transfixed by where he slid inside her. She felt the waves build until she couldn't hold back.

"Dane," she cried as her body clenched around him.

"Fuck," was the last word she heard before her ears began to ring. When they cleared, she found Dane's arms shaking from holding her. His breath came in pants, and his eyes were the most brilliant blue she had ever seen. "Fuck," he said again.

"Yeah," she agreed. Her heart was racing, keeping time with his.

"I love you." Slowly, he eased her to her feet. The second she was steady, he pulled her against his chest.

"I love you, Dane." With one arm still wrapped around her, he took the shampoo from the shelf.

"I like the smell of this stuff." He poured some in his hand and began messaging it into her scalp. She had never had a man wash her hair before. Sure, she had it done at the salon often enough, but this was different.

"That feels amazing," she moaned.

He hummed in agreement before easing her back under the water. When the water ran clean, he found her bath gel and poured a handful. She debated falling asleep standing in the shower when he massaged it around her shoulders. His large hands worked down the muscles of her back releasing the knots of the day.

Time slowed as he lathered her up, rinsed her off, and turned off the water. She was wrapped in a soft towel before being led to the bed. He settled behind her as he worked at drying as much of the water from her long tresses as possible.

"Dane?"

"Hmm."

"What if he never stops?" she asked. "What if he just keeps coming until he finally catches me?"

"He'll have to kill me first."

"Don't say that." She pushed up and turned until she was straddling his thighs. "I couldn't bear it if anything happened to you."

"I will do whatever I have to to protect you," he said. His hand cupped her cheek. "You understand that, right? As long as we still draw breath, we will keep you safe. It's not just you and your dad anymore. You're mine, so my family is in this fight."

"I'm yours." She said it as a statement, not a question. She liked how it sounded.

"Until they lay me in the ground." His lips slid against hers. "Even then, I will still love you. Into the next life."

"For all of eternity," she agreed. She rolled her hips, grinding her heat against his cock. It hardened in response.

"Until Ragnarök ends with the death of the gods."

"You grew up in the same church I did." She laughed. "You know better."

"Yeah, but it sounds sexier."

"Dane, everything out of your mouth sounds sexy."

Slowly, she slid down his shaft until he was seated fully inside her. She rocked her hips. He moaned in response. "That, however, is my favorite sexy sound."

He leaned back with his hands bracing him on the mattress behind him. His gaze never left hers as she rose and lowered on him. As her pace increased, his eyes closed. He was beautiful with his long hair falling behind him and his face smoothed in concentration. She couldn't remember ever feeling this whole before.

She knew she didn't need a man to be complete. It was a truth she believed until now. She didn't need just any man; she needed this one. The man who never saw her as anything less than amazing. The one who waited all these years because he knew they belonged together. That together they would be stronger, braver, and tougher than she ever thought possible.

"Dane," she whispered as her body tightened around him.

"I love you," he answered.

They came together, a perfect symphony. Her hands traced down his body before she leaned into him, her remaining strength leaving her. As exhausted as she was, she couldn't help but want more.

He wrapped his arms around her, holding her against him. She would have remained this way forever if she could. But they had to work tomorrow, and they needed rest.

"I'll hurry in the bathroom," she said, climbing from the bed. When she emerged from the bathroom, the sheets had been straightened and the comforter pulled up. Dane held them for her as she slid onto the bed.

"Get some rest," he said. "I'm going to run through the

shower, then I'll join you." He kissed her forehead before walking into the bathroom.

Tani sighed. This was a good day, even with everything that had happened. At the end of the day, she got to fall asleep in Dane's arms. Any day she could do that was a good one. Slowly, she felt herself drift off. It was hard to believe this would be her life now. She felt the first flutter of a baby kick. He knew how good his life was becoming as well.

"You're right, baby. We are blessed." She fell asleep with a smile on her face.

TWENTY-THREE

"Good morning," Tani called, walking into Freja's kitchen the next morning.

"You are just in time," Freja said, sliding a stack of pancakes off the griddle.

"That's what we were hoping for." Dane sat in the chair closest to his father. "I assured Tani there'd be more than enough if we hurried. Where's Arne? I figured he'd already have eaten half the stack."

"I'm sure he's out wreaking havoc already," Sten mumbled. He sat at the head of the table, sipping his coffee.

"He's already been through," Freja said. She set a mounded plate of pancakes on the table. "Something about fences. Didn't sound like he got much sleep last night." She laughed when Tani blushed. "Speaking of, do you have to work today?"

"No, today is my day off," Tani answered.

"How do you feel about helping me in the shed today?"

"Ohh, are we spending the day in your she-shed?" Thrya asked, walking into the kitchen. She sat across from

Dane and swiped two of his already prepared pancakes from his plate.

"Brat," he growled.

She grinned at him knowing full well he was all bark and no bite where she was concerned.

"I thought if Tani is ready, it's time to teach her some spell casting," Freja said.

"She's ready," Dane answered.

"Eeeeee," Thyra squealed. "I finally have a sister."

"I think I'll head outside. The table conversation certainly seems to have taken a turn." Sten stood and kissed Freja's forehead.

"I'll go with you. The swather isn't going to fix itself," Dane said. "Seems like for every hour I use it, I have to put in two screwing it back together." The men walked out the door leaving the women to plan their day.

"I should dress," Thyra said, jumping from her chair. "Thanks for breakfast, Mom." She placed her plate in the sink and ran up the stairs. They listened to her feet pound down the hallway overhead.

"I swear she's twice as loud as all the boys combined," Freja said with a laugh. She stood to clean up. Tani started to stand also but was waved back into her chair. "You sit and talk to me while I clean up. It's going to be a long day for you."

Freja listened while Tani told her about her day before at work. She laughed hearing how Arne and Dane ganged up on Thyra's pie. She noticed Tani skipped over the attack on the truck. Whether it had taken too much of a toll on her, or she felt it wasn't to be shared even with family, Freja had no idea. Either way, Tani was a good choice for her son.

She marveled that it was Dane to find his mate before his brothers. There was a time she thought Roar was settling down with his college girlfriend. But that had ended abruptly with her leaving him overnight. Even Arne, the supposed lady's man, seemed like a more likely choice for finding a mate.

Dane had always had his sights set on Tani, though. It was no wonder he beat a path to her door the moment he heard she was back in town. Freja had always liked her. Even in high school, Tani was a beautiful girl both inside and out. She was looking forward to her becoming Dane's wife. Before that, however, there were a few things she needed to know.

"Are we ready?" Thyra asked, bounding back down the stairs. She had changed into a pair of jeans, boots, and a T-shirt.

"We are," Freja answered. "Lead on."

Tani joined them as they walked into the yard. The shed was set out back at least a couple hundred feet from the house. There was a stone pathway leading to it that was installed several years ago. It didn't appear, though, that anyone had used the shed in years. Freja had already taught Thyra everything she knew about casting spells.

Freja unlocked the door and pulled it open. The room was dusty, but nothing seemed to be missing. Not even the mice had found their way inside this winter. Thyra stepped inside and began arranging the table. Tani simply walked around the room studying the dried herbs along one wall.

"So what do we do first?" Tani asked.

"It's really up to you," Freja answered. "You can start with meditation, a cup of tea, a prayer. However, you need to get in the right mindset."

"What do you do?"

"When I started, I had two little ones. Just a moment of

quiet meditation was good for me. I had to watch so I didn't fall asleep."

"I get that," Tani said with a smile. "I think just a prayer will do for me. Can we join hands?"

The two women moved to her and clasped hands. They formed a connected circle while Tani offered up a silent prayer. Freja watched Tani's lips move for a minute before closing her eyes.

"Okay, what's next?" she asked when the prayer was over.

"Now we have to find what speaks to you to make charms from," Freja said.

"We all have silver barrel charms," Thyra said, showing her the charms. "Dad said they had rocks or something."

"That's it," Tani said. "I've been collecting gemstones since I was a child. I never knew what drew me to them until now. Maybe they were choosing me for this very reason."

"Where are they?" Freja asked.

"They're in my room in town." Tani's shoulders slumped.

"That's not a problem." Freja pulled her phone out of her pocket and pressed a number. "Dane, I need you to run to Tani's for something." She hung up and moments later, Dane stuck his head into the shed.

"What am I after?" he asked.

"In my nightstand is a sack full of gemstones," Tani said. "If you can grab it. Also, you might look around for any that are loose in the drawer."

"I'm on it." He took the keys to her house from her hand. "Mom, where's your shotgun?"

"In the corner within reach."

"Good. Arne is in the pens, cussing at one of the water

troughs, and Dad is in the shop. If there's trouble, just yell." He wrapped an arm around Tani's waist and pulled her against him. Bending, he pressed his lips to hers.

"I don't think we're the ones you have to worry about," Thyra teased.

He glared at her as he walked from the shed. "Thyra, why don't you help Tani get the rest of the supplies together."

"Okay. First, we need the ridiculously huge book of charms that none of us can read." Thyra pulled the old book out from a nearby bookshelf and dropped it on the table. "Good thing someone along the way thought to translate it or we'd all be lost."

Tani pulled it closer to her, leafing through the pages. "What is this?" she asked.

"Something between modern Danish and Norse, I think," Freja answered.

"Huh. I don't know how to pronounce any of this."

"Yeah, no one does," Thyra said. "I think that's the point. Anyway, you need to make at least a protection, a health, and a binding charm."

"I'll go collect some sticks," Freja said, picking up a bucket.

She left the shed as the two women discussed the different herbs behind them. It was an odd sensation to hand over something she had been doing for most of Dane's life. She was turning his life over to the woman who held his heart. Only Tani's charms would keep him safe now.

She remembered being skeptical of the entire ritual the first time she did it. Now, she had seen her family survive too many close calls to doubt the power the small charms had.

It was the responsibility of each generation of women to pass the ritual down to the next. Tani was only the first of her daughters-in-law she would train over the coming years. Next time it was taught, she would be by their side as a teacher instead of a pupil.

It was powerful to know each woman held their mate's life in their hands. Her job was to show the women how important they were in the family. How much they would be relied on.

"Mom, what is that herb for protection I never can remember?" Thyra shouted out the door.

"Angelica?"

"That's it. Thanks." She disappeared back inside the shed.

Freja chuckled. Thyra had been the hardest of her five children to have. She had labored for many long hours before the doctor finally called for a Cesarean. The first thing she heard when Thyra was pulled from her body were the screams of a mad infant. She had been vocal ever since.

Of course, having four older brothers made her tougher than most teenage girls. Most of her life skills they had taught her over the years. She pitied that poor boy from Texas who dared to sneak glimpses of her. All four of her brothers had their hackles raised over it. She would have to find a man eventually who could stand up to them or suffer at their hands forever.

"Woman," Thyra said, walking out of the shed. "What is taking so long with the sticks?" Freja raised an eyebrow at her. "Kidding, of course. Here, let me get that." Thyra hoisted the bucket and carried it next to the shed.

An old fire ring remained in the dirt outside the door. Thyra sat the bucket down. She arranged the sticks, with

Tani's help, in the form of the rune for protection. Dane arrived as they were finishing.

"Bag of rocks," he said, handing a medium bag to Tani. "I also grabbed a couple of pizzas."

"They'd better have loads of meat," Thyra warned.

"One meat-a-tarian and one with a little more finesse."

"I knew you had my back."

"Always, tiny tot." They grinned at each other.

"Thank you," Tani said, drawing his attention away from his sister. "These will be perfect."

"Anything you need." He pulled her into a kiss. This time he ignored Thyra catcalling them. "I also grabbed you an iced tea from Donna's on the way by."

"You really are a catch, aren't you?" Tani teased. With one last kiss, he returned to the equipment shop. "I didn't realize how hungry I was." She took a bite of a ham and pineapple pizza. "This little one hogs the groceries."

"Just wait," Freja said. "Soon, it'll inflict heartburn just thinking about pizza."

"There's a good reason for birth control," Thyra mumbled.

"True." Tani laughed. "What are the next steps?"

"This is the hard part," Freja continued. "No one charms an object the same way. For me, I had to have Sten spit in the bag of items and throw it on the fire just right. It took me days to figure them all out. You'll just have to find what works for you."

"Okay. Well, it makes sense that I would need something from Dane if the charm is for him. I'll be back." She left the shed and headed toward the equipment barn.

"Do you think it'll work?" Thyra asked as soon as Tani was out of earshot.

"I'm sure it will," Freja answered.

"It's so exciting. I've never actually seen a real spell cast. Without someone to cast them for, none of mine work. It's just practice."

"I'm sure you'll get your turn someday. Just not too soon." Freja smiled at her daughter. She was always in such a hurry. A hurry to grow up, to keep up with her brothers, to move on. If only she would stay young just a little longer.

"We're going to try hair," Tani said, stepping back around the corner. "Dane wasn't thrilled, but I figure he has plenty of it. A little less won't hurt him."

"Perfect," Freja said. "Now to add everything else. Don't forget the dirt. It has to be from Denmark."

The women bent over the table as they carefully measured the herbs. Everything was secured in a small bag. A smooth piece of jasper was added before the bag was tied. Thyra had the fire pit built with the sticks in the shape of a protection rune. The words from the old book were practiced carefully. They didn't exactly roll off the tongue.

"Heill sé þú ok í hugum góðum! Þórr þik þiggi, Óðinn þik eigi," Tani tried for what felt like the hundredth time. "Those don't even look like real letters."

"It loosely translates to: may Thor protect you and Odin keep you. Try again," Freja encouraged.

Tani raised an eyebrow at her, but she tried the words one more time. "Are you sure I can't translate this into something else? I could at least call on Chitokaka instead of Thor and Odin."

"I'm not sure if it works in another language, but if that's what you want, we can give it a try." Freja watched as Tani held the bag over her head and began to chant in a language that could only be Choctaw. It was beautiful to listen to her asking for protection for the man she loved in her native language.

Then Tani tossed the bag onto the sticks. At first, nothing happened. Then the bag began to hiss. They all stepped back as the hissing turned to smoke. The bag flashed with fire that devoured it in seconds. Tani's gaze reached Freja's. She shrugged back. It either worked, or it didn't. If not, they just had to keep trying.

Thyra wasn't as hesitant. She grabbed a stick and began sifting through the ash in the fire pit. "It worked." They all squatted to see the small piece of jasper with the rune emblazoned on it.

"But how do we know for sure it works?" Tani asked.

"If the rune appears, it worked. You just need to string it so Dane can wear it around his neck. I think we have an old drill in there somewhere," Freja answered. She picked up the gemstone. "Well done, Tani. Dane is going to love this. Now just a couple more, and you'll have it licked."

"What do you think?" Tani asked.

"I think they're amazing," Dane answered. He turned the necklace in different directions as he studied the stones. He recognized the jasper and onyx, but the rest escaped him. They all had a rune etched into them. She had them hung on a piece of cord to tie around his neck. "You did all of these today?"

"Yeah. Once I had the first one figured out, it wasn't hard."

"That must be some kind of a record. Mom always told us it took her days to get them all done."

"She also had more to do."

"That's true I guess." He slid the cord around his neck and tied it off in back. The stones were a little heavier than the charms he had been wearing, but he knew he'd get used to them soon enough. "Thank you."

"Just doing my due diligence." She smiled up at him as he pulled her closer.

"Still. This means everything to me."

"And you mean everything to me. Can't have you running around out there unprotected."

"All willy-nilly," he said with a grin.

"Exactly." Pushing up on her toes, she pulled him down for a kiss. Her arms circled his neck as he wrapped his around her waist. He would never get tired of kissing her. His tongue swept into her mouth to tangle with hers. His heart pounded in his ears. Her body pressed flush against his begging for more.

"Seriously, we're in public," Arne teased as he walked by.

"We're in the driveway," Dane responded.

"Exactly," Arne said, walking backward toward the house. "There are children present." He pointed at Thyra following him.

"Don't drag me into this. I think it's awesome," she said.

"Ass kisser."

Thyra opened her mouth to reply, but Dane cut her off. "Knock it off. Both of you," he growled. Why he still had to jump between his siblings regularly, he didn't understand. They reached the house and stepped inside.

"Do you want to practice more after lunch?" Thyra asked Tani.

"Maybe after I have a chance to rest. This little one is wearing me out."

"That sounds like a great idea," Freja added. "I could use some rest, too."

"That's just from advanced age, though, right?" Dane slapped Arne on the back of the head. "Hey, just kidding. Mom knows I'm just teasing." He leaned down to kiss his mother's cheek.

"You're an idiot," Dane grumbled.

"Dane, don't call your brother an idiot," Freja scowled. "Even if he is one on occasion."

"Ouch," Arne complained. "That hurts, Ma. You know you're still the hottest mom on the block."

Dane just shook his head as he carried a bowl of salad into the dining room.

As much as he would love to spend the afternoon snuggled against Tani, he had too much work to do. The west field wouldn't plow itself. Nor would it tend to its own planting. He didn't worry about her staying here without him. His mother had proven time and again that she was one tough customer.

"Neighbor called," Sten said, stepping out of his office. "We've got cows out."

"You don't even have to tell me," Arne answered from the kitchen doorway. "I bet it's the water gap in the West Martin pasture."

"Didn't we just fix that?" Dane asked. He moved to help Arne finish setting the table.

"Yep, but that doesn't seem to deter them. I'll take the feed truck down after lunch and see if I can call them back."

"I'll be in the lower west if you need help."

"Thanks. I might take you up on that."

"Everyone ready for something to eat?" Freja asked, walking into the room.

"Always," Arne admitted, sliding into a chair. The food was placed on the table, and everyone found their seats. They discussed everything but the largest of the problems looming over their heads.

Arne announced the date for spring roundup, Dane reported on the millet he was putting in the ground, and Thyra informed them her softball team was certain to make the playoffs. The best, however, was Tani's addition of how well her last doctor's visit went.

"I should get back to work," Dane said finally. He rose from the chair and kissed Tani on the forehead. "Take it easy this afternoon. I'll be back later to get you."

"I will. Be careful," she said as he walked toward the door. "You too, Arne."

"No worries," he answered.

He parted ways with Arne in front of the house. Arne headed to the feed room to get the feed truck out, and he walked to the equipment barn. He climbed into the largest tractor and backed over to the disk. Once everything was hooked up, he drove out to the field. If the millet he was planting did what he wanted, he'd have a very busy summer.

Dane looked at the house one last time before he dropped over the rise into the bottom. Everything looked quiet. He hoped Tani got some rest this afternoon. Pointing the tractor through the gate, he slowly made his way west.

Every pasture had a name on the ranch. The one he was working in this afternoon was technically called the Fifty-Five pasture. No one knew why it was named that exactly. Perhaps that was its original acreage, but it had been fenced several times over the years so that was no longer the case.

When he reached the corner of the field, he unfolded the disk. He would turn up the soil with the disk, break up the clumps with the attached harrow, and then plant the seeds.

It wasn't a hard process, just tedious. It wouldn't all get done this afternoon. But at least the ground would be ready for the next day. If he could just get his father to see the reasoning behind upgrading some of the equipment, it would take less time.

He was halfway across the field when the disk sunk into the soil. "Son of a bitch," he groaned, climbing down from the tractor. Walking to the back, he found one of the hoses that ran the hydraulics dangling from the tractor. The fitting was still attached, but the hose was no longer attached to the fitting.

At least he didn't have to walk back to the shop. He could unhook the disk and drive the tractor back. It wouldn't take him long, hopefully, to put a new fitting on the hose. He released the remainder of the hose and tossed it inside the tractor. Returning to the back, he began to unhook the equipment.

As silent as it was with the tractor turned off, he still didn't hear the bear running at him until the last minute. He stepped out from the back tire only to be hit full force in the chest by a charging Jakub.

Landing in the dirt near the disk, he was surprised to find himself still breathing. The massive beast rose on his hind legs over him. His only hope was to roll as best as he could under the disk.

Dane fought to crawl between the rows of metal. He felt the bear grab his left leg before he could get out of the way. He tried desperately to hold on to the disk as Jakub dragged him closer.

Dane kicked out, but it was no use. The bear was much larger, and he hadn't had time to shift into a wolf. He had no defenses that would protect him from death. Jakub raised onto his back legs with a roar. If he came down on Dane's chest, that would be the end.

He was positive this was where he died when a shotgun blast reached his ears. The beast screamed and turned to look at where the shot came from. Without hesitating another second, the bear loped toward the edge of the tree line. Another boom echoed through the bottom, but the bear had placed the tractor between him and the shooter.

"Dane!" Arne screamed, running across the field.

Dane dropped his head back into the dirt. He was half under the rake and unwilling to crawl back out. Arne dropped to his knees when he reached him.

"Dane." Wrapping his hands around Dane's ankles, he pulled him out much like the bear had. "Dane, say something." He gripped the shotgun between his hands. His eyes drifted between Dane and the field where the bear had disappeared.

When he just lay there, Arne started feeling for injuries. He put up with it for a second, then batted his brother away. "Please stop," he wheezed. "I feel like I've been kicked in the chest by a horse." Arne jerked his shirt up to check the extent of the damage. His brother pushed on different parts of his chest until he finally shoved him into the dirt. "I'll live."

"Shit, I thought he had you for sure this time," Arne said. "I'm glad I came to get some help with the gap. He would have killed you." He helped Dane sit with his back against a tire.

"Thank God for little brothers," Dane agreed. "Even if their aim is for shit."

"Hey, I think I winged him, and I don't have my contacts in." Arne slid down to sit next to him.

"Where are your contacts?"

"I ordered new ones. Those were killing me."

"Where are your glasses?"

"At home where I forgot them. I had on sunglasses this morning when I left."

"I guess I should be grateful you didn't shoot me." His little brother had been half blind since he could remember. He wore glasses until he was old enough to handle contacts. Always a good-looking guy, but with the glasses on, women seemed to swarm to him.

"There's always next time."

Dane chuffed out a laugh. "Oww," he moaned, holding his chest.

"Come on," Arne said, pushing off the ground. "We're leaving the tractor here. I have a panel covering the hole in the fence for now. I think we've had enough excitement for today. Let's get you back to the house so we can see who's hauling your sorry ass to the emergency room."

"I don't need to go to the emergency room." He stifled a gasp when Arne hoisted him off the ground. "Nothing's broken. You might have to work on my ankle, though. I'm pretty sure his claws made it through my jeans."

"Oh, yeah," Arne answered, peering at Dane's leg. "Blood is oozing down your boot."

With Arne's help, he managed to hop to the feed truck. He wrestled his way into the passenger seat while gritting his teeth. He knew if he let out so much as a yelp, Arne would tell their mother who would haul him to town for x-rays. All he really wanted was a good night of sleep snuggled against Tani.

"I think it's time for another family meeting," Arne said as they bounced out of the field. "We have to do something before he kills you. I know we keep talking about it, but this time we need to take action in some form."

"I agree, but not tonight. Erik has a televised game. It can wait until tomorrow."

"Yeah, I think Mom was making chicken and dumplings so we can eat while we watch the game," Arne said. "I'll still take you to town, though, if you think we need someone to take a look at you."

They pulled up to the house. Tani and Thyra were sitting on the porch swing laughing. He could think of nothing worse than breaking up a perfectly good evening getting x-rayed. "I'll be fine," he said, sliding out of the truck. He limped slowly to the gate. Tani took one look at him and immediately sobered.

"What happened?" she asked, meeting him on the steps.

"I got ambushed."

"How? Where?" Her hands worked over his body hunting for injuries. When they grazed his chest, he flinched. Carefully she peeled his shirt up. "Dane," she whispered.

An angry bruise had begun to form over his sternum.

"His ankle is pretty bad, too," Arne added, walking up behind them. "Help me get the hard-headed ass inside so I can bandage it up."

"We should take you to the hospital," Tani said.

"She's right," Thyra said. "You could have something inside bleeding. You could die in your sleep, and we wouldn't even know it."

"Thank you, Thyra," he said with a smirk. He turned back to Tani. "I'll be fine. Arne can fix me up. We don't want to miss Mom's dinner or Erik's game."

"You're right, Arne. He is a hard-headed ass," Tani said. "Come on, let's get you inside." She wrapped an arm around his waist and helped him limp into the kitchen.

"What happened?" Freja asked. They got him into a kitchen chair with his foot propped up on another. He knew this was a scene they were all growing weary of. His jeans were pulled up almost to his knee on his right leg. "Those are claw marks."

"Jakub ambushed him while he was behind the trac- tor," Arne explained. "Glad I needed his help right then, otherwise it would have been too late."

"Where was your gun?" Sten asked from the doorway.

"In the tractor," Dane said. "I can't exactly hold a gun at the ready and take the hydraulic hose off."

"No, I guess your little brother will just have to follow you around constantly. God forbid you multitask," Sten snarled.

"Speaking of, can someone text Roar to grab my glasses from my nightstand on his way by?" Arne asked.

"I guess you should say a prayer of thanks that he didn't shoot you. Son, how do you forget your glasses? I swear he'd forget his head if it wasn't attached," Sten mumbled as he turned back to the living room.

Arne rolled his eyes at Dane. "I wasn't going to shoot you. Not by accident anyway." He bent over Dane's ankle, almost close enough to touch it with his nose. A towel was placed under it as Arne cleaned it with antiseptic. The skin was shredded, so instead of sewing it back together, he simply bandaged it. "I'd still have this checked tomorrow."

"Maybe," Dane answered. "Now how about I hop into the living room, and you bring me some of Mom's world- famous chicken and dumplings so we can watch the game."

"Suck-up," Arne teased, helping him from the chair with a grin.

TWENTY-FIVE

They were back at his parents' house the next afternoon. Last night had been nice. Erik's team won the game, dinner was exactly what Tani needed, and Dane's condition never seemed to worsen.

It was a much-needed break from the violence that had settled around them. She had hauled Dane off the couch around eleven, and they had slept until almost noon. It was the first time she felt fully rested in quite a long time.

Dane, Tani, and Arne walked into the Ulvman family living room that afternoon. They had retired to their house after the game. Roar decided to sleep upstairs in his old room instead of driving home only to drive back out the next day. They were surprised, however, to find Erik sitting on one end of the couch watching television.

"Hey, man," Arne greeted him. "When did you get here?"

"I drove down this morning."

"Why?" Dane asked.

"Mom said there was a family meeting this afternoon. I figured being family, I should be here."

"Well, I'm glad you are," Tani said, flopping down next to him. She hugged him and kissed his cheek. "Your game was amazing last night. Do I get your autograph?" She laughed when his cheeks turned pink.

"Thanks," he mumbled.

"Lunch is here," Freja called, walking into the house. Tani pushed herself off the couch to help in the kitchen. She found Freja and Thyra in their Sunday best, moving fried chicken onto a platter.

"There're sides in the bag," Freja said, motioning with her head. "Can you put them in bowls? Set some plates on the counter, Thyra. Everyone can just buffet it."

When the food was ready, Freja called everyone into the kitchen. Plates were filled, and everyone moved into the dining room. Sten let them eat in peace for a few minutes. Tani watched him out of the corner of her eye knowing he was biding his time until he could bring up the attack on Dane the day before. Setting down his chicken, he cleared his throat.

"It doesn't look like he's going to give up and drift on," he began.

"From what I can see, it seems he's turned his focus more on Dane," Roar added. "Have you seen him near the diner at all?"

"Not since this escalated," she answered. "Donna said she hadn't seen him either. She's been keeping an eye out. He hasn't shown up at our house since Dad moved back in. No one has even mentioned seeing him around town. I think Roar is right. He seems to be focused on Dane now."

"What happened exactly yesterday?" Erik asked.

"I didn't see him coming until he was on me," Dane said. "He steamrolled me behind the tractor while I was removing the hydraulic hose. I crawled under the disk as far as possible, but he dragged me out. He would have killed me if Arne hadn't blindly winged him."

"Hey," Arne argued. "At least I did something."

He had on his glasses today. Tani had to admit, he was even better looking with them. Still not as hot as his brother, but not bad either.

"And I am grateful," Dane answered.

Tani was too. Without Arne, Dane would no longer be in her life, and that was something she couldn't bear. She squeezed Dane's hand under the table. He smiled at her. She knew he felt the same.

"So what happens now?" Thyra asked. They grew quiet as thoughts turned to a solution to the problem. It was a few minutes before anyone spoke.

"We need to bait him," Roar said. "Draw him out. But, on our terms where we can control the situation."

"What if that works? What do we do about him then?" Erik asked.

"We end this," Sten said. He looked at each family member for a moment. Even Tani felt the seriousness of his gaze as he met her eyes. "In whatever way it takes." She nodded in agreement with him; this couldn't continue.

She was struck suddenly with an idea. Did she say it out loud? Would they listen? If she was truly part of this family now, she needed to act like it.

"A wedding," she blurted out. Everyone turned to stare at her. "Think about it. He won't be able to stay away if we get married. We can have it here where it's controlled and have just family attend. The rumors are already flying around town, so they'll just think it's a shotgun wedding." The room remained quiet.

"I thought you'd never ask," Arne said, breaking the silence. Some of the tension eased from the room.

"Fuck off, she's mine," Dane growled.

Arne shared a grin with her before turning to argue with his brother. More voices joined in the fray until Sten had heard enough.

"Quiet!" he bellowed. "Dane, apologize to the women."

"Sorry," he mumbled. He didn't sound very sorry to her ears. She realized she should have run the idea by him first. He might not be ready to tie the knot. "You know what, I'm not sorry. It makes perfect sense. There's no reason for us to wait anyway," he added, turning to her. "Is there?"

"No, no reason." She shook her head.

"Then it's settled. We get married next weekend."

"Can it be Sunday?" Erik asked. "I have a game Saturday."

"Sunday works," she agreed.

Talk turned to wedding plans. Duties were divided out. Dane would buy a ring tomorrow, Freja would take Tani dress shopping, Sten would finish the planting, and Arne would oversee getting the yard ready. Roar began to draw up a plan on how to handle Jakub when he arrived. Much to Erik and Thyra's dismay, they were relegated to school.

"Are you sure you're okay with this?" Dane said quietly in her ear.

"Yes, I think this is our best chance to move on with our lives."

"This isn't exactly what I had in mind."

"Me either, but hopefully the result will be the same. Jakub will be out of our lives, and we can live in peace. Together," she said. "I guess I need to sit my dad down, though, and have a long, hard talk."

"Do you want me there?"

"No, I think it's best if I do this alone."

"I'll take you," he said. "I'll wait outside just to keep an eye out. Any questions he has, I'll be there to answer. I should also ask permission to marry you."

"Maybe we should lead with that before dropping the other bomb on him."

"Whatever you think."

They turned their attention to the cacophony around the table. It seemed everyone had something to say about the wedding.

"You know, I can think of something I'd much rather be doing with my fiancée than this." He waggled his eyebrows at her. "To celebrate," he added.

"How are we going to sneak out?"

"Follow my lead." Dane yawned loudly. "Does anyone mind if we head back to rest? I'm still pretty sore, and I know Tani is tired."

"Are you feeling alright?" Freja asked her.

"I'm good, just still trying to catch up on my rest," she said.

Dane pulled her up from her chair.

"Okay, take care," Freja said.

"We'll drift over later to hang out. Much later," Roar added with a wink.

She should probably be embarrassed that Dane's brother seemed to understand exactly what they were going to do, except she just didn't care anymore. It was no secret they couldn't keep their hands off each other.

"Sounds good," Dane mumbled as they headed for the door.

They hurried to his truck and raced for his house. He helped her out after checking that everything was clear. She made it just inside the door before he was on her.

His lips met hers as he pressed her against the door. Tongues fought for control only giving in when he pulled her shirt over her head. His shirt quickly joined hers on the floor. Then his mouth was back on her. He worked down her neck to her collarbone. She lifted her leg to hook over his hip. She needed him closer.

Taking her ass in his hands, he lifted her to his waist. A moan slipped from her lips when she felt the ridge pressing against the zipper of his jeans. Using the door to hold her up, she let her hands trace over the muscles of his chest. They stopped at the mottled bruise that fanned over his ribs.

"Are you sure you want to do this?" she asked. Her fingers traced the scars left from the last time Jakub attacked him.

"There is nothing else I want more in this world."

"Okay, but I think you should set me down. Your ankle is injured, and my weight can't be good on your chest."

"Your weight is nothing," he growled, but slowly he returned her to her feet. Taking her hand, he led her to the couch. He shoved his jeans down and pulled her onto his lap.

"What if your brothers come back?" she asked. Her body was already sliding against his, begging for the release she knew only he could give her.

"Then they'll know better next time." His hands pushed the skirt she wore above her waist. He slid aside her panties, testing if she was ready for him. She knew by the rumble in his chest that she was wet and more than ready. Freeing his erection, he slid slowly into her. They moaned at the same time at the feel. He filled her so completely that it was almost too much. Her hips rocked as she tested what rhythm she wanted.

His icy gaze met hers as she rose and sank on his cock. A hand moved to worry her aching nipple. It was both agony and ecstasy in equal measure. "You feel like a fantasy," he murmured before his lips began to suck gently on her shoulder.

"Dane." Her body tightened as she rocked her hips harder. She could feel every nerve tingle as the wave of her orgasm rose. His hand worked between them until his thumb pressed against her clit. It was all she needed to explode. She clamped around him, riding his cock sporadically as she finished.

Her eyes finally opened to find his gazing back. She could feel his length still hard inside her. "You didn't finish?"

"Not yet," he answered with a smirk. "There's more I want to do to you."

Carefully, he eased her off his lap. She stood in front of him, her mind swirling in self-doubt. He bent forward and untied his shoes. He eased them off, followed by his jeans. Leaving them in front of the couch, he stood and took her hand.

He led her through the house to the room they shared. "Get on your hands and knees," he said, pointing to the bed. Slowly, she crawled onto the end of the bed. He gripped her hips and slowly reentered her. His hand moved to grip her shoulder as he pushed deeper. The angle pulled a moan out of them once again. "How's that feel?"

"Right there," she begged.

He slammed into her harder and harder. How was it possible that she could already feel the next orgasm building? "There." The wet sounds of his hips slapping against her only made her beg for more.

Behind her closed eyes, she could visualize Dane. He was completely nude with his muscles bunching as he made love to her. His eyes would blaze a brilliant blue, and his eyebrows would be creased in concentration.

"Come for me, Tani."

She opened her mouth to scream as the waves crashed over her, but all she managed was a mewl. Her voice felt ripped from her as his hips stopped moving behind her. It was the most beautiful thing she had ever experienced. Every time just got better with Dane. She couldn't wait to marry him.

"I love you," she whispered.

His hand ran up her spine. He pulled her up gently until she was on her knees.

"I love you too." He turned her until they faced each other. His lips pressed against hers, gently this time. "Forever."

He helped her off the bed and into the bathroom. She finished cleaning up before returning in one of his T-shirts to the bed. The covers had been pulled back. She slid between them and drifted to sleep.

The last thing she felt was his strong arm wrapping around her. He was the love of her life, and by this time next week, he would be her husband. He would swear an oath to love her forever. It was a dream that she hoped she never woke from.

TWENTY-SIX

"You know what I was just thinking about?" Arne asked, breaking the comfortable silence Dane was enjoying. They were sitting on the tailgate once again watching Thyra's softball practice. Tani was across the street visiting with everyone at the diner. They would swing by to pick her up as soon as practice was over. Dane was smart enough to bring the crew cab truck Arne used to haul cattle this time.

"I'm afraid to even ask," he said.

The week was already half over. Wedding rings were sitting in his parents' safe, his suit was ready at the cleaners, and he had convinced Uncle Oscar to perform the ceremony. He would also be backup if they needed help with Jakub. Not that Dane would admit it to Arne, but sitting here on a quiet weekday evening seemed miles away from what awaited them.

"I was thinking I have to find somewhere else to live."

"What's wrong with where you live now?"

"Are you kidding? I don't want to stay with my brother and his wife. All the noise, the moaning and screaming."

Dane slapped him in the stomach. Arne laughed. "Not to mention you're going to need my room for a nursery. Or did you forget there's a baby on the way?"

"No, I didn't forget," Dane growled. "Where will you go though?"

"I've been thinking about buying a trailer and parking it on the rise in the Robb pasture. There's electricity and water. It's also quiet over there. Until then, I'll move back in with the folks," he answered. "You'll owe me. Living with them again is definitely going to cripple my social life."

"I guess you can always live with Roar until the house is ready."

"That's even worse. Don't want to trade one lonely asshole brother for another."

"You know I was perfectly fine before you moved in," Dane said, cutting a side-eye at Arne.

"No, you weren't. Life is always better with my magnanimous personality around."

"You're a twat." Dane laughed. Arne was funny if he was nothing else.

"Speaking of being a twat. How did your visit with Tani's dad go?"

"About like you'd expect. I asked to marry her; he said yes. Then we told him the wedding was this weekend, and he kicked me out. Tani explained about...the other thing. He called me back inside, asked two questions, and then kicked me back out. I think he just wanted to slam the door in my face twice."

Arne burst into laughter. "Damn, I wish I'd been there," he said between bouts. Dane was about to punch him when softball practice let out.

"What's set the hyena off?" Thyra asked, walking up to the truck. Arne was still laughing.

"Nothing." Dane hopped off the tailgate. Shoving Arne off, he closed it. "Get in, and we'll pull over to get Tani." Arne and Thyra climbed into the back seat. He pulled over to the diner. "Wait here." He slid out of the truck and walked into the diner.

"Hi," Tani greeted him. "Give me like two minutes." She swept into the back to gather her things.

"Dane," Donna called. She walked around the counter. "Congratulations are in order, I hear."

"Thank you."

"Just FYI, I tried to get her to take the rest of the week off. She's the one insisting on working through Friday."

"She is obstinate."

"Hey," Tani said, walking back into the dining area. "Who are you calling obstinate? That's a little like the pot calling the kettle black." He grinned at her and pulled her against him. Brushing his lips over hers, he gave the locals something to truly gossip about this time. He led her to the door. "See you tomorrow," she called as the door closed behind them.

"Save something for the honeymoon," Arne teased as Dane helped Tani onto the passenger seat.

"Jealous," Dane said.

"Always," Arne agreed.

"Before y'all get wound up, I have some news," Tani said.

"Hold that thought." Dane walked around the hood of the truck and slid into his seat. "Now, what's your news?"

"Mr. Dunlap came into the diner."

"The high school principal?" Thyra asked.

"The very one. Anyway, he said one of the science teachers is leaving at the end of term and asked if I'd be interested in interviewing for the job," Tani continued.

"And you said?" Arne asked.

"I said yes," she said, looking at Dane. "Though with the baby, I don't know."

"We have all summer to figure that out," he answered. "You've been waiting for something to open up. There's no way you should pass this up. Trust me, we'll be just fine. Everything will work out."

"You think?"

"Yep, right now, all we have to worry about is Sunday. After that, life will be a breeze."

"Buddha, you are not," Arne pointed out. Thyra began to laugh, and they all joined in. Dane wasn't lying though. If they could survive Sunday, nothing could stand in their way.

DANE WOKE EARLY SUNDAY MORNING. He hadn't seen Tani since Friday night when his mother summoned her to the house. There were dress fittings, final plans to make, and an early start that morning on hair. He spent his Saturday evening sharing a beer with his brothers. Even Erik made it late that night to toast him.

Pulling a pair of pajama pants on, he stumbled to the kitchen. Roar was snoring on the couch, and Erik was stretched out on the floor. If he was a good brother, he'd be quiet and let them sleep.

His head was pounding though. He filled the coffee pot with water, dumped it into the back of the machine, added several heaping spoonfuls of coffee to the filter basket, and pressed the red button.

There was a groan from the couch as the smell of coffee filled the house. Arne stuck his head into the kitchen. Dane imagined he looked as bad as his brother. Arne's hair stuck up in all directions, his eyes were bloodshot behind his glasses, and he had an uncharacteristic scowl on his face.

"I thought it was understood that I make the coffee," he said.

"You were asleep, and I can make coffee."

"Yeah, but yours tastes like burnt plaster. Has the consistency of it, too."

"Both of you shut up," Roar grumbled from the couch. "It's too fucking early to listen to you two girls bickering." He rolled over and resumed his snoring.

Dane rolled his eyes and held the coffee pot up to Arne. Arne shrugged before fishing a cup out of the cupboard. They carried their coffee to the table.

"Jakub has been weirdly quiet this week," Arne said.

"I wish I knew what he's planning," Dane said. "I don't think he's moved on, but I have no idea what his next move is." He took a sip of coffee. "I mean, today could just be a simple wedding day or a bloodbath."

"It's not going to be a bloodbath. We have a plan."

"Jesus," Roar growled. Throwing the blanket off, he stood and stomped into the bathroom.

"I think he's lived alone too long," Arne said with a smirk as they listened to him in the bathroom. "Obviously he doesn't know how to use a door anymore."

They watched in silence as their oldest brother stomped into the kitchen. He slammed a cup of coffee on the table before joining them.

"He's right," Roar said, nodding at Arne. "We stick to the plan. With any luck, nothing happens, and Tani takes you off our hands. But, if Jakub shows up, we're ready."

"I noticed Mr. Johnston wearing a set of charms when I was finishing up yesterday," Arne said.

"Can't hurt," Dane admitted.

"No, can't hurt," Roar agreed. "Well, I guess we should get this day going. Someone slap Erik awake."

"I volunteer," Arne said, jumping up.

Dane moved through the day like he was in a daze. There was no question that he wanted to marry Tani. He just wished it was under different circumstances. Watching his brothers banter through breakfast and then for the rest of the morning as they milled around the house made him realize his life was about to change drastically.

Mid-morning, Arne packed the rest of his clothes to move into their parent's house. He had already talked to someone about moving his new mobile home out to the location he had picked out.

As excited as he was for Tani to become a permanent fixture in their house, Dane knew he'd miss having his brother around. He was certain he'd see Arne even less once the baby came home. Everyone had to begin the next chapter of their lives sometime, though. Now was his turn. Everything would turn out fine, or so he hoped.

"Your turn in the shower," Erik said, stepping into the hallway with a towel wrapped around his waist. Whoever thought it was a good idea for the four of them to get ready at a house with one bathroom was out of their mind.

"Did you leave any hot water?" he asked.

"I think that ship sailed with Roar."

"Great," he said, stepping into the bathroom.

After a lukewarm shower, shaving, and deodorizing everywhere he could think of, he returned to his bedroom to dress. Tani had agreed that the groomsmen could wear dark suits instead of taking the chance on destroying rented tuxedos. His was new. He had paid extra to have the alterations done in time.

"There he is," Arne announced when he walked into the living room.

"There's something we want to do before heading down the hill," Roar added.

He picked up a bottle of high-end bourbon Dane hadn't noticed earlier. Sitting on the table were four glasses. Roar poured two fingers of the bourbon into each one. His brothers picked up the glasses. Erik handed him one of them before turning to Arne.

"We don't know what's going to come at us once we leave this house," he began. "So before we hand you over to your new wife, we want to say a few words. Dane, you're the brother I harassed the most growing up. I was your shadow; you were my hero. I couldn't have picked a better hero if I tried. Thank you, brother." They touched glasses and drank.

"My turn," Roar said. "I don't remember asking for siblings, but then you came along. Even though you've been a grump for your whole life, I wouldn't want you any other way. Fighting for Tani is the best thing you've ever done. There's no doubt in my mind that this is just the beginning of a long life of happiness. To you, brother."

Again, they touched glasses and drank.

"That just leaves me," Erik said. "Dane, I was always too little to do what you did. Too small to keep up, but that never seemed to matter to you. You taught me everything I needed to know in life. I loved hanging out with you after you finished college when it was just the two of us. Thanks for everything, brother."

"Damn, guys. All I can say to that is—" Dane said. He took a moment to wipe a stray tear away with his handkerchief. "I would never want to do this life without all three of you by my side. Hell, I wouldn't even be here without you."

He finished the rest of his bourbon before the knot in his throat grew too big to do so.

"We'd better go," Arne added. "We don't want Tani to suddenly come to her senses and flee." Dane smacked him on the back of the head. "Hey, hair."

"Don't worry," Roar said. "I told Thyra to keep an eye on her. Watch that she doesn't try to climb out a window."

"You're a dick," Dane answered.

"Yeah, but you're going to miss us."

"I'm not going anywhere. I'm just getting married."

"Maybe, but none of us want to put up with someone's smug ass getting it on the regular," Erik added.

"Get in the truck," Dane growled.

"Look at it this way. Maybe he'll get nicer once he's domesticated," Arne said.

His brothers were laughing when they walked out the front door. Dane took a second to look around the living room. They had cleaned up any evidence they had been here. It even smelled half decent. He slowly pulled the door closed behind him. The next time he opened it, he would officially be a family man.

TWENTY-SEVEN

Tani turned back and forth, checking herself in the floor-length mirror. There was a prevalent baby bump, but overall, it wasn't too bad. She had chosen a soft peach-colored dress instead of traditional white. It was simple but elegant with an A-line flare. Very little had needed to be altered on it. The florist had woven a simple crown of flowers for her hair that complemented the color of the dress.

"You look amazing," Thyra said.

She had been attached to Tani's hip since the Ulvmands insisted she move in until the wedding. Freja had cited something about traditions and all. It wasn't that she minded. She adored Thyra, and Thyra acted like having her for a sister was the best thing since sliced bread. She just missed Dane. He was the only one she truly needed.

"Thank you. Can you help me hook my necklace?"

Her father had moved into one of the empty rooms the night before so he could be in the middle of the festivities. He had insisted on handling the flowers, and from what she had seen, they were amazing. The necklace was a wedding gift from him. She cried when she learned it was her grandmother's necklace given to her on her wedding day.

"There. All done." There was a knock on the door. Thyra opened it to find Royal on the other side. "Perfect timing." She opened the door further so he could see Tani.

"Wow," he said. "You look beautiful." He pulled out his handkerchief to wipe a few stray tears away. She kissed him on his cheek, careful not to smear her lipstick. "It's almost time. Are you ready?"

"I'll see you outside," Thyra said. She closed the bedroom door quietly behind her.

"I am. It's just hard to relax when I'm so worried about Jakub showing up. You remember what you have to do if he does show up, right?"

"It's been drilled into me. You just focus on getting married and leave the rest to us."

"I'll try." Turning back to the mirror, she adjusted her hairpiece one more time. "Shall we?"

She took his arm as they left the room. He helped her downstairs where they waited by the side door for their cue. She took a quick peek outside at the yard. The Ulvmands and her dad had outdone themselves. Flowers lined the path from the door to an arch where Dane and his brothers stood. A cake sat in the middle of the dining room table. To the side were tables covered with food for a reception.

"I think that's our cue," her father whispered.

The music changed as they stepped outside. Her gaze caught Dane's as she walked down the flower-strewn path to the arch. She only half listened as her father did his part and sat down. Thyra took her bouquet so she could take Dane's hands. It was perfect.

Then it wasn't. She said her vows, and then Dane said

his. As his uncle opened his mouth to pronounce them married, the loudest roar she had ever heard ripped through the ceremony. Dane jerked her against him as he scanned the area. Everyone who had been sitting rose to their feet as if on cue. Sten stepped away from his chair to grab Thyra.

"Uncle Oscar," Dane pleaded.

"I pronounce you husband and wife. Now, kiss her quickly and get her inside," Oscar answered.

Dane laced his hands into her hair as he pulled her against him in a kiss. Mayhem broke out around them. Freja grabbed her hand, dragging her away from him. It took all of her courage to let him go.

"Wait," he called. Racing over, he held out his fist. She opened her hand, and his charms fell into it.

"No, Dane," she began.

"This ends now. I'll need all of my strength. Promise me you'll not come outside no matter what happens. You won't come near me until they have me down." Tani nodded.

She would promise no such thing, but she understood what he was saying. Without the charms, he could not control the wolf inside of him once he shifted. He could easily forget who she was and attack her.

"I love you," he said.

She had one last look at him before she was pushed inside the house. Thyra was right behind her. The door was locked and barricaded by her father. So far, their plan was going smoothly. Everyone inside was accounted for.

"Upstairs, girls," Freja barked. Thyra raced up behind her. They dropped down next to one of the windows and pushed it open. The view of the front of the house was the best from here. They each picked up a gun and waited.

Downstairs, she knew her father and new mother-in-law were standing guard at the doors.

Normally, all of this would seem like overkill. Tani, however, had seen the destruction Jakub could leave in his path. Drastic times called for drastic measures. If he got past Dane and his brothers, she would do what it took to save the young girl next to her. Her family was all that mattered.

"Tani, look," Thyra said, breaking into her thoughts. She followed where Thyra was pointing to see two tawny-colored wolves prowling the yard. "It's Dad and Uncle Oscar."

It had been agreed that while the younger men pursued Jakub, the two older men would keep sentinel at the house. If he managed to elude the brothers, they would try to stop him before he could get inside.

"Do you see Dane?" Tani asked.

"Not yet, but I'm sure everything is fine. It has to be," she added quietly.

Tani clutched his charms in her fist. She wasn't sure she believed that everything was fine. Especially since she held the one thing that protected Dane from harm in her hand. All she could do was pray he was careful. Right now, that didn't even seem like enough. They heard another roar coming from the other side of the house.

"Come on," Thyra said, pulling her shotgun from the window.

She raced across the hall with Tani close on her heels. Throwing open the window in Roar's old room, they stared down at a terrifying scene. The white wolf, blood smeared on his beautiful coat, stood snarling at the bear. He was surrounded by his brothers trying to keep the beast distracted. They snipped at his heels to keep him off balance.

Tani could barely stand watching them, but she was too afraid to look away. What if she turned away, and it was the last time she saw Dane? If only he had his protection charms. She understood why he didn't though. The wolf she watched was so much fiercer than she had ever seen him. He was so much more vicious than the first time he took on Jakub.

Dane lunged toward Jakub with a snarl. Tani held her breath as Jakub swung at him. Roar darted forward to bite at the bear's back foot. The moment of distraction let Dane dance under the paw before any damage was done.

Shaking Roar off, Jakub tried to flee into the pasture. He only managed a couple of steps before he was outmaneuvered by the pack. This time, it was Erik who latched onto the bear's flank.

The bear rose up to try and pull the wolf from his flank only to expose his neck doing so. The white wolf took the opportunity to lunge. Dane sunk his teeth into Jakub's throat.

Then the pack attacked, taking the bear to the ground. Tani sank with her back to the window. She knew it had to be done, but she couldn't watch as her husband fought a life-and-death battle. Whatever happened, someone wasn't getting up again.

THE WHITE WOLF held on with all of his strength. His brothers pounced, helping him pull the beast to the ground. He latched on to the beast's throat tighter. In the back of his mind, he knew he had to finish this fight for the last time. Only one of them would get off the ground. He couldn't remember, however, why. This wasn't food; it was war. He couldn't remember what had caused such strong feelings inside him.

He wrestled onto his feet without turning loose the beast. His paws braced against the ground as he pulled backward. The beast screamed and writhed around trying to throw him off. Finally, the life slowly eased from him, and he lay prostrate on the ground. The white wolf backed away from him. He watched until the beast stopped twitching. Finally, it was finished.

His brothers came to mill around him. Two older wolves from his pack ran up to check on him. He sat on his haunches to clean the red off of his coat assuming that the rest of the pack would take what meat they needed. Instead, they suddenly fled across the pasture to a house. He watched as they disappeared around the corner. He waited for them to reappear for a few minutes before following.

He rounded the corner of the house expecting to find his brothers wrestling in the grass. Except it wasn't his brothers standing in wait for him. Five men threw something over him. He became ensnared in a net, and no matter how hard he struggled, he couldn't get free. The men pounced on him trying to pin him to the ground.

"Dane," an older man said. "Calm down, Dane."

He snapped at the man's arm in response.

"Come on, buddy," another, younger, man said. "Try to remember who you are." He didn't understand what the man was talking about. He knew exactly who he was; he was the white wolf. He snarled at the man.

"The danger is gone. You can come back now," someone else spoke.

He already knew the danger was gone. He had watched the life drain from the beast himself, tasted his blood in his mouth. Snapping his teeth at anyone near him, he fought harder at the net that entrapped him. Then a woman stepped through a door. Slowly, she walked to where he was struggling on the ground.

"Turn him loose," she said.

"Tani—" the older man started.

"He won't hurt me. Turn him loose and step back."

The men argued among themselves but finally untangled him from the net. When it fell away, he sprang to his feet with a snarl. The men moved away, leaving him and the woman facing each other.

She stood still as he sniffed the air near her. She was familiar, but he struggled to understand why. His nose inched forward until it rested on her belly. He nudged it before looking up to lock gazes with her. Her warm eyes reminded him of home.

"Come back to me, Dane," she said softly. She sank to her knees until they were face-to-face. He took one last breath before he was kneeling in front of her. A great sob escaped her throat as she threw her arms around him. "I thought I had lost you." He felt her tie the charms back around his neck.

"I thought you promised not to come out here," he said.

"Never ask me to choose myself over our family again." A blanket was draped around them as they clung to each other in the middle of the yard. He now recognized the men as the same brothers who stood by him as he wrestled Jakub in the pasture. Arne and Erik helped them off the ground. Sten handed Dane a pair of pants.

"Why don't we go inside and have some cake while we wait for Victor and his sons to arrive for Jakub," Sten said.

"That's a good idea," Freja said from the doorway. "Though this might be the most casual wedding reception ever." She nodded toward the men, none with more than a pair of pants on.

"We'll go clean up and meet back downstairs," Arne said. He led them inside. Dane stayed back with Tani until they were gone.

"Are you okay?" he asked.

"I am now," she answered.

"I killed him."

"You did what you had to do. I don't know what other choice you had." She slid her arms around his waist. "I'm sad it came to this, but he made the decisions he did on his own. You had no say in them. He should have just moved on."

They stood holding each other until his mother stuck her head back outside. Holding her for a few more minutes, he turned her over to his mother once again. This time, though, he knew it would just be for a few minutes. Then they would begin the rest of their lives together.

"Please cut the cake," Arne begged when Dane returned downstairs. He was cleaned up and wearing slacks and a dress shirt. "I'm starving." Dane took note of his plate of food.

"Yeah, looks like," he said with a smirk. "Shall we?" He held his hand out to Tani. She took it, and he pulled her into a kiss. Everyone cheered as he dipped her backward. They made it to the table finally to cut the cake. They each fed the other a small piece before turning it over to Freja to serve.

"You know," Dane said in Tani's ear when he managed to finally get a moment alone with her an hour later. "My family is going to be tied up most of the evening. If you're done, I can sure think of somewhere I'd much rather be." He watched as a slow grin spread over her face.

"All I can say is, lead on, Mr. Ulvmand."

"You'll follow?"

"Always and forever." With a smile, he slipped his hand in hers as they snuck out of the house. She followed him to his truck. She would follow him anywhere. There was nowhere else she would rather be.

EPILOGUE

Arne rolled out of bed on a cold workday morning. He didn't so much mind the early morning or the cold, but when you could see your breath, it was too cold, in his opinion. He stumbled through his home naked to the bathroom. That was the best part of living alone: not a lot of incentive to wear clothes.

It had been eight months since he moved out of Dane's place and six since he moved into his new home. Two months living back in his childhood room down the hallway from his parents had been a lot. Not for the faint of heart. Even at twenty-three, he had rules he had to follow similar to when he was seventeen.

Life had settled into a steady routine after the wedding last spring. Dane and Tani's baby was born, but it had gone smoothly. Aksel was a typical four-month-old, nothing on his mind but eating, sleeping, and pooping as far as Arne could tell.

It was nothing short of a miracle how fast an eight-pound baby could secure the most adored spot in the family. Even Arne found himself snuggling the little guy whenever he was near.

He finished in the bathroom, pulled on his clothes, and walked to the kitchen for coffee. Fortunately, the breakfast strudel he attempted last night turned out edible. He cut a piece and tossed it in the microwave.

If life got any more settled, he might go mad. His brother rarely had time to hang out anymore, Erik was still in college, and Roar...well, who knew what Roar did in his spare time. To say it simply, life had become boring.

After rinsing his dishes, he pulled on his coveralls, grabbed his keys, and walked outside. All he had to do today was ride some fence lines and check that the cattle had hay. He drove the two miles around to his parent's house and parked his truck next to the tack room.

His horse, Elmo, snorted in the cold air in his pen. He grabbed a halter on the way through the room. He had to wade through the other horses to catch Elmo. They usually kept four or five horses just to help when they gathered cattle twice a year. He tried his best to rotate through them whenever he rode into the pasture, but Elmo was his favorite.

Although this morning, he might have to rethink that. Elmo had spent the night rolling in every mud hole he could find. The horse was covered from head to hoof in dried mud. It took another twenty minutes to finally get the majority of it brushed off. He slid a saddle pad on the freshly brushed back and slung his saddle on it.

He cinched up the saddle, traded the halter for a bridle, and swung up.

"Okay, boy, let's get this done. I'm already jonesing for another cup of coffee." Elmo snorted in agreement as they trotted past the equipment barn. He noticed Dane hadn't made it in yet. He was probably still trying to get Tani out the door. She now worked as one of the high school science teachers. Aksel stayed at the daycare next to the school.

It didn't matter to him when Dane showed up. It wasn't like they worked together that often. The cattle were all his concern, and Dane dealt with crops. The division of labor worked perfectly for them. On occasion, they worked together, but not enough that they got on each other's nerves.

He veered Elmo off the dirt road toward the fence line. Somewhere, there had to be a break. The cattle kept showing up in the next pasture over without explanation. If he could find the break, he could mark it and come back later in the UTV with supplies to fix it. With any luck, it wasn't on the side of the rocky hill at the back of the pasture.

The first problem he found was on top, almost in the corner where the fence turned. Several of the barbed strands had been torn from the post. No doubt a herd of wild boar had done the damage running through the pasture. He doubted this was where the cattle kept getting out though, but he might as well fix it while he was here.

Stepping off his horse, he opened one of the saddlebags. He learned long ago there were certain things, like fencing pliers and stays, that you always carried with you.

He pulled the strands back into place and secured them with the stays. Each stay was tightened using the pliers and the extra cut off. It only took him fifteen minutes to finish.

He swung back on Elmo and continued down the fence. Soon, they'd have to slide down the rocky hill to the bottom. As obnoxious as Elmo was, at least he was steady on his feet. His old horse, Bart, had lost his footing on the same hill when Arne was in high school. He almost had a heart attack thinking the large horse was going to land on him.

"Alright, buddy, do we feel lucky?" he asked, reining the horse in at the top of the hill. "Well, do we?" The horse snorted before throwing his head. "I think you're the only one that ever appreciates my jokes. Okay, lead on."

He pointed Elmo over the side and gave the horse his head. They walked down parts of the hill and slid down others. Finally, they were almost at the bottom.

He was just thinking about how they'd gotten better at sliding down the hill when he felt the air around him change. It was just for a moment, but Elmo must have sensed it also. The big, red horse reared up tossing Arne unceremoniously on the ground. Something must have seriously spooked him. Elmo was about as calm as they came. Arne lay on the ground in a daze for a second until he caught his breath.

"Whoa," he yelled as the horse trotted a couple of steps away from him.

Elmo stopped, but his whole body quivered as he pranced around to face something in the trees. Arne sat up and squinted at where the horse was looking. Lying not a hundred feet away was a young deer with a bolt from a crossbow in it.

"Oh, hell no," he growled. Every year they had problems with people poaching on their ranch. The game warden did the best he could to curb it, but he couldn't be everywhere all the time.

He crouched behind one of the trees hunting for where the bolt had come from. Suddenly, he saw someone stand from the brush and run.

"You'd better fucking run," he shouted.

Arne took off after the runner. He had been fast enough in high school to anchor most of the relay teams in track. A couple of years had done nothing to slow him down.

He crashed through the undergrowth in pursuit. Pushing through to the open field beyond, he saw the runner just a couple of lengths in front of him. He could catch them. No one was going to get away with not only poaching one of their deer but almost shooting him in the process.

Closing the distance, Arne managed to get his fist in the back of their coat. He dragged both of them to the ground. They landed hard, but he kept a grip on the other person as they kicked to get free.

A small boot landed a blow to his chest before he could pin their legs down. Fists rained down on his head until he managed to flip them face down on their stomach. Then an elbow slipped out making contact with his face.

"Son of a bitch, hold still," he snarled.

Straddling the poacher, Arne rolled over until he was on his back with the other person in a headlock. He tightened his grip around their neck and placed a couple of punches to the side of their head until he felt them go slack on top of him. He fished a piece of tie rope off a belt loop to bind their hands behind their back.

He dragged the poacher back to his horse. Finding another piece of rope in the saddlebag, he bound their legs at the ankles. Grabbing them by the front of their coveralls, he hoisted them onto his horse. It was a little harder than usual to secure them to the billet straps with his horse still dancing around.

"I think that dude broke my fucking nose," he said to Elmo. He wiped the blood from it with the back of his glove. "Give me a second to field dress that deer. No reason for it to go to waste." He walked to the deer and made quick work out of it. Dragging it back across, he tied it to the back of his saddle.

"Now, where in the hell am I supposed to sit?" Elmo stomped his foot on the ground. "I guess we should make sure our poacher is still breathing first." Holding the reins, he walked to the other side of the horse. "Hey, buddy. You still alive?"

It was hard to tell how they were doing under all the layers of clothes. Arne reached up and pulled off the balaclava the poacher was wearing. Long dirty-blond hair fell out of it. He stared at it as it cascaded down the side of his horse's front leg.

He slowly squatted next to the horse. Gently, he held up their head.

"Shit, Elmo. I've knocked out a woman. Now what are we supposed to do?" The horse bent his head until he could nudge Arne with it. "Wait here," he ordered. He walked back to where he saw her rise from the bramble. Poking around in the bushes, he didn't find anything but some extra bolts.

"Where did you come from?" he mumbled.

Taking a slow look around, he didn't see any ATV or other way she got here. It was a long hike from the edge of their property. Rarely, did someone just poaching a deer venture quite this far in. They mostly stuck to the edges of the property where it was easier to disappear after they got their game.

He walked halfway back to where he tackled her to collect the crossbow. She had tossed it during the chase to get away. There were no identifying markings on it. He slung it over his shoulder and walked back.

"This makes no sense, Elmo. She has to come from somewhere, but damn if I can figure out where."

Now, he needed to decide what to do about her. No way was he cutting her loose, but he didn't want to turn her over to the warden either. Something about her intrigued him. There had to be a story there. He didn't know of any women who randomly hiked cross country shooting deer with a crossbow.

He swung up on his horse. No easy feat considering he had two bodies strapped to it and a crossbow on his back. Elmo turned back toward home. Arne agreed with his choice, except they were heading for his home, not his parents.

Until he got to the bottom of what was going on, he was taking her home. He'd let her try to talk herself out of this if she woke up. He nudged her in the side. She moaned before growing quiet again. At least she was still alive.

The ride back took longer than normal. He couldn't push Elmo into a trot with so much extra weight banging against him. The horse was already unsure about having a gutted deer strapped to his hindquarters. The last thing Arne needed was to be tossed on the ground again in protest.

By the time they stopped outside the mobile home, it was time for lunch. He swung off the horse and untied the deer. He hung it from a tree limb before turning back to Elmo. The crossbow, he propped next to the door of his house.

He just had to do something with the woman on the front of his saddle. He untied her from the billets and slid her into his arms. Wrestling her into the house, he laid her on the couch. How much longer would she remain unconscious?

Arne left her on the couch to return to Elmo. He had a small pen near the house he could put the horse in until he took him back. He slung the saddle over one of the pipes next to an old well and turned Elmo into the pen. The horse immediately rolled in the mud. Arne shook his head. The horse was a menace.

His stomach growled as he walked back inside the house. He checked on the woman to guarantee she was still breathing. She seemed to be alright for now. If she didn't wake up soon, though, he'd have to take her to the city emergency room. Until then, he could at least make some lunch. He pulled ingredients out of the fridge and turned to the stove.

He was just finishing up his homemade macaroni and cheese when he noticed her breathing had changed. He scooped some into two bowls and set them on the table.

"I know you're awake, you're holding your breath." His breath caught in his throat as two of the most beautiful blue eyes sprang open. They narrowed in spite as she began to struggle with her bindings.

She struggled until she fell off the couch. Arne left the food on the table and crossed to her. He lifted her back up to the sofa. Sitting on the coffee table across from her, he crossed his arms over his chest. She wrestled some more trying to free herself.

"By all means, keep fighting. I have all day. Whenever you want to tell me what you were doing, I'm happy to untie you. I can't wait to hear this."

THANK you for reading Dane and Tani's story. If you enjoyed it, please leave a review wherever you read books.

Watch for Arne's story in the continuing saga of the Ulvmand family and Sköll Ranch. Will he be able to save the golden-haired beauty that almost shot him? Get the second book in the Sköll Ranch Shifter series here: https://book s2read.com/u/4AXVpk

Also by A Samson

<u>The Sköll Ranch Shifter Series</u>

Sten

<u>Dane</u>

<u>Arne</u>

<u>The Inhuman Protector Series</u>

Intangible

Invincible

Combustible

Justifiable

Inevitable

Writing as Avery Samson

<u>The Sideswiped Series</u>

Hers to Take

Hers to Keep

Hers to Win

Hers to Tame

Hers to Crave

Hers to Forget

Hers Always

<u>The New England Romance Series</u>

Nothing Ventured

Best Laid Schemes

In For a Penny

Actions Speak Louder

<u>The Dansboro Crossing Series</u>

Overdue

Upshot

Brazen

ACKNOWLEDGMENTS

I think most writers will tell you that this is the hardest part of writing a book and the most important. There are no words that can ever be enough to thank all of the readers, ARC reviewers, and bloggers who continue to choose my books to read. Whether you've been with me the entire time or this is your first book, thank you.

I thank Ellie at My Brother's Editor in every book. But, I could never do this without her. Her team is indispensable when it comes to writing. They catch all of my mistakes while leaving my southern roots in place.

This time I get to thank a new to me photographer for the gorgeous photo. Emma at Emma Jane Photography captured the essence of Dane perfectly.

This was a full-on family participation book. It helps to have a farmer and cow herd manager in your family when you write a book with cowboys and farmers in the family. My family has been in the business for over 150 years in the U.S. and no telling how long in Scotland before that. The Ulvmand ranch terrain is based on two of the ranches we live on. I'm also a small town expert in case you wondered.

A special thanks to my amazing daughter, Rachel, for all she does for me. I hope you have the chance to meet her at one of the book signings we attend. I couldn't do this without her and the rest of my family.

ABOUT THE AUTHOR

Avery Samson grew up on a ranch outside of a small west Texas town. Since she could remember, she's had her face stuck in a book. High School graduation found her leaving ranch life for the big city.

After living all over the state of Texas, she now finds herself back on one of the family ranches near Dallas with her husband surrounded by cattle. A lot of them. They're everywhere! When not traveling or reading, she spends her time writing.

Avery would love for you to follow her. She's everywhere (just like those damn cows.)

Join my newsletter for all the latest news.
averysamsonbooks.com/newsletter

Visit my website for my current book list.
averysamsonbooks.com

Join my reader group.
https://www.facebook.com/groups/216191437248096

Like me on Facebook.
https://www.facebook.com/averysamsonauthor

Follow me on Instagram.
https://www.instagram.com/averysamson91/

Watch my videos on TikTok.
https://www.tiktok.com/@averysamson91

Check out my Pinterest page.
https://www.pinterest.com/averysamson91/